Praise for Willia~~m~~

Last Will

'A Scottish crime thriller with a great lead in lawyer Robbie Munro and a cast of reprobates to keep you guessing, laughing and on the edge of your seat - a cracking read.'

Gregor Fisher (*Rab C. Nesbit*)

'McIntyre's outstanding mystery featuring Scottish defense counsel Robbie Munro perfectly blends humor and investigation. Readers will want to see a lot more of the endearing Robbie.'

Starred review, *Publishers Weekly*

'*Last Will* is a reminder of how good Scottish crime writing is ... Robbie Munro, defence lawyer, struggling Dad, always flying by the seat of his pants, is great fun to be with.'

Paul Burke, *NB Magazine*

'A clever, absorbing and funny book ... an addictive page turner. I loved it!'

Mrs Bloggs' Books

Present Tense

'Crime with an edge of dark humour ... could only come out of Scotland.'

Tommy Flanagan (*Braveheart*, *Sons of Anarchy*)

'Page-turning read, helped by a clear and crisp writing style. A fresh take for the Tartan Noir scene and I look forward to seeing where McIntyre takes Robbie next.'

Louise Fairbairn, *The Scotsman*

'This is dark humour, ironic humour, the kind you need when dealing with the things lawyers deal with.'   *Liz Loves Books*

'This is an entertaining novel with enough of a mystery threaded through it to keep crime fans gripped, and characters well rounded enough to carry a series.'   *Shots Magazine*

Good News, Bad News

'Take a large measure of Spencer Tracy and Katherine Hepburn in *Adam's Rib*, add a plot that would knock John Grisham for six, season with a picaresque cast of supporting characters, garnish with one-liners that Frankie Boyle would kill for and you have a recipe for a page-turner of the highest quality.'

Alex Norton (*Taggart*)

'Dry and pleasing wit which will surely see Robbie taking his place alongside Christopher Brookmyre's Jack Parlabane soon.'

Sunday Sport

Stitch Up

'A compelling, well-plotted mystery.'

The Herald

'This new release does not disappoint in bringing his trademark nail-biting, dark-humoured writing, with twists and gut-wrenching surprises that leave you thinking, "just one more page please".'

Scottish Field

'A cracking read: cleverly plotted, engaging characters, humorous and McIntyre knows his subject matter well.'

Grab This Book blog

'A deft slice of Caledonian crime... rings viscerally true, thanks no doubt to McIntyre's lifelong experience in criminal law.'

The Times

Fixed Odds

'Yet another terrific outing for Robbie Munro... Fast paced and witty.'

The Journal of The Law Society of Scotland

William McIntyre is a partner in Scotland's oldest law firm Russel + Aitken, specialising in criminal defence. He has been instructed in many interesting and high-profile cases over the years and now turns fact into fiction with his Robbie Munro legal thrillers. He is married with four sons.

Also in the Robbie Munro series

FIXED ODDS

A Robbie Munro Thriller

William McIntyre

SANDSTONE PRESS

First published in Great Britain by
Sandstone Press Ltd
Dochcarty Road
Dingwall
Ross-shire
IV15 9UG
Scotland

www.sandstonepress.com

The publisher acknowledges subsidy from Creative Scotland
towards publication of this volume.

ISBN: 978-1-912240-72-2
ISBNe: 978-1-912240-73-9

Cover design by Two Associates
Typeset by Iolaire Typography, Newtonmore
Printed and bound by CPI Group (UK) Ltd, Croydon, CR0 4YY

To my grandson, Archie Taylor McIntyre,
welcome to the world – sorry about the mess.

ACKNOWLEDGEMENTS

I, like any other right-minded thinking human being, was profoundly affected by a recent visit to the former concentration camp at Auschwitz. It would be trite of me to dedicate this frivolous work of fiction to the millions who died at the hands of the Nazis; however, in this story I have taken the liberty of naming one of the characters after Aurelia Bienka, prisoner no. 17545 'the smiling lady of Auschwitz'. I am sure, like me, other visitors passing by the row upon row of prisoner photographs in the corridors leading to the displays of human hair, shoes, spectacles, suitcases etc. will have noticed that hers is the only face smiling - and will have wondered why? Was it simply the learned behaviour of a polite young woman to smile for the camera? Or was it a subtle two fingers up to her captors? I'd like to think it was the latter. Aurelia was thirty years old when she entered the death camp and she survived less than three months. How I wish, like the Aurelia in this book, she'd gone on to be a feisty ninety-year-old.

1

It all started with a dog. Well, really, it started with two dogs.

I met the first dog by the reception desk of HM Prison Addiewell while I was passing through the security check. Having removed my jacket, belt and cufflinks, I was leaning against the frame of the metal detector, holding up my trousers with one hand and trying to untie my shoelaces with the other, when I was approached from the rear by a couple of cops. They were dressed in the sort of black combat gear one dons before abseiling down the front of the White House and assassinating the President.

'Do you have any objection to being sniffed, sir?' Wasn't a question I had been expecting, so I thought it only reasonable to seek some clarification on who exactly would be doing the sniffing.

The answer was Sam, the big black Labrador they'd brought with them, and, just in case I held hopes of clinging to a shred of self-respect, the sniffing would be swiftly followed by a search of my oral cavity. Whether this examination was to be undertaken by man or dog was something I didn't bother to ask, because I refused and brought the whole humiliating process to a halt.

Thereafter, I was visited by a series of prison officials of increasing rank and better suits, each making it very clear that I would not be allowed to visit my incarcerated client unless Sam was permitted to sniff my gentleman parts and some, as yet unidentified, individual had a look inside my gob for rope ladders, nail files and getaway cars. It was at this juncture I granted myself early release and returned, dignity almost intact, to the office.

'So you never saw him?' Shannon Todd was the partner of George 'Genghis' McCann, the inmate I'd decided not to see. Like Genghis, Shannon was a drug addict. She was also a proficient pickpocket, an occasional prostitute and handy with a knife.

I told her about the sniffing-dog scenario. She wasn't impressed. 'Who cares? Dogs sniff. That's what they do. You've got a dog, haven't you? Are you telling me it never sniffs you?'

Shannon clearly didn't understand the principle of the thing. One day the prison authorities wanted to X-ray your briefcase, the next they had a dog trying to stick its cold, wet nose where it shouldn't. If no one took a stand, before long the screws would be snapping on rubber gloves and cracking open tubs of Vaseline.

'It was a stupid mutt that started all of this,' Shannon said, introducing dog number two. 'I wish I'd never bought the thing.'

'You bought a dog?'

'Aye. I paid a hunner and fifty for it.'

Like most heroin addicts, Shannon had to steal, deal and do all sorts of other unpleasant things to feed her habit. We both knew that if she had a spare one hundred and fifty pounds, there was no way she was using it to buy a dog. Not while there was a tenner-bag left in West Lothian.

'Not a hunner an' fifty *quid*. A hunner and fifty *skoobies*.'

The skooby, or diazepam tablet, is a currency as yet

unrecognised by the International Monetary Fund but on the streets it's as good as gold.

'I got a script a while back and been saving them up,' she said.

'Okay. Let's backtrack a little.' I picked up my copy of Genghis's charge sheet and read it again. Nope, there was definitely no mention of either dogs or drugs. It was a straightforward charge of housebreaking. I squinted at Shannon across my desk. 'What's the dog got to do with anything?'

'That's what I'm trying to tell you,' she said. 'It was all the dog's fault.'

'Are you saying the dog's a thief? What is it? A pinscher?'

But my comedy genius was wasted on Shannon, as it is on a lot of people. 'Naw. It was a nice wee, white fluffy one. Would you just listen for a minute?'

And I did – for the next ten minutes – while she rambled on as to why her partner should be pleading not guilty to a charge that had all been down to a terrible misunderstanding. Over the many years I'd acted for Genghis McCann, I knew just how many times Her Majesty's Advocate had misunderstood him.

'I was at the chemist getting my methadone script and Genghis and the mutt were waiting outside. Then this woman came up to Genghis and said it was hers.'

'And was it?' I thought it only pertinent to ask.

It had been. Even the dog had thought so.

'Genghis said the thing was all over her, barking and yelping.' Shannon coughed, sniffed up a snottery one and continued. 'The woman telt him if he didn't give her back the dog, she'd call the cops. When I found out what had happened, I went mental. I telt Genghis he was getting my dog back, or my skoobies, or else.'

3

I could understand why Genghis had agreed. Well acquainted as she was with various bladed and/or sharply pointed instruments, Shannon Todd was not a woman whose benzodiazepine stash I'd have wanted to play fast and loose with.

'Who'd you buy the dog from?' I asked.

'Davie Bell. Genghis went to see him to try and get my gear back.'

Davie Bell was a bigger fence than the US/Mexico border. As far as I knew, he didn't offer a refund policy. 'How'd he get on?'

'How d'ye think? He told Genghis where he'd got the dog from and said if he wanted it back, he'd huv tae get it himself. That's why Genghis went there an' broke in.'

'You might want to avoid words like "broke" and "in" if you come to give evidence on Genghis's behalf,' I said.

'But he broke in for a reason.'

'You're doing it again, Shannon.'

'It was hardly even a proper break-in. He got in through a windae.'

'Careless of someone to leave it open,' I said.

'I'm not saying it was open. Not exactly.'

Upon further clarification, it turned out Genghis had cunningly overcome the security of the house with a half-brick. We weren't talking *Mission Impossible*.

'An' after all that, it turned out it wasn't even the right house.'

Okay, now we were getting somewhere. I mulled it over. Breaking into a house was only a crime if something was stolen, or if it could be proved the accused had intended to steal. There might be some mileage in a not guilty plea right enough. With Genghis's record, what was there to lose? First off, we'd have to jettison the dog story. A jury would take one look at Genghis and feel sorry for the animal. But poor wee misunderstood George McCann, full of drugs and accidentally stumbling into somebody's house – if I could take that material and stitch it up into a defence, the jury might wear it.

Shannon wasn't slow on hitching her wagon to my alternative scenario. 'That's right, Robbie. He was in the wrong place at the wrong time.' She laughed. 'It was just a stupid mistake.'

I laughed too. 'Doesn't sound too bad. With a bit of luck, I can turn the whole thing into a Section 57 or, at worst, a vandalism. At least there was nothing stolen...' I stopped laughing because, I noticed, Shannon had.

'Was there?' I asked. 'Anything stolen?' I glanced again at the charge sheet. There had been: three bottles of whisky, some cash and a cell phone. A load of other bits and pieces had also gone missing, so much in fact, that it looked like Genghis must have accidentally stumbled in and out of the wrong house several times, removing items as he went.

'How do you know so much about it all, Shannon?' I asked. Shannon and Genghis were something of a double act when it came to stealing stuff, and had been found guilty art and part on a number of occasions. 'Were you keeping edge for him?'

'Naw. Genghis telt me about it when he got back. He said the stuff was sitting there in a cardboard box, an' he just lifted it and bolted.'

'But why would he do that? Why steal anything at all? I mean, if it was the wrong place...'

Shannon screwed her face up. 'Ach, you know how it is, Robbie. He'd gone to all that bother and, well ... he was there anyway, wasn't he?'

'Where's the stuff he took?' I asked.

'He sold most of it to Davie.'

I wondered. 'Think there's any chance of buying it back? It might help me do a deal with the PF, and Genghis would definitely get less of a sentence if the property was recovered.'

Shannon looked doubtful.

I stood up. 'See what you can do.' It took Shannon a moment or two to realise the meeting was over. 'I'll speak to the PF and see if I can sort something out,' I said. 'I can't promise anything. I'll let you know how I get on, and you can visit Genghis and tell him what's happening.' The Legal Aid Board only paid enough for one pre-trial trip to prison and, thanks to my high principles, I'd used up mine. I showed Shannon to the door and down the steps leading to Linlithgow High Street, even though it was for her, like the road to prison was for her partner, a well-trodden path.

2

'You're late.'

The third trimester. No one could say I hadn't been warned. Hormonally, the first six months of Joanna's pregnancy had been no trouble at all. At least not for me. Then the mood swings started. Some days when I came home from work, my wife was all cuddles and kisses. Other days she was distant and tearful. Once or twice I'd had to check behind the front door to make sure she wasn't standing on a stool clutching a meat cleaver. Today, everything seemed perfectly normal. Friday evening was Tina's dance class and my wife was busy ironing our daughter's little pink outfit.

'Are you remembering Malky's coming for dinner?' she asked.

How could I forget? My brother lived in Glasgow but was a creature of habit, especially on a Friday night. Living soccer legend that he was, late afternoon he recorded his football phone-in for the radio, then came through to Linlithgow to play five-a-sides with his pals. After that he would pop in to see his niece, drink any beer I had carelessly left lying inside in my fridge, meet those same pals in the pub later, then round off the evening by crashing at my dad's. Tonight was different, though. Tonight my brother was introducing us to his latest girlfriend. I gave

Joanna a kiss and rubbed her stomach. 'How's second-in-line to the Munro throne coming along?'

'Alive and kicking.' She put the iron down and pressed my hand to her bump. 'I think we're expecting a cancan dancer.'

'Sit down,' I said, leading her away from the ironing board. 'I'll make you a cup of tea and then I'll do the... You can finish the ironing later.'

Joanna lowered herself onto a kitchen chair. 'I don't want tea. I want Ovaltine.'

Ovaltine? Had people not stopped drinking that shortly after the Blitz? I pulled open one of the wall cupboards. 'I think there's a tin of cocoa somewhere.'

'Is Ovaltine now called cocoa?'

'No ... I don't think ... but—'

'Then I don't want it. I want Ovaltine. If you go into a pub and ask for a pint of lager, would you be happy if someone brought you a pint of Guinness?'

To be honest, I wouldn't have been all that bothered. Anything vaguely alcoholic would've been fine. I couldn't remember the last time I'd had a drink. I was always driving somebody somewhere or looking after Tina. Right at that moment, I'd have settled for just about any fermented brew. I found a tin of hot chocolate powder at the back of a wall unit and held it up to her. 'Come on, Jo. Same thing, isn't it?'

'If it was the same thing it would be called Ovaltine, and not Cadbury's Hot Chocolate, don't you think?' she replied in that sweet tone of voice which we men with pregnant wives know to be extremely wary of. I assessed the situation and realised I was left with two viable options: debate the similarity between brands of chocolate-based milky-drinks with my enormously pregnant and

8

potentially homicidal wife, or head immediately for the supermarket.

Tesco was surprisingly busy for a Friday night. Not that I had much experience of supermarkets on Friday nights. I tried to avoid shopping any night, but of all nights, I tried to avoid Friday nights most.

Somebody who seemed right at home was Hugh Ogilvie, the local Procurator Fiscal, a man compared to whom the tinned fish aisle seemed interesting. Still, what better chance to have a word about Genghis McCann's plight?

'If you've come to talk to me about one of your clients, you can forget it,' Ogilvie said, realising the can of sardines he was holding in front of his face wasn't going to cut it as camouflage. 'If you want to discuss business, communicate with me during business hours.'

I laughed at the very suggestion. 'Communicate with you during business hours, Hugh? You work for the Crown Office and Procurator Fiscal Service. I'd have better luck trying to communicate with Houdini's mum. When have you ever taken one of my calls or answered an email? And, by the way, I know you've got a wastepaper racket going on, and that the letters I send are shredded and sold for hamster bedding. How am I supposed—?'

'Okay. Okay . . .' He dropped the can of sardines into his wire basket, then changed his mind and exchanged it for a tin of mackerel in a spicy tomato sauce. It was an adventurous side to the PF I never knew existed. 'Just shut up and ask me whatever it is you're going to ask anyway.'

So I did. 'It's about Genghis . . . I mean, George McCann. He's been charged with—'

'Housebreaking. Like he always is. I know.'

'You've remanded him on petition, and I was wondering if—'

'*Please* don't ask me to reduce the charge to a summary complaint. You always do, and I always don't.'

'Come on, Hugh. He was drunk and accidentally stumbled into the wrong house. It was an innocent mistake. He never actually stole anything ... much.'

'I don't care if he came down the chimney and left gifts,' Ogilvie said. 'It's a housebreaking.'

'What if he returns all the stuff?'

'You mean all the stuff he didn't actually steal?'

'Okay, let's agree, without prejudice and purely for the purpose of these negotiations—'

'We're not negotiating, Robbie.'

'That he might have mistakenly removed a few things ... A bottle or two of whisky ... Some money ... Possibly a mobile phone ... A few other odds and ends, maybe...'

'There's no *possibly* about any of it. According to the witness statement I have, he cleaned out a whole room: all the items you've mentioned plus ornaments, a clock, pictures off the very wall ... If it wasn't nailed down, he—'

'Okay, Hugh. I get it. Maybe he helped himself to a few bits and pieces, but at least he didn't do any damage.' The PF took a deep breath. I could tell he was going to try and muddy the water with facts. 'Unless you're going to count a wee hole in a window as damage.'

Ogilvie showed me the upraised palm of his hand. 'I am no longer listening. The man's a menace. He's on petition for housebreaking and he will be going on indictment for housebreaking in due course. The householder is in her nineties. Vulnerable people like that need protection from people like George McCann. And that goes for his psycho-girlfriend too. If I find out she was involved,

10

she'll be joining him. It's about time the public was given a break and that pair were put away.' He put his hand in the basket, removed the tin of mackerel, swapped it for the sardines, and then he and his tinned fish set off down the aisle like they were being chased by a school of hungry orcas.

I let him go. I had more important matters to consider. Joanna would be waiting for me to bring back ... What had I come for again?

3

'Are you really telling us you forgot what you'd gone for, Robbie? Why didn't you take your phone with you?'

I wasn't sure what to make of Kimberley Ironside. First impressions, some people said, were lasting impressions. Motown even had a song about it. Then again, other people said first impressions could be deceptive. Whichever, I couldn't help but think there was something not quite right about my brother's new girlfriend. She was different from Malky's usual squeezes. She was pretty and she was blonde. Nothing too unusual there. The difference was that Kim wasn't made-up pretty. Most of Malky's girlfriends had faces you could have marked with a pickaxe without hitting flesh. Kim wore scarcely any make-up, and I was quite sure her hair was the colour Mother Nature had intended. Not only that, but she wore clothes that covered those parts of her body that polite society thought best not uncovered, and which the sort of women with whom Malky normally associated liked to put very much on display. I suppose the best way to describe Kim was normal. What was a *normal* woman doing with my brother?

'Well?' she said. 'Why didn't you take your phone with you?'

Kim's normality wasn't skin deep. No, her cross-examination technique, like that of most normal females, if more bludgeon than rapier, was extremely persistent.

'Robbie's always forgetting his phone,' Malky said.

'That's right,' I said, adding, 'and it was only the name of what I went for that I forgot . . .' As pleas in mitigation went, it wasn't my finest work.

'What you're saying is, you went to Tesco for only one thing and forgot the *name* of it?'

Honestly, I didn't know what the big fuss was about. It wasn't like I'd gone for a chocolatey, milky-drink thing and come back with a boiled ham.

Kim was unrelenting. 'You went for Ovaltine and brought back Horlicks. What was Joanna supposed to do? Write you a shopping list with a single item on it? That's not really a list, is it – one thing?'

Joanna, having already given me a hard time, seemed happy enough to let another woman in on a piece of the action. I glowered across the kitchen table at her, but my wife refused to acknowledge said glowers, content to prod at the vegetarian dish she'd made and which Malky and I had skilfully avoided in favour of my homemade spaghetti bolognese. Cooking? I didn't know what all the fuss was about. All it took to whisk up authentic Italian cuisine was a pound of mince, a jar of sauce and some spaghetti – or, on this occasion, oven chips, since I'd discovered too late we hadn't any pasta left. 'How about we drop the subject?' I said. 'I'll go to Tesco's in the morning and get you a jar of . . . er . . .'

Kim was a woman with not enough eyes to roll. 'Ovaltine!'

'I know, I know. I'll get some *Ovaltine* tomorrow.'

'No need,' Joanna said. 'I've phoned your dad and asked him to pick up some on the way back with Tina.' At which point, Tina, dressed in her little pink dance outfit and clutching a large orange jar, came skipping into the kitchen, my old man close behind.

'Thank you very much, Tina.' Joanna brushed our daughter's hair back and planted a kiss on her forehead. 'Now, will you bring me a teaspoon, pet?'

She did, then jumped up on my lap and stole a chip; the crispy one I'd been saving for last. 'So, Kim,' I said, trying to make myself heard over the sound of Tina crunching my dinner and my wife munching mouthfuls of Ovaltine granules. 'Malky was saying this is going to be your last season.'

Kim who had been staring open-mouthed at Joanna, turned to me again. 'What's that? Oh, yeah. Looks like it. I'm thirty now. The oldest player in the team by a good few years. It's time to retire before I start embarrassing myself on the pitch.'

'Three hundred and twenty-six games for Hibernian and their all-time top scorer,' Malky said proudly. 'Kim's already notched up fourteen this season.' He had obviously been studying his girlfriend's statistics, but then, when it came to women, my brother had always had a head for figures. He gave her a nudge. 'Don't sell yourself short. You've got a couple of good seasons left in you. Every team needs someone with experience. Someone who's been there and done it.'

'I don't know,' Kim said, modestly. 'I'll see what my agent says. Maybe it's time to hang up my boots.'

'Well, don't do anything too hasty,' my dad said. 'You're a long time retired. Make the most of your playing days.' My dad greatly approved of his older son's new relationship, and the prospect of another professional footballer in the family. By the way he studied the two lovebirds, I could tell he'd already assessed the genetic advantages

14

of such a union when it came to grandchildren and the future of the beautiful game in Scotland. It made a nice change. My old man's opinion of Malky's girlfriends was usually pretty scathing, and, in the main, filed under the heading 'hing-oot', a category reserved for young woman too obvious in appearance, too generous with their affections and too free with the cash that Malky, as a former football star and now sports pundit, earned. Kim was different. She'd not only trained as nurse, she'd done all right financially from her career in sport. She was sponsored by a firm of medical suppliers and was one of the few female footballers to be on a professional contract with her club.

Kim smiled modestly. Setting down her cutlery, she leaned her head on Malky's shoulder. 'Despite what this man says, I think it's time to call it a day. I'm hoping for a coaching job or maybe Malky can get me a spot on the radio with him. There's a lot of interest in women's football these days.'

Tina started tickling me and I laughed.

'What's so funny?' Malky asked.

'It's Tina, she's—'

'Do you find women's football amusing?'

'No, I'm not laughing. Well, I am but it's Tina, she's—'

'It's okay, Malky.' Kim put a hand on my brother's arm and froze me with a smile as she did. 'Not everyone is as enlightened as you are. There are still a few dinosaurs out there.'

My phone buzzed on the worktop next to the microwave. Tina jumped down and brought it over to me. It was Genghis McCann phoning from prison.

'Should you not be tucked in bed for the night?' I said, taking the call through to the living room.

Genghis was tucked up all right. Tucked up in a cell with a smuggled mobile.

'I thought you were coming for a visit?' he said.

'I tried to see you today, but there was a problem.'

'Aye, so Shannon tells me. I'm stuck in here and you're doing bugger all to get me out.' Bouncer, the dog, wandered over and lay across my feet. Perhaps I shouldn't have been so prissy about the sniffer dog. It wasn't as if my principles were so terribly unsullied. A lot of worse things had happened to them over the past fifteen years of criminal defence work than the unwanted probing of a cold wet nose.

'All right,' I said. 'I'll try and come out to Addiewell after court on Monday, but if they've no appointments left, it will need to be Tuesday or maybe Wednesday. That do you?'

He grunted in reply.

'And I've not been doing bugger all. I've spoken to Shannon *and* I've spoken to the PF to try and work out a deal to get you out.'

'I'm getting out? When?'

'It's not completely sorted yet.'

'When?'

If you do the crime, you do the time. It's something a lot of people say, but never those who actually have to do the time.

'It looks like you'll have to wait until the First Diet,' I said.

'When's that?'

The Crown had eighty days to serve the indictment and the First Diet was a procedural hearing held within one hundred and ten. The amount of times my client had been on remand, you'd have thought he'd be familiar with the timescales by now. 'You've only been in a fortnight, so you're looking at another fourteen weeks unless I can get the PF to agree a Section 76 to a reduced charge.'

'Fourteen weeks!'

The line went dead at that point. I switched off my phone in case he tried to call back and went through to the kitchen to see my dad sitting in my vacated chair, smiling up at me.

'Kim's getting us tickets to the League Cup Final.' Was he sounding excited about women's football? My dad? The man whose previous highest praise for the ladies' game had been, "*Ach well, it's good exercise for them.*"

'It's on the twenty-eighth of next month,' he said. 'An Edinburgh Derby. What do you think about that?'

'Great,' I said, 'though if there's not enough tickets, I wouldn't want to—'

'Don't worry,' Kim said, 'there's plenty to go around. Joanna can come along too if she likes.'

Joanna pressed a hand against her bump. 'Hopefully, around about then I might be busy doing something else.'

'Can I come?' Tina asked.

Kim smiled. 'Of course. But make sure your dad takes his mobile with him — just in case.'

Everyone got up from the table and our guests moved through to the living room while Joanna and I stayed behind to clear away. She put a hand on my shoulder. 'You will be there, won't you, Robbie?'

'I'm not sure. It's kind of Kim to get us the tickets, but, women's football? I mean ...' She gave me a punch on the arm. 'Not that I think the women's game is a load of old rubbish or anything,' I said hurriedly. 'I'm sure they're very skilful and they try really hard, and—'

My words were interrupted by a second punch, harder

17

than the last. 'I'm not talking about a stupid football match.' It seemed that when it came to football, my wife didn't discriminate between the sexes. It didn't matter who was kicking a ball about a field, it was all a waste of time so far as she was concerned. 'I'm talking about the birth of your child. You will be there, won't you?'

'Of course,' I said.

'You won't be stuck in some *really* important trial or something?'

'No,' I said. 'And even if I am, I'll unstick myself pronto. There's no way I'm missing our baby being born.'

She smiled and gave me a cuddle. 'Promise?'

I crossed my heart. 'Hope to die.'

'Correct answer,' she said, releasing me and lifting a pile of plates from the table. 'Because, miss this baby being born, and you'll wish you *were* dead.'

4

What was the point of employing a secretary if she wouldn't tell clients you were out when you were in?

'Ah, Shannon, glad to see you,' I said, as Grace Mary, ignoring my dagger-like stare, closed the door behind her. 'Come away in and sit down. I can guess why you're here.' Tuesday afternoon and not only had I not visited her remanded boyfriend, I hadn't even booked an appointment. It would be Thursday, or more likely Friday now, before there'd be a time available at the prison. 'I've been up to my eyes in it, but I promise you . . .' Why was she smiling?

'I'm just here to tell you Genghis says cheers, Robbie.' Shannon said.

'For what?'

'For getting him out, of course. He says he knew you'd do the business for him.' Shannon thumped a carrier bag onto the desk, disturbing some of my case files, many of which were already quite disturbing enough. Smiling like a piano, showing mostly sharps and flats, she put her arms out wide and twirled around. 'What d'ye think? How am I looking?'

In appearance, Shannon was usually something of a *Walking Dead* tribute act. Today, there was a slight improvement. We weren't talking front cover of *Women's Health and Fitness*, but there was a sparkle in her eye, and an unmistakable tinge of colour about her cheeks.

'You're looking great,' I said.

She couldn't bring herself to deny it. 'I know! Genghis too. Me and him, we're both aff the kit. That's us forever.' Like most heroin addicts, Genghis would have benefited from his couple of weeks in the slammer. After his prison detox, he'd be waxing evangelical on the wisdom of staying clean, and continue to do so until one of his mates came round to his place with a couple of score bags. Hotel Heroin. You could check out any time you liked ...

Shannon dropped into the seat opposite, almost slipping onto the floor in the process. She was temporarily off the drugs and very much onto the drink if the smell on her breath was anything to go by.

'So, Genghis got out okay, then, did he?' I wanted rid of a drunk Shannon, but not before I found out more about her boyfriend's unexpected release from prison.

'Aye, he got off the bus about twelve. I was just on the way to cash my Giro and said to myself, why not drop in and say thanks to Robbie?'

'You're very welcome ... Did Genghis happen to say why they let him out?' I asked, casually, not wishing to give the impression that his emancipation wasn't all down to me.

'Naw, he just telt me it was a PF release. GNLE.'

Grounds no longer exist? In my lengthy experience as George 'Genghis' McCann's lawyer, grounds always existed in any crime in which he was involved. It was what came of attempting audacious break-ins whilst off your face on smack or skoobies. Genghis was so inept, he could break into a bookie's and still lose a tenner.

'He says he doesn't know what shit you told the PF, but it must have worked.'

I stood up, hoping Shannon would take the hint. She

didn't. The nick she was in, a hint would have had to have been tied to a half-brick and thrown with some force.

'Anyway ...' she said with a leer and an attempt at a wink, 'what I'm here for is to say thanks and to bring you a wee present.' She reached for the carrier bag and, after a few goes, managed to remove a large maroon box. It said, 'Gordon & McPhail' on the front and carried the independent bottler's distinct stag's head logo. What most caught my eye was the name of the distillery, gold-embossed, slap-bang in the middle. That and the date.

'Shannon,' I said. 'Tha ... that's a bottle of Brora.'

She seemed taken aback, the smile momentarily wiped from her face. She studied the box. 'Naw, Robbie, it's definitely whisky. You take a wee drink of whisky now and again, don't you?'

There was certainly a rumour going around to that effect.

'Well, here. You can have this for getting Genghis out.' She popped the large gold stud near the base of the box and slid the cover up to reveal a hessian interior into which the bottle inside fitted snugly. She prised it out and set it in front of me. There was barely an inch of golden liquid in the bottom.

'Where's the rest of it?' I asked.

'Me and Genghis have been celebrating. But there's enough there for a dram,' she added defensively.

I wasn't sure if Genghis and his girlfriend drank their whisky neat or even if they used glasses. I preferred mine with a drop of water, and absolutely no saliva other than my own. I also preferred not to be charged by the police with the receipt of stolen goods.

'Where did you get this, Shannon?'

The wrinkling of her face confirmed my view that this

was one of Genghis's grounds; the ones that for some reason no longer existed.

'Shannon, this is one of the rarest whiskies in Scotland, which means in the world. It's thirty-two years old!'

'Aye, but you can still drink it,' she said. 'It's awright with a wee drop Irn Bru.'

I gripped the arms of my chair, gritted my teeth and continued. 'No, you don't understand. This bottle would have been worth at least a thousand pounds.'

What little colour there was in Shannon's pasty-face drained faster than 70cl of fine single malt whisky does if placed in the wrong hands. She snatched the bottle back from me and gave the contents a shake. 'How much will I get for this? There's easy got to be fifty quid's worth left in there.'

'That's not how it works, Shannon. Once the bottle is open the value's gone.'

'But you said—'

'You can't sell an open bottle. Once it's open, how would anyone know what was really in it?'

Shannon slammed the base of the bottle down and hunched over in the chair, forehead resting on my desk.

I took a closer look at the bottle. 'This is one of the bottles from the break-in, isn't it?'

She didn't answer. I'd acted for Shannon on many occasions and had never known her to say anything that might incriminate her or anyone else.

'How many more are there?'

'Two,' she mumbled.

'The same as this?'

She sat and straightened quickly. 'Naw ... not exactly.'

'What's different about them?'

'It's the boxes that are the same. The writing's different. It's not that Brora thing.'

'What does it say on the other boxes?'

'One says something about roses.'

'Rosebank?'

'Could be.'

'What about the other?'

She thought about it for a while. 'It's a name. Helen, I think.'

'Is it Ellen? Port Ellen?'

'Maybe ... Aye ... Why?'

Brora, Rosebank and Port Ellen. The royalty of Highland, Lowland and Islay single malts. Three whiskies from silent distilleries, and each worth a small fortune.

She stood up, suddenly keen to leave.

'Take the bottle with you,' I said.

'That's all right, Robbie,' she said, magnanimously. 'You keep it. Not every day you have a fifty-quid dram, is it?'

'No, it's not,' I agreed. 'And it's not every day I get done for resetting stolen goods either. So, put the bottle back in the box, put it in the bag and say hello to Genghis for me.'

The grin was back, wider than ever. 'I will. Wait 'til he hears we've got two grand worth of whisky.'

She paused in the doorway. Befuddled with alcohol though her brain might have been, we both had the same thought at the same time. Drug-free Genghis McCann, newly released from prison and in celebratory mood. He'd have quite a drouth on him, and he was sitting at home with two full bottles of whisky.

I didn't need to show Shannon down the stairs to the High Street. She was halfway down them before I'd reached the top landing, screaming as she went, 'If he's opened one of those bottles, I'll bloody kill him!'

5

'But what possible reason would she have to kill him, Hugh? They've been partners for years.'

Wednesday morning, Livingston Civic Centre, I intercepted Hugh Ogilvie as, gown draped over a shoulder and carrying a big red plastic box of case folders, he climbed the flight of stairs to the Sheriff Court.

'Because she's a junkie,' he said, trying to push past me. 'That's what they do. We all have our different roles in life. Mine is to prosecute criminals and yours is to annoy me. A junkie's job is to take drugs, steal and occasionally commit murder or else be murdered. The whole thing's probably for the best.'

Typically, Ogilvie had found an upside to the previous night's brutal slaying of the recently released, now very much deceased, George 'Genghis' McCann. I didn't know a great deal about it, except I'd heard there'd been a lot of blood.

The Procurator Fiscal shimmied around me and expanded on his silver lining theory as we made our way onwards and upwards to Courtroom 2. 'Overdoses, ulcerated limbs, septicaemia, blood clots, HIV, Hep C – need I go on? Your average junkie ends up on a slab long before his three score and ten. You should know that. At least this would have been quick and painless.' He paused on the stairs before continuing. 'Well, it would have been quick. They say an ambulance wouldn't have made it in time, even if one had been called. So, you see, your Miss Todd has saved both the NHS and the DWP a fortune. Shame the money is going to be spent on keeping her in prison for the next eighteen years.'

Inside the courtroom, there were no other lawyers. The early birds had already been in to put their names on the list for that morning's cited court. It was more out of habit than anything else. The recent drop in prosecutions meant that the court rarely sat past noon. The Government's decision not to prosecute people, providing they were willing to sign up to drug or alcohol rehabilitation courses, had cut a swathe through criminal business. It was a policy I thought tough on the teetotal criminals and meant most clients in-the-know declared themselves a junkie or jakey even if they touched nothing stronger than vitamin C supplements or wine gums.

'Any chance you could fill me in on some of the background information?' I asked.

Ogilvie dropped his pile of case folders onto the table in the well of the court. 'Oh, I'm sure your client will be able to fill you in on all the little details when she's sober enough to be interviewed. I wouldn't want to spoil the surprise.'

'She's not drunk,' I said. 'She's in hospital with alcohol poisoning. It could be ages before I get to see her.'

'Well, if she will drink those expensive single malts ... What was it she had in her bag? Port Ellen?' He slipped the black gown from his shoulder, climbed into it and sat down. 'Strange, isn't it, that they found a bottle of Rosebank, Falkirk's finest, next to her dead boyfriend?'

'About the whisky ...' I said, tentatively. 'Any idea where it came from?'

25

'Hmm ...' Ogilvie glanced at the names scribbled on the cited court list, removed a yellow folder from the centre of his bundle and pulled out a sheaf of papers held at the corner by a treasury tag. 'Let me see. Your late client was in receipt of Universal Credit. What's that? A couple of hundred a fortnight?' Ogilvie tore a schedule of convictions from the green string of the treasury tag and set it aside, ready for the first case of the day. 'No, I just can't see your Mr McCann, the known thief, or indeed his homicidal partner, saving up to buy a couple of thousand-pound bottles of Scotch. Not when they could have had two hundred tenner-bags, so ...' he said, extracting the next case folder from the pile, 'I'm going to go out on a limb here and say that he stole it.'

'Wasn't there supposed to have been whisky stolen during the break-in McCann was remanded for?' I asked. What did it matter now? Sentence-wise, Genghis was already serving eternity.

Ogilvie pulled the contents from the folder and studied them while he spoke. 'You know, I think there was. All a terrible mistake, though.' He looked up at me. 'Ironic, isn't it? For once, your client was accused of a crime he didn't commit, and yet if he'd stayed in prison, he wouldn't be dead. It's truly tragic.' Ogilvie's tone suggested he'd come to terms with the tragedy of it all quite quickly.

'But how do you know for certain he *was* innocent of the break-in?' I asked.

'Apart from you accosting me in Tesco on Friday night to tell me he was, you mean? As I've already told you, the house the late Mr McCann broke into, accidentally, of course, was owned by an elderly lady. Her carer phoned the office yesterday morning to say nothing was stolen. The old girl got herself confused. Turns out a window was smashed, nothing more. I'm not splashing money on a trial for a Section 57. I ordered McCann to be released pending service of a JP summons for vandalism or maybe a fixed fine.' The PF glanced up at me with what he probably classed as a smile on his face. 'Looks like one of your clients was telling the truth for once, and now, unfortunately, he's not one of your clients anymore. Still, you've got his girlfriend's murder case to console you. Unless you think there would be a moral conflict there.'

I might have thought that. My bank manager wouldn't.

'Then, what can I tell you?' Ogilvie said, still managing to see the cheery side of things. 'Every cloud ...'

6

'I don't know why it is, but you don't get many proper murders these days.' Detective Inspector Dougie Fleming was in nostalgic mood on the way from reception to the interview rooms in the bowels of Livingston Police Station. He'd already asked me how my dad was, and seemed happy to learn that his former colleague was still doing my head in on a regular basis. Fleming and my dad went way back. It was Sergeant Alex Munro who had shown cadet officer Fleming the ropes — as well as how to tie them so as not to leave marks. Until the advent of video recordings, I suspected they'd also each employed the same technique when it came to interviewing suspects: get the answers down in your notebook, ask questions later.

'It's always either a domestic or drug related,' Fleming continued, as he opened a series of doors. 'Take this Shannon Todd of yours. A junkie who stabs her junkie partner. A drug-domestic. It's ticking all the boxes, but the whole thing is a waste of time. She's a woman. Your QC will say it was because her man was violent, or controlling or something; the AD won't care because the dead guy was a junkie. There'll be a deal done on a culp hom and some soft-sentencer will dish out four years to keep the women's liberation front happy. After that, your client'll be sent to one of the new female-only holiday camps and be out on a tag inside twelve months. Where am I supposed to find the job satisfaction in that? It's all Maggie Thatcher's fault for closing the pits. There used to be fights every weekend down at the miner's clubs. There was always someone getting their head stove in, *and* there's not so much bigotry nowadays either. The Tims and Proddies spend all their time hating Jews or Muslims instead of each other now. Used to be, after any Old Firm match, you were practically guaranteed a bloodbath. Ask your dad. Nowadays, they don't go down the pub after the game looking for trouble. They just go home and call each other names on Twitter.'

'Talking about happier times,' I said, 'murder or not, I'll bet my dad never did an interview after seven o'clock on Champions League semi-final night.'

Fleming grunted. 'Tell me about it. It's this new DS they've lumbered me with. Dead keen. We'll be lucky to catch the highlights.'

Our arrival at the interview room brought an end to Fleming's nostalgic reminisces. Shannon Todd was already there and waiting for us in the company of a female detective sergeant who looked too young to be up this late on a school night. They were sitting opposite each other on the bolted down metal seats that were arranged in pairs either side of an equally bolted down metal table. The female officer was in plain clothes. Shannon was wearing a white paper suit that had a long orange stain down one breast, and which may have been the source of the sour smell in the room. Her lank, greasy hair was pulled tight into a ponytail and secured by a black plastic electrical tie. When I sat down beside her, she dragged her gaze from the table to look sideways at me. 'Thanks for coming, Robbie,' she said, sending a wave of puke breath wafting over me.

'Right, then.' Fleming clapped his hands together while his colleague fiddled with the DVD recorder. 'You both know the script.'

'Are you not going to write it for us?' I said. 'Like in the good old days.'

'I've a better idea,' he said, through a bitter slice of a smile. 'How about you shut up and listen, and we can have this whole thing wrapped up in no time?'

The DS typed the necessary details into the recording apparatus. 'Would your client like some time to consult with you before we begin, Mr Munro?' she asked.

Fleming took it upon himself to answer on my behalf. 'No, she wouldn't, Sergeant. Mr Munro's client has been through this procedure more times than you have, and she was formally advised of her rights when she was booked in. We could sit around while he tells her to say nothing, but that's what she's going to do anyway. Isn't that right?' For once, I was on Fleming's side. Even a no comment interview would take the best part of an hour. If we moved things along, with a bit of luck, I might make it back for the second half of the match.

'Start asking your questions,' Fleming said.

His colleague's face flushed. 'I don't think so, sir.' This might have all been run-of-the-mill to Fleming, but the young DS didn't look like she'd sat in on too many murder interviews, and was going to make the most of it. So, even though Shannon and I both agreed that a consultation was unnecessary, the detective sergeant reminded my client of the right to remain silent, started the recording device and went through the whole SARF process word for word, while Fleming leaned back grim-faced and arms folded.

'... but anything you do say will be recorded and may be used in evidence. Do you understand, Miss Todd?'

Shannon nodded.

'Good,' the DS said.

'For the tape,' Fleming said.

His young colleague looked confused. 'Tape?'

'Answer the question out loud,' Fleming snapped at Shannon. 'Do you understand you don't have to say anything?'

'You don't have to answer that,' I told Shannon.

Fleming sighed.

'Aye,' Shannon said, 'I understand.'

'Good.' Fleming turned to his colleague. 'Let's get this over with.'

The DS cleared her throat and picked up the first page of an alarmingly thick sheaf of papers covered in her handwritten questions. 'Miss Todd, did you murder George McCann?'

She might have been a modern police officer, but the opening bombshell question designed to shake recalcitrant suspects was a technique as old as Robert Peel's sideburns.

'No. I never,' Shannon said. 'I wasn't there.' I looked across the table at Fleming. He stopped picking his fingers and looked at me. We both looked at Shannon. It took a few seconds for my brain to unscramble the words she had uttered and realise that there was no order into which they could be reassembled to come out as: 'no comment.'

I turned to brave the stale vomit fumes. 'What are you doing, Shannon?'

She stared at the table. 'I'm answering the questions.'

'Well, stop it,' I said. 'You never answer questions.'

She lifted her head and glared at me. 'That's because I'm always guilty. This time, I'm not.' As replies went, that would be something of a two-edged sword if ever presented to a jury. 'I never killed Genghis. I wasn't even there. I don't know nothing about it.'

I just knew that some smart-arse QC would jump all over that double negative at the trial. 'You might think you are, but, trust me, you're not helping yourself,' I told her.

The young officer shuffled her papers, trying to find a follow-up question to that unexpected answer. Fleming leaned forward.

'So, if you weren't there,' he asked, suddenly interested. 'Where were you?'

I sat back. Maybe the match would go to extra time and penalties.

7

'Your dad was here,' Joanna said, when, having eventually made it home, I collapsed onto the couch, almost impaling myself on the leg of one of Tina's dolls that was wedged between the cushions in a most unladylike position. 'He thought you'd be going down to the Red Corner Bar to watch the football. He waited for you, but you never showed so he stayed and watched it here. He's not long away.'

'Do you know the final score?'

'Four-three to someone. I don't think it was all that much of a game. Your dad said there was a big fight and some of the players had to get sent off.'

'So, just a boring old seven-goal thriller with a few sendings-off? Did the Swedish women's netball team happen to do a half-time streak?'

'You missed one football match,' Joanna said. 'Get over it, there'll be another along in five minutes. I've just got rid of one grumpy Munro man. I don't need another one kicking off. No pun intended.'

'What was my dad being grumpy about?'

'I don't know if he was being grumpy, but he was doing some amount of yelling at the telly. I stayed out of the way in the kitchen helping Tina do her school project on Italy. Though, when I say helping ... She sat watching the football with her gramps while I stuck dried pasta and pictures of the Colosseum in a jotter.' Joanna came over and gently lowered herself down beside me. 'By the way, next time you're making your signature pasta dish, the jar in the cupboard without a label is bolognese sauce. The label is now part of Tina's project. Bolognese comes from Bologna, doesn't it?'

'You're really after that gold star, aren't you?' I said.

Joanna laughed. 'Why are you so late? I had your dinner ready.'

'Sorry. For once, Shannon Todd decided she was going to help the police with their enquiries. I couldn't get her to shut up.'

'Landed herself in it, has she?'

'That remains to be seen,' I said. 'Let's just say she's painted herself into a corner. She gave the cops an alibi.'

'Oh.' Joanna recognised the significance of my client's decision. A burst alibi was the legal equivalent of a burst aneurysm, and fatal to most defences. Once their alibi had haemorrhaged, it was no good an accused changing their mind and asking if they could swap it for a better defence. In any criminal case, it was best for the defence to keep its cards close to its chest and let the Crown show its hand first. Even if an alibi were true, it should only be sprung on the prosecution at the last minute. Now, Shannon had given the cops several months to find different and possibly highly imaginative ways to discredit it.

'Where's she saying she was on the night of the murder?'

'Trying to flog stolen whisky, and after that getting steaming with one of her pals.'

That was Shannon's story and she was sticking to it. She had returned home after her meeting with me to discover Genghis had opened the Port Ellen. It had only taken him a sip or three to decide he didn't like its extreme flavour and so he'd opened and drunk most of the unpeated Rosebank. There'd been a few cross words, but, according to Shannon, nothing more than that. She'd gone to see Davie Bell to try and sell him the almost full bottle of Port Ellen, and when he'd not been interested, she'd taken the bottle to a friend's, where they'd forced down the Islay malt before switching to vodka. The only crime she'd committed that evening was to kill the taste of a rare Islay malt with a bottle of Scotland's other, fizzier national drink. She didn't know her partner was dead until she was arrested for the crime.

'Well, she's definitely capable of murder,' Joanna said.

'She's a pickpocket and a thief,' I said. 'She's not a murderer.'

My wife didn't see it that way. 'Says who? She's got pages of PCs for assault, and remember when I was working with you and she got charged with that Section 49?'

I did. Shannon had been caught with a pair of nine-inch scissors in her bag and we'd run a defence that she was training to be a hairdresser, and therefore had good reason to have them in her possession.

'You made me do that trial.' Joanna still harboured a grudge over some of the less than seaworthy cases I'd asked her to do when she'd been my employee, and occasionally dredged up the wreckage.

'And because of that, you think she's capable of murdering her boyfriend?' I said.

'Why else carry a huge pair of pointy scissors unless you're prepared to use them? For cutting hair? I never believed that for a second, and neither did the jury.'

'Well, I could hardly have you say she kept them in her handbag for cutting the price-tags off designer goods,' I said.

'You *knew* that and still let me run the stupid hairdresser defence? Why didn't you tell me?'

'I didn't think knowing the truth would have helped.'

'Robbie, the truth *always* helps. That's the purpose of a trial: to get to the truth of the matter.'

I held her stare for a moment. She didn't flinch. She meant it. Had my wife learned nothing during her time working with me? Yes, criminal law, whichever side of the fence you were on, was a search for the truth. However, if you did manage to find it, it was often best if the jury didn't get to hear it. A little ignorance went a long way. Something recognised by most lawyers, both Crown and defence.

'If I'd told you the truth, what would you have done?' I put to her. 'It was better you didn't know. Keeping scissors in your handbag for shoplifting purposes is not exactly a statutory good reason.'

'Then she should have pled guilty,' Joanna said.

'Why? Section 49 was brought in to prevent violent crime — not to stop folk snipping tags off the clothes they're nicking.'

'I'll bet she did kill him,' Joanna muttered.

'You would say that.'

'Because I'm a PF now, you think I'm biased?'

Unlike Shannon Todd, I knew there were times when it was best to make no comment.

'What do you *really* think?' Joanna pressed. 'Is she guilty or innocent?'

'What I think is of no relevance.'

'Oh, I see. That's how it is, is it? I'll bet she told you she did it.'

'No, she did not,' I said emphatically. Perhaps too emphatically. Joanna took my jaw in her hand and put her

36

face up to mine so that our eyes were inches apart. I was first to blink. 'Not in so many words, she didn't. All right, she may have mentioned to me in passing something about *wanting* to kill him,' I added in response to a jaw squeeze.

'When?'

'Tuesday afternoon.'

Joanna let go and recoiled, I thought, over-dramatically. 'Tuesday afternoon? She told you a few hours beforehand she was going to kill him, and you did nothing about it?'

'*I'll kill him*,' I scoffed. 'People are always saying stuff like that.'

'Yes,' Joanna agreed. 'Murderers.'

'Get a grip. It's a turn of phrase. You said you'd kill me if I wasn't present at the birth.'

'That's different.'

'How?'

'Because that was *me* saying it and, unlike your client, I don't have previous convictions for carrying pointy scissors around with me. *And* I've never stabbed someone before.'

'Neither has Shannon.'

'Yes, she has.'

'Okay, okay, I'll grant you she was *charged* with stabbing that bloke who annoyed her outside a pub, but it was a flesh wound, and, if you remember, I got her a not proven.'

'Only because a self-defence is easier for a woman stabbing a man than the other way around.'

'Or maybe,' I said, 'that's why I'm a great defence lawyer and you're back prosecuting.' It was a cheap shot, but then it had been quite a sore jaw-squeeze. I stood up smartly and walked through to the kitchen. The raising of Joanna's bump from the couch delayed her arrival.

'Let's look at this rationally,' she said. This from a woman who ate Ovaltine straight from the jar. 'Shannon Todd habitually carries a weapon, she told you she was going to kill her partner and now he's dead.'

'There you go, getting away ahead of yourself. You don't even know how Genghis McCann died.'

'He was stabbed.'

'You're speculating he was stabbed. You don't know that for a fact. You're worse than the cops. Jumping to conclusions based on a biased and highly prejudicial opinion of my client's character.'

'How did he die then?'

'Look, I don't want to argue about this any longer. I've had nothing to eat since a bacon roll at lunchtime and I'm starving.'

'This isn't an argument,' Joanna said. 'I'm just explaining to you why I'm right.' She waddled past me in the direction of the fridge, returning with a plate of curry and rice. She put the plate in the microwave and set the timer for three minutes. 'Well? Was he stabbed, or wasn't he?'

'It's early days,' I said. 'You know the cops don't like to go into too much detail at interview in case they accidentally give away some special knowledge and spoil the chances of a self-corroborating admission.'

'But?'

'Okay, there are certain indications that there may, perhaps, have been some kind of ... I don't know ... a cut ... or laceration or ...'

'Stab?'

'It's possible.'

'There you are, then. She did kill him. After you've eaten, make me a cup of tea, will you? Decaf.'

A few weeks into her pregnancy, Joanna had gone off coffee because it now had a horrible metallic taste. She'd changed to tea. Then she'd heard somewhere that caffeine was bad for the unborn child. Unfortunately, it wasn't quite so simple a problem to solve as changing from normal to decaffeinated teabags. Joanna didn't like the taste of decaffeinated teabags or, rather, their lack of taste. This meant I had to make two cups of tea using the same caffeinated teabag because she had heard somewhere else that caffeine came out of a teabag early on in the tea-making process, and therefore it was safe to drink the second cup.

'Are you in the huff, just because you know I'm right?' she asked, when eventually I joined her in the living room. 'Or is it about you having to take the late-night caffeine hit again? I know how it delays the onset of sleep for you by a good thirty seconds. You could always pour it down the sink. You don't have to drink it.'

I handed her the mug of tea that I was pretty sure was the caffeine-free one. It was hard to tell. I'd been so busy thinking about Shannon Todd's case that by the time I'd put the milk away and picked up the mugs, I couldn't remember which was which. Still, the odds were good: fifty-fifty.

'You know what the problem with you is, Joanna?' I said.

'You mean apart from the cannonball in my stomach, perpetual heartburn, swollen feet and piles? No, go on, tell me.'

'You've always got to be right about everything.'

'No, I don't.'

'There you are at it again,' I said.

She sighed. 'Are we back onto the subject of Shannon Todd?'

I never heard the back door open. 'Shannon Todd, the murderer?' Malky asked, striding into the room. 'She one of yours, Robbie? The bint who stabbed her boyfriend? They were talking about her down at the pub tonight.'

'You were in the pub?' I said.

Malky sighed. 'Yes, I know the radio station's sponsoring me to do that Sober October thing for charity, but I wasn't drinking. I collected Kim from training and we stopped off to watch the end of the semi-final at the Red Corner Bar. Not really Kim's sort of place, but I thought you might be there with Dad. Did you see it? What a game!'

'Is Kim with you?' Joanna asked. It turned out Malky's girlfriend was waiting in the car. 'Then don't be so rude. Tell her to come in.'

Malky shook his head. 'Can't. I don't want her to know why I'm here. I've told her I've only jumped in to see Robbie about something important.'

'What important thing is that?' Joanna asked.

'Something I can't tell her. Any chance you could you think up a good lie about why I'm here, Jo? You can think about it while I talk to Robbie.'

'What's the big secret?' I asked.

'I've got you a new client.'

I managed to fight off the excitement. Malky had brought me a number of new clients over the years; mainly pals of his looking for legal advice on minor road traffic infringements. They all came with great expectations, except that they might have to pay a fee.

'You remember Peter Falconer?' he asked.

I remembered him all right. Peter Falconer had been a goalie and former team mate of Malky's at Glasgow Rangers back in the day. Peter was six-foot-nine with hands like frying pans and looked like he could gather low flying aircraft, let alone corner kicks. His problem had been with low shots. It was said Peter had once tried to commit suicide by throwing himself in front of a bus, and the bus had gone under him. He'd made a few inauspicious appearances for the first team before being put on the transfer list and ending up in the Highland League. After an undistinguished career in professional football, Peter had fallen in with Aloysius Kenyon Quirk, former small-time bookie, now online gambling magnate, whose son I had once represented. Peter had managed to get himself in on the ground floor of Honest Al's new venture, Bet AKQ, which had funded his foray into sports agency, and where he was now ensconced as one of the dodgiest in a dodgy business.

'Peter's got a client who's in a spot of bother and needs a new lawyer.'

'A *new* lawyer? So, what you're saying is they've got a lawyer already?'

'Aye, some balloon from Glasgow. Liam somebody or other. They call him the Loophole. You heard of him?'

'Liam Tait?'

'Could be.'

Liam 'the Loophole' Tait was a great lawyer. Whoever Peter's client was, it seemed to me he was in safe hands.

Joanna interrupted. 'Why exactly am I having to think up a lie for you?'

Malky winced. 'It's complicated.'

'Try me,' she said.

'Okay, I don't want Kim to know I've been talking to Peter Falconer because I said I'd sound him out about a deal for her.'

'What kind of a deal?' I asked.

41

Malky sighed. 'In ladies' football, hardly anybody gets paid. Kim's one of the lucky ones. She was put on a four-and-a-half-year contract with Hibs four years ago when they thought ladies' football might be a money-spinner and really take off. But she's worried. She gave up her work at the hospital to go full-time and now she's looking for a deal with another club.'

'How much do women players get paid?' I asked. Not very much was the answer. In Kim's case, it was the combination of being one of Scotland's top female players and a nurse that had attracted sponsorship from drug companies.

'That's where the real money is,' Malky said. 'Even her car is sponsored. If Hibs drop her, she'll just be another amateur and the sponsorship cash will dry up, which is definitely not good because she's built up a fair bit of debt over the years. I've offered to help her out, but she's too proud and already thinking about signing on with the NHS Nurse Bank.'

'I thought Kim was retiring from football, anyway?' Joanna said.

'No, she's just saying that to save face. She's only got until the end of the season with Hibs. After that, there won't be a queue to pay wages to a thirty-year-old centre-forward. You know what you women are like, Jo. Your backsides don't get any smaller once you hit the big three-oh.'

'Joanna's thirty-one,' I said, 'and her backside is … well, it's been smaller, but she's having a baby, and I think Kim's bottom is quite small, pert in fact.' Joanna gave me a nudge. 'Not that I've been looking at it. Anyway, as I was saying, it doesn't make sense. What about all the goals she's scored this season? Sixteen—'

'Fourteen,' Malky corrected.

'Still, it's a lot.'

'Five were penalties, and what you need to understand, Robbie, is that in ladies' football—'

Joanna butted in again. 'Would you stop calling it ladies' football. You don't call men's football gentleman's football, do you?'

'No,' Malky agreed, 'I just call it football. So, as I was saying, Robbie, *girls*' football is not like the real thing. I'll admit there's some with a rough idea of how to play the game, but most of them couldn't kick doors at Halloween.'

Joanna inhaled sharply as my brother continued. His view on the women's game seemed to be directly proportional to the distance he was from his hot new girlfriend.

'You see that game on telly tonight?' he continued. 'Seven goals. When was the last time there were seven goals scored in the Champions League? In women's football, there's usually seven goals before they've sliced the half-time oranges. And as for bookings and red cards, it's practically a non-contact sport when the girls play.'

'You can think up your own lie,' Joanna said. 'I'm going to bed.'

'What's wrong with her?' Malky asked, watching my wife depart. 'She doesn't even like football. Anyway, I've spoken to Peter about Kim. He's not interested, and I don't want to break the news to her yet. That's when we got talking about this client of his who's in bother. Peter says their present lawyer, you know, this Liam guy, he's hopeless apparently. Keeps telling Peter's boy to plead guilty.'

'If that's Liam's advice, then I think maybe he should listen,' I said.

'How can he? If he pleads guilty to match-fixing, he'll

be banned for life. Peter wants to hire someone who'll at least put up a fight, and I said that's what you were: a fighter.'

Match-fixing wasn't a run-of-the-mill type of a case. There was only one on the go that I knew about, and that was because the whole world knew about it. 'Peter's client . . .' I said. 'He's not Oscar Bowman by any chance?'

'Aye, that's right, the snooker player.'

Although there were periods when it never seemed to be off the telly, and I couldn't help but watch it, snooker wasn't really my thing, either to spectate or to play. As a man who'd been known to hit himself with the heavy end of a pitching wedge after a shanked approach shot, I'd always thought it better not to be left in charge of a long, pointed instrument while in the company of others in the close confines of a snooker hall. Still, I knew who Oscar Bowman was. Everyone did. At a ridiculously young age, he'd won the US Open 9-Ball Pool Championship before turning to and mastering the game of snooker. For years he'd been recognised as one of the world's top sportsmen – if a game you could play in a dinner suit while sipping a G&T could be called a sport.

'Will you speak to him or will I tell Peter he's better sticking with this Liam the Loophole guy?'

'*Loop*-hole? I think you may have misheard what people really call him behind his back,' I said. 'If Peter is looking for a fighter, tell him I agree; Liam couldn't fight sleep. Tell Peter to bring Oscar to my office tomorrow afternoon. Better still, I'll go to his.'

8

Shannon Todd appeared on petition for murder at nine-thirty next morning. Surprisingly, the court started on time, something I thought only happened when I was running late. Less surprisingly, Shannon was refused bail and remanded in custody pending further enquiries. A decision would be made within the next eight days as to whether she should be fully committed for trial or released due to lack of evidence. The hearing took less than ten minutes, so I was able to jump on the train and be early for my meeting at Peter Falconer's Edinburgh office, near the foot of the Royal Mile. I arrived at eleven-thirty. They arrived at noon: Peter, his sports star client and a woman dressed in a black suit that contrasted with Bowman's trademark white attire. Peter attempted an introduction, but grim-faced Bowman walked straight past me and through a door at the far end of the hallway. Instead, I was introduced to the woman in black. I didn't catch her name. She was the snooker player's close-protection officer: Asian, very pretty and just the sort of person most men would choose to protect them closely.

'No need for that,' she said with a smile and a hint of a bow, when having stepped forward to take a look at me, I'd raised my arms and assumed the position.

Peter took me aside and lost one of my hands in his. 'Thanks for taking this on at such short notice, Robbie.

You know the trial is due to start the week after next, don't you?' I didn't, but, with a change of lawyer, it wouldn't be difficult to seek an adjournment. 'That's not a problem for you, is it?' Peter slapped my back. 'Didn't think it would be. Your brother, Malky, speaks very highly of your capabilities. Would you like a drink before we get started? We've got mineral water, still or sparkling?'

'*Sparkling* water?' I said. 'What are we celebrating? No thanks. I came on the train. I'll have a bottle of beer. Anything's fine. I'm not fussy.'

Peter's face set like a jelly. He backed slowly down the hallway. Not taking his eyes off me, he closed his office door. 'Did Malky not tell you?' he asked on his return.

'Tell me what?'

'Oscar's a Mormon,' he hissed. 'You know, Church of the Latter Day what's-its.' Peter whacked his forehead. 'I knew he'd forget to tell you. Alcohol is a strict no-no. The boy thinks coffee's a sin, so no more talk about beer, okay?'

'And gambling?' I asked.

'It's just another reason why this case is potentially disastrous for Oscar. As if a life ban from snooker wouldn't be bad enough, the Mormon church can be very unforgiving, not to say vindictive, when its name is brought into disrepute. You'll have heard the stories.'

I hadn't. 'What about your link to gambling through Al Quirk and Bet AKQ?' I asked. 'Does your client know about that?'

'No, he doesn't, and he doesn't need to, understand? The reason you're here is that when Malky told me about you, he said you'd acted for Al's son once and I checked you out with him. He said you were a royal pain in the arse, but worth it.'

As client feedback went, I'd had worse.

'That was good enough for me,' Peter said, setting off down the hall again. 'Now, come on. Oscar doesn't like to be kept waiting.'

I pulled him back by a tree branch of an arm. 'Peter, before we go any further. Any chance you could fill me in on some more of the background?'

He could, though only quickly. Peter, it transpired was Bowman's UK tournament agent. The snooker star was very particular about who represented his interests, and he had a great many interests that needed representing. He had advisers, both sides of the Atlantic, looking after his fashion range and endorsements for sports equipment, while a media company took care of his TV appearances and an upcoming autobiography entitled *Front of the Cue*. He even had people taking care of his deal with the confectionery company that made his favourite brand of mints. The man had more agents than the CIA and, according to Peter, was quite capable of giving underperforming employees the bullet just as fast as any Government hitman. 'He might look like a choirboy,' Peter said, 'but when it comes to business he's an astute little bugger. Whatever you do, don't balls this up or we're both for the chop. You need to be extremely careful not to upset him. That's why there can't be any chat about drinking or gambling.'

No talk about gambling? Wasn't that why I was here? What kind of match-fixing didn't involve gambling?

Peter led me down the hallway. 'I just hope you're as good as Malky says you are. You get Oscar off with this and I'm going to owe both the Munro brothers big time.'

Was this the reason Malky had been bigging me up? If I secured an acquittal, the agent would owe him a favour. A new contract for his girlfriend, perhaps?

47

'You all set?' he asked, when we reached the door to his office. 'Sorry about the lecture, it's just that this is very important for everyone. If Oscar's found guilty, he'll be banned for ages and every Mormon-based sponsor he has will drop him like a hot toddy.'

'No pressure, then,' I said.

'That's the spirit.' Peter gave me a friendly slap on the back that would have sent me into the door if he hadn't pushed it open at the same time. 'And don't scrimp when it comes to the bill,' he whispered, as I went to meet my new client. 'Just because you're Malky's wee brother, I'm not expecting any favours.' He needn't have worried. My meter had started running the moment I stepped on the train to Edinburgh.

Peter showed me to a seat on the circumference of a highly polished walnut conference table. His client didn't acknowledge my presence when I walked in, or when Peter forced an introduction. Even when I stood up and offered my hand, the man in the white suit stayed at the window, staring out across the street at the Scottish Parliament building.

'Okay, then, I'll leave you pair to get on with it,' Peter said. 'If you need anything, just give me a shout.'

'Stay.' Oscar Bowman was American, which is one of the things I look for least in a client. American clients don't have mere problems, they have issues and nothing's ever easy with them. He turned from the window and pointed to the chair across from me. 'Peter, you're my agent. You should stay and listen to what this guy has to say.'

Without a word, Peter pulled out the chair and sat down, looking at me over the top of the few bottles of mineral water that were standing to attention in the centre of the table, surrounded by crystal tumblers. Each table setting had a pad of paper embossed with the logo of Peter's company and a pen similarly branded. I pulled my stationery over, clicked the plastic pen and smiled at my new client. 'Let's start at the beginning,' I said.

Bowman pulled a slim blue tin from the breast pocket of his jacket, opened the lid and popped a mint in his mouth. 'Let's not.' He replaced the tin and began to pace up and down, hands clasped behind his back. 'Let's cut to the chase. This time next week, I'm standing trial. I have no intention of being found guilty and I want to know how you're going to prevent that from happening.'

It sounded like this wasn't so much a legal consultation as an audition.

'First of all,' I said, 'this time next week you're not standing trial. Not if I can help it. We're going to put the trial date back. A week isn't long enough for me to prepare what could be a fairly complex defence.'

Bowman steepled the hands that were insured for ten million pounds, put them to his lips and tapped his index fingers together, as though exercising great patience.

'*First of all*,' he said at last, in an exaggerated Scottish accent, that I took to be his impersonation of mine, 'we're not putting the trial off. The trial will go ahead as planned. I've had it hanging over me long enough. Move on to your second of all.' Crunching his mint, he planted his hands and leaned across the table at me. 'Well?'

'Well,' I said, 'if we're getting down to it, I need some instructions on your defence.'

Bowman closed his eyes tightly and began to massage his forehead with both hands. Eventually, he revolved his head slowly to face Peter. 'Have you not filled him in?'

'Peter's given me some background information,' I said

before the big man could answer. 'But, as for the defence? If it's all the same, I'd prefer if you filled me in on that yourself.'

Bowman went over to the window again and looked left towards Holyrood Palace. 'It isn't all the same to me,' he said. 'Speak to Peter. I'm tired talking about the whole thing.'

I put down my pen and reached for a bottle of still mineral water. 'I'd speak to Peter if he was my client. He's not. You are.' I twisted the lid off and tossed it to the side. 'So, tell me why it is you think you should be found not guilty, and I'll tell you how best we go about establishing your innocence.'

Bowman came around the table and sat down on the chair next to mine. He flicked a strand of blonde hair out of his eyes, the better to stare straight into mine. 'You know? I don't think I like you. Who is he, again, Pete?'

'He's Robbie Munro, a highly experienced criminal lawyer,' Peter replied obediently.

Bowman absorbed that information for as long as it took him to stand up again. 'Get rid of him and find me a new one.' His close-protection officer appeared from nowhere. The two of them walked to the door where they were intercepted by Peter.

'Oscar . . . wait.' Peter put an arm around the shoulder of the white sports jacket. The snooker player was tall but enveloped by the big man's embrace. 'Mr Munro comes highly recommended.'

Bowman pouted like a two-year-old and stared at the thick pile carpet. 'I don't care. I don't like him.'

'But you've only just met the man, and he's your fourth lawyer, not counting the two QCs you've also sacked. You should have stayed with Mr Tait. No offence, Robbie.'

'Tait wanted me to plead guilty, and I'm not pleading guilty.' Bowman's eagerness to take the matter to trial was like music.

'There's one week to the trial,' Peter told his client. 'By the time we find another lawyer, one you actually like . . .' He tailed off.

Bowman wrestled himself out from under his agent's arm. By the time he looked my way again, the childish expression was gone, replaced by a crooked smile. 'You think I'm guilty, don't you?'

'You haven't told me why I should think otherwise,' I replied. 'But it's irrelevant if I think you're guilty. It only matters if the jury believes that beyond a reasonable doubt.'

'And you'd like me to give you such a doubt?'

'It would definitely help,' I said.

Bowman walked around the table until we were face-to-face again. 'I should be found not guilty because I'm Oscar Bowman. That's all you need to know.' He about-turned and walked to the door his close-protection officer was holding open for him. 'You want a reasonable doubt?' he called to me from the doorway. 'Then do your job and find one.'

9

My mind was whirring as I made my way back up the High Street and down to the Cowgate. After my brief encounter with Oscar Bowman, I'd spent half an hour in Peter's office viewing the video evidence. It wasn't good. The alleged offences had occurred when Oscar had been at the very peak of his game, three or so years previously. Those were the days when the bookies didn't give odds on who would win a tournament, only on who'd come second to Oscar 'The Showman' Bowman. For the allegation wasn't that Oscar had ever deliberately lost a snooker match. It was that he had thrown certain frames against weak opposition in the early rounds of several prestige competitions. Those particular lost-frames happened to coincide with a spate of high-value bets being placed in the Far East and Las Vegas. Whether any of the money was laundered back to Oscar was something the Crown hadn't thought merited the expense of making international banking enquiries. Instead, the prosecution relied on experts who would opine that the important shots missed by my client had been inexplicable, other than if they had been deliberate. I had to identify a line of defence that would neutralise the evidence of those witnesses, and I had only a few days in which to find it.

But before all that, I had to return my thoughts to

another equally pressing matter. Oscar Bowman wasn't my only client. After the initial court appearance of a murder accused, the first thing a defence lawyer does is obtain an additional opinion on cause of death to ascertain if there are any adminicles of physiological evidence that might support the accused's version of events. The organisation of a defence autopsy involves lawyers grovelling to the Scottish Legal Aid Board for money to pay doctors. And it isn't as simple as filling in some online forms and making a few phone calls. There aren't that many forensic pathologists around. For a case in the West Lothian jurisdiction, the Crown would already have instructed the Edinburgh contingent, the Glasgow lot were always far too busy, the chaps in Aberdeen seldom ventured south for fear of sunstroke and the precious ones in Dundee wouldn't go near the defence side of a prosecution in case they contaminated themselves. Add to that the logistics of trying to arrange an autopsy slot at the morgue that suited your slicer-and-dicer, and it could take days to arrange, and yet all that time and effort was work the Scottish Legal Aid Board classed as 'administration', and therefore not worthy of a fee. So, on this occasion, I thought I'd save myself the trouble. If my client insisted she wasn't there at the time of his murder, what difference did it make how Genghis McCann died? All I wanted were a few basic facts and I hoped I might get what little I needed for free.

'No, Robbie. Go away and obtain your own autopsy report.'

I didn't expect someone who'd spent the morning cutting up dead people to be skipping around, singing the opening number from Oklahoma, but I did think Professor Edward Bradley was being exceptionally boorish, even by his own extremely high standards. I'd phoned ahead to check that he was down at the City Morgue and lain in wait for him to come out at lunchtime, which he did in the company of his colleague, the diminutive Dr Yasmin Ashmat.

'What's the big problem?' I asked, as the professor tried to make his way along the narrow Cowgate footpath that I was determinedly trying to block.

'The problem is, as it is ever with you, Robbie, that you want something for nothing.'

'I only want to know the cause of death,' I told him.

'Then pay for your own forensic pathologist. I'm being paid by the Lord Advocate.'

Another good reason not to instruct my own expert was the five hundred pounds to hire the morgue's facilities, plus another one thousand pounds for a forensic pathologist. It was money I'd have to pay upfront and the Legal Aid Board would later find a reason not to pay me. It was a large outlay for the small amount of information I required.

This time the professor succeeded in pushing past me. 'It's always about money with you lot,' I said.

He turned. 'Oh, I am sorry. I forgot how altruistic you lawyers are.'

'Yeah, but us lawyers are *supposed* to be money-grabbers. You angels of the NHS, with your giant taxpayer funded salaries, bit of private work on the side, you're supposed to be above all that and working for the common good.'

'I *am* working for the common good,' he called back. 'That's why I'm not doing anything to help you get one of your murderers off.' I wasn't prepared to run after him. Not while I could turn instead to his colleague, young Dr Yasmin Ashmat.

'He's touchy today,' I said. 'I suppose, because all your clients are dead, you pathologists aren't used to criticism. Whatever got you into this job in the first place? Did they shout, "*All those who don't want a career dissecting dead people, stand up!*" and they never noticed you were?'

'That's right, Robbie,' Yasmin said, as I fell in step beside her, 'making jokes about my height is a sure-fire way to get me on your side and have me divulge the confidential information you're undoubtedly angling for.'

She was on to me. 'But seriously – pathology?' I said. 'When did you first see that as a vocation?'

She sighed. 'What can I say? There are a lot of doctors and only so many jobs in each field. I'll let you into a secret. Fifty per cent of doctors finish in the bottom half of their class in medical school.'

She needn't have put herself down. I hadn't made the top fifty percent of my law year, but, liked to think I had made it possible for there to be a top fifty percent.

'And so here I am,' Yasmin said. 'With pathology, just like proctology and gynaecology, there are always plenty of openings.'

I bent at the knees and gave her a shoulder bump. 'Good one. Nice bit of medical black humour there.'

She smiled.

'So, anyway, tell me,' I said, 'how *did* George McCann die?'

Clearly the woman needed more buttering-up, for, at the question, she stopped smiling and quickened her pace.

'Come on, Yasmin. Why can't you tell me?' I called after her.

'You heard Professor Bradley. Our report is confidential,' she said, when after a couple of strides I'd caught up with her again. 'The Crown will send you a copy of the full report in due course. You'll just have to be patient and wait for it to be released.'

She continued onwards, eyes fixed on the figure of Professor Bradley marching downhill heading either for the vegetarian restaurant on St Mary's Street, or the new burger joint on the corner of Holyrood Road. The clever money was not on the stuffed aubergine.

'Oh, go on, tell me,' I said. 'I don't need the full feature. Just give me the trailer. You know, *coming soon to a courtroom near you*. How about it?'

She didn't reply. Professor Bradley disappeared into the burger bar.

I tried again. 'Like you say, I'm going to get the information anyway. I'm only asking for it a wee bit earlier than normal.' Still nothing. 'Okay. You're right. I shouldn't have asked. A professional relationship should be based on trust and you haven't reached that stage with me yet.'

'Has anyone, Robbie?' she asked with a scalpel slash of a smile. 'You do, shall we say, retain a certain reputation.'

We'd reached the foot of St Mary's Street. I stopped. 'I think I'll head back for the train.' Sincerity is something all court lawyers learn to fake at an early stage in their careers, but righteous indignation adds another string to one's bow, and I'd been practising it in the mirror. 'I hope being seen with me hasn't tarnished your public image.'

Yasmin put a hand on my arm. 'I didn't mean it that way, Robbie, and I'm really sorry you've wasted your time. You know I'd help if I could, but it's Prof B He'd go crazy if he found out, and he would find out. He's always hanging about me, asking how his girl's doing today, and if I'm ...' She made quotes with her fingers. '"*Coping*". He treats me like a child. And the pressure ... He makes me so nervous, sometimes I can hardly hold a scalpel without shaking.'

There are moments during the preparation for any court case when inspiration strikes. Sometimes it brushes by. Other times it slaps you in the face. I looked down at the young woman at my side. She was no longer just Dr Yasmin Ashmat, Fellow of the Royal College of Pathologists. She was about to become the stone I'd use to kill two birds.

'That's all right,' I said, doing my best to exude an air of nonchalance. 'I was through in Edinburgh anyway. I had to consult with Oscar Bowman.'

'Who? *The* Oscar Bowman? The snooker player?'

'Yes, he's been charged with—'

'Match-fixing. I know. My mum's devastated.'

'Your mother a snooker fan, is she?'

'More of an Oscar Bowman fan. Good, clean-living lad like that, those big cow eyes and that blonde quiff. I think it's something to do with the son she never had or the husband I haven't got. She even loves his Oh So Cool Cue-Ball Mints, though they're choking hazards, if you ask me. Why was he consulting with you? I thought he had a proper ... I mean ... you know ... some big-shot lawyer. You've not taken over the case, have you?'

I winked and tapped the side of my nose with a finger.

'You *have?*' Yasmin stopped. 'What's Bowman saying about it? Did he lose all those frames on purpose? Promise, I'll not say a word.'

'I shouldn't really be telling you this because it is highly confidential,' I said allowing the hook to embed itself.

'Aw, go on, Robbie. Promise, my lips are sealed.'

'Well, it seems that in moments of high pressure, Bowman's cueing action loses its normal smoothness. A bit like you when Prof B is looking over your shoulder. He gets a bit shaky, snatches at the shot and misses, which in turn—'

Yasmin was way ahead if me. 'Makes it look like he's missed on purpose?'

'Exactly. All I need is an expert witness to confirm it.'

'Sounds psychological.'

'I was thinking it might be more of a physiological problem,' I said.

Yasmin took a moment. 'Could be ... I suppose ...'

'That's why I'm looking for someone with an in-depth knowledge on anatomy, nerves, muscles, that sort of thing. But if you think it's more of a psychological issue ...'

'No, no, not necessarily. You see, Robbie, the brain sends the message, but the fault often lies with the synapse between nerves endings. That can cause involuntary muscle fibre twitches, even spasms.'

'So, there's the basis of a defence there, you think?'

'Undoubtedly.'

'In that case, maybe I'll come for lunch and sound Professor Bradley out about it,' I said.

'Do you think that's wise? He seemed a bit annoyed with you.'

I waved Yasmin's concerns away with a flap of my hand. 'He's always annoyed with me. Wait 'til you see how *unannoyed* he gets when he hears Oscar Bowman will be paying him an exorbitant fee, and you know how much he loves the publicity of a big court case.'

'Yes ... Of course. You could ask Professor Bradley,' Yasmin said, her voice wavering slightly. 'Or ... if I can be of any assistance at all?'

'You? No, you're busy enough. I wouldn't want to prevail upon you,' I said.

'No, really, prevail,' Yasmin said, growing more excited by the second. 'I'd be pleased to help. I could study the evidence, provide an opinion, whatever you need.' She'd taken the bait so well, I doubted if she'd be hungry for lunch.

I screwed my face up and scratched my chin.

'Is it my lack of experience?' she asked.

'Well ... you are quite new.'

'I'm probably more up to date than Professor Bradley when it comes to myoclonus.'

I had no idea what that was, but let it go. 'Seriously, it wouldn't be fair on you.' I walked on, but not too quickly.

Yasmin was right at my heels. 'Robbie ...'

I turned to face her. 'Whoever takes on the role of defence expert in this case is going to have to put up with a lot of media attention; radio, TV interviews, that sort of thing. They'd forever be known as the man, or woman, who saved Oscar Bowman's career ...' Dr Yasmin Ashmat was a small woman who had spent her short professional career in the shadow of a very large man. This was her chance to step out and into the limelight. I shook my head. 'I couldn't let you go through all that. There'd be newspapers, TV companies, women's magazines, all wanting to speak to you. The publicity would be intolerable.'

Yasmin breathed in and pulled herself up to her full height. 'I could cope with that,' she said.

'And,' I said, 'I'm looking for an expert I can trust. Someone who's prepared to stand up in court and stick by their opinion. I can't have anyone buckle under pressure.'

Yasmin snorted a laugh at the very idea of buckling.

I pretended to think about it. 'All right,' I said. 'You're hired.'

Yasmin beamed at the news. 'Thanks, Robbie. Probably

best if you don't tell the Professor you were thinking of offering the job to him. Let me break it to him gently.'

She thrust out her hand. I didn't take it. 'I've just had a thought,' I said. 'The trial is next week, so I'm going to need your report ASAP, and if you're going to be tied up with Bowman's case, that's bound to delay the PM report on George McCann, and I really do need to know the cause of death urgently.'

Yasmin took my hand and squeezed it. 'Now that we trust each other, I think I might be able to help there too.'

10

'So, he *was* stabbed? What did I tell you?'

Joanna was in triumphant mood, not only because she'd been proved right – I wondered she didn't get tired of that – but she'd also been for her final check-up. The baby was doing fine and the ETA was Halloween, thirty days and counting. Not only that, but she'd somehow managed to rope me into attending an antenatal class, arranged especially for dads-to-be. Up until then, there had been other opportunities to attend, and I'd skilfully evaded them all. Why did I need to go? Over the months of Joanna's pregnancy, we had talked about the end game and, though keen to help, I believed I could handle the mopping of my wife's brow while administering liberal doses of gas and air in between words of encouragement without wasting time at a training seminar. Joanna thought otherwise and, like in so many of our domestic arrangements, we had reached a compromise – we'd do things her way.

To allow us out for the evening, my dad had come over to our house to watch Tina. The Italian project was due for submission at the end of the week, and the two of them were at the kitchen table making a paper maché model of the Leaning Tower of Pisa, actual size, if the amount of old newspaper and wallpaper paste was anything to go by.

'It was more of a slash than a stab,' I said, helping my wife into her coat.

'Slash, stab, what's the difference?' she said. 'Now, let me think ... Who do we know who stabs or slashes people?' Joanna pressed an index finger against her cheek and cocked her head. 'Oh, what about Shannon Todd?'

'Not proven – remember?' I said. 'And she has an alibi.'

'Oh, yes, she was with that notorious thief and receiver of stolen goods, Davie Bell. Who's *not* going to believe a man with a record of dishonesty longer than the intro to "Bat Out of Hell"?' My wife had become very cynical since she'd gone back to the Fiscal Service. I could understand that, but dissing Meatloaf? There had to be limits. 'Where'd she give him it? In the neck? Under the ribs? The armpit is always good for a quick kill. Lots of major blood vessels all hanging around in there. Makes it very difficult to apply pressure to stop internal bleeding too. It's one of the kill blows in the martial art of Kendo.'

I'd always thought a career in criminal law had given my wife far too much of an insight into effective methods of murder.

'You're not even warm,' I said.

'So how *did* he die?' Joanna asked. She attempted to button her coat over the bump, came to a quart/pint-pot realisation and decided to leave it open.

'Femoral artery. Just below the groin. It's the second largest artery in the body. Yasmin Ashmat reckons he'd have lost consciousness very quickly and, without immediate help, be dead within minutes.'

My dad came through holding a wooden rolling pin. 'Keep it down, will you? I don't want to spend the rest of the evening explaining groins and arteries to the bairn.'

'All right, all right,' I said. 'Point made. You can put the rolling pin away now.'

He came over and made to hit me. When I instinctively

raised my hands up to protect myself, he stuck the rolling pin between my legs and made a slashing motion, drawing it out across my right thigh.

'That's how they do it,' he said, cheerfully.

I backed away. 'That's how who do what?'

My dad held the rolling pin up to me. 'Imagine this isn't a rolling pin, it's a combat knife. And I'm not me, I'm a commando. That's how they teach us to kill folk in a knife fight, or when taking out sentries. Going for the neck is risky. The target is too small, and a person reacts instinctively to protect themselves, so it's hit and miss. A slashed inner thigh is unexpected, and all the blood gushing out causes a victim to go immediately into shock. No screaming, they just collapse and bleed out. Your great uncle Jim taught me that. Killed his fair share of Japs before they caught him and made him build that railway.'

Joanna wasn't quite so sure. 'You'd need to know what you were doing to kill someone that way.'

'My point exactly,' I said, or, at least, it was my point now. 'Shannon Todd might carry a blade occasionally, but I don't think she's been SAS trained.'

'She could have got lucky,' Joanna said, not wanting to dismiss her theory of Shannon as the murderer quite so easily.

'She'd also have needed a bloody sharp knife,' my dad said. 'Those commandos can shave with theirs.'

More grist to the defence mill. Where was Shannon Todd going to get a knife sharp enough to cut through a pair of jeans before it got to flesh? Yasmin Ashmat had said the cut was bone deep. I thought I'd lob another ingredient into the mix. 'One of the Crown pathologists reckons it could have been an accident. A broken bottle, something like that.' It was a possibility Yasmin had reluctantly conceded when I'd pressed her on the point. I'd yet to persuade her that perhaps Genghis could have rolled onto said broken bottle in a drunken stupor, but I'd work on it if, as I suspected, Shannon's alibi didn't hold water.

'*Were* there any broken bottles at the scene?' Joanna asked, trying to patch up the wound she'd unintentionally created in her imaginary Crown case.

'I don't have that precise information yet,' I said, hoping there were – so long as one of them wasn't a broken bottle of thirty-two-year-old Brora with my fingerprints on it.

'Are you two going or not?' my dad said, as if he and his rolling pin weren't responsible for our delayed departure.

Joanna gave me a peck on the cheek and took my hand, either out of affection or to make sure I didn't make a bolt for it. 'Let's go. It won't take long. Just a wee lecture from a midwife and a short film.'

'Enjoy yourselves,' my dad said. 'I was at Malky's birth. I wouldn't have missed it for the world.'

'What about mine?' I asked. 'Were you there?'

He threw my jacket to me. 'There was a break-in at the paper mill that night.'

'Oh, I see. You wouldn't have missed Malky's birth for the world, but you missed mine so that someone didn't make off with a pallet of A4?'

'Ach, your mum had the whole thing sussed by then, and,' he said summarising the field of obstetrics and midwifery, 'if you've seen one birth, you've seen them all.'

'Well, I've not seen one yet and neither has Robbie,' Joanna said, which was perfectly true. When Zoë Richards had abandoned me for Australia, over seven years before, little had I known she'd been carrying more than just her

64

suitcases. Halfway around the world from my daughter, I'd never known I was a father, not until after my ex-girlfriend's untimely death, when I'd found myself the single parent of a three year old. 'But ...' Joanna emphasised her words by tightening her grip and escorting me towards the front door, 'in four weeks' time, we're *both* going to.'

11

Grace Mary was waiting for me when I stumbled into the office the next morning. Joanna hadn't slept well. She'd tossed and turned with heartburn, and I'd had to get up in the middle of the night to spoon indigestion mixture into her. After that, she still couldn't sleep because she was too uncomfortable. It was a problem only resolved by commandeering my favourite pillow and placing it between her knees, while I was pressed into rubbing the small of her back for what seemed like hours.

'I don't suppose you actually went to the hospital last night,' my secretary said, setting a wire tray of mail on my desk. 'What excuse did you come up with this time?'

I could have feigned death and Joanna would still not have let me miss the antenatal tutorial, even if it had turned out to be more or less what I'd expected: a lecture from a midwife about breaking waters and contraction intervals, interspersed by warnings for mothers-to-be not to panic and advice to prospective fathers to offer support, but keep out of the way up at the speaking end. There was absolutely no mention of towels or kettles of boiling water. After that, there had been a video. I'd seen worse on the *Countryfile* Easter lambing special. 'I think I'm all set for the big day,' I said. 'What's in the diary?'

'Nothing much. Your two trials were both adjourned at their intermediate diets. Other than a five o'clock appointment, you're in the clear. It'll give you time to catch up.'

Five on a Friday. Great. 'Who's the appointment with?'

'A Mr Wallace.'

'Who is he, what does he want and why does he have to see me about it on a Friday afternoon?'

'He's a new client. I don't know. And because he finishes work early on a Friday.'

'Then phone him back and tell him so do I.'

Grace Mary made an executive decision to overrule me. She made several of those daily. 'I'll start cancelling clients when there are fewer red numbers on our ledger book.' With that, she left my room and returned to reception.

'Then you'd better buy us a new bottle of black ink,' I called to her. 'And while you're at it, score all my business out of the diary for the week after next.'

Grace Mary returned to my room bearing a puzzled expression and the big court diary. 'Score out an entire week? You're not taking another holiday, are you? Did you not have one of those a couple of years ago?'

I leaned over the desk and mimed a snooker shot. My cueing action may not have been entirely authentic because Grace Mary pulled me upright with the aid of my shirt collar and looked me in the eye. 'Have you been sniffing the yellow highlighters?'

I stepped away and straightened my shirt. 'We are now . . .' I said proudly, 'instructed in the case of Her Majesty's Advocate against Oscar Bowman.'

Once I'd confirmed that I was indeed referring to the person described by my secretary as *that nice wee lad on the telly who wins all the snooker games*, she drew a pen across the diary with a flourish. 'Will he be coming here to consult?' She glanced around the room, from the

67

ceiling with its fluorescent tubes in their yellowed-with-age casings, to the heaps of dead files stacked in a corner of the floor, to my rubber plant still stubbornly refusing to die at the side of my desk. 'Probably best if you met somewhere else.'

But I'd had all the meetings I was planning to have with the arrogant snot who was darling of the snooker world. The next time I planned on seeing him was in court.

'Who are you getting to do it?'

Grace Mary lifted the phone. I took it from her. 'I'm doing this case myself.'

'Don't you want me to give Miss Faye's clerk a call to see if she's available?'

I replaced the handset. Fiona Faye QC was my first choice in any High Court case where I could sweet talk the Scottish Legal Aid Board into sanctioning representation by senior counsel. But this wasn't a High Court case. These days – unless it was murder or rape – just about the only cases that made their way to the High Court of Justiciary were allegations of historical sex abuse, where elderly men tried to remember where they were, what they'd been doing and who they'd been doing it to, forty years previously. Oscar Bowman was to be tried before a sheriff and jury, and I believed there were some very good reasons why a solicitor like myself was preferable to a member of the Faculty of Advocates. It was horses for courses. The High Court was all wigs, white bow ties and brass collar-studs. Everyone held a great respect for one another. It was, '*If it please your Lordship this,*' and, '*My learned friend that.*' The place positively stank of good manners, chivalry and fair play. The Sheriff Court, where ninety-five per cent of Scotland's criminal cases were tried, was different: the trenches of Flanders as opposed to the playing fields of Fettes College. In the Sheriff Court, two sides, each regarding the other with ill-concealed disdain, shredded the evidence and pulled every stroke in the book to win, no matter the odds, the rules of procedure or the law. All done before a Sheriff who usually didn't know any better or couldn't care any less. When it came to a dogfight, you wanted a junkyard mutt, not Crufts' best of breed.

'It's really just so you can charge a big fee and keep it all to yourself, isn't it?' Grace Mary said, unsubtly suggesting a more mercenary reason for not employing counsel. I handed her a folded sheet of Peter Falconer Agency stationery. 'These are my consultation notes. Use them to start a new file.'

Grace Mary stared at the few lines of handwriting. 'This scribble is your consultation note?'

'You call it a scribble, I call it encryption. That's highly confidential information. I don't want just anyone reading it.'

'No fear of that,' she said, taking a cardboard folder from a drawer, punching a hole and clipping my notes inside. 'Now what?'

'Send a mandate to Liam Tait asking him to bundle up the papers for the Bowman case and send a courier for them, then draw up a witness list with Dr Yasmin Ashmat on it and send her a citation. After that, send the client a letter. Address it to his agent's office, the address is on that piece of paper. Tell him not to worry, defence preparations are underway and going well, blah, blah, blah. Tell him I'll see him in court nine-thirty sharp a week on Monday.'

Grace Mary looked at the folder. 'That it?'

'No. Remember to enclose my terms of business letter.'

'What hourly rate shall I say you're charging?'

I led her to the door. 'You're the one who knows how much red ink we have on the ledger. I suggest you dredge the extremes of your imagination, and when you've come up with a figure so ludicrous it makes your eyes water – double it.'

12

There wasn't much more I could do in either the Bowman case or Shannon Todd's, without sight of the prosecution evidence. There was, however, one thing that had really been bugging me about the latter. If Genghis McCann had been killed during some drunken argument, and Shannon's remarks to me on the day of his release from prison were anything to go by, it was all down to the valuable whisky he'd stolen. Or, rather, not stolen.

"Machseh" was a large detached country house on the outskirts of town, heading east. It was separated by large gardens from a couple of smaller properties that looked like former outbuildings converted into bungalows. One of them was empty, a for sale sign in a window that nobody could see from the main road. I lived just a mile or two away, and never even knew the place existed. It wasn't surprising that Genghis had become lost trying to track down Shannon's dog. It was hard enough for me to find the address I was looking for, and I wasn't stuffed full of benzodiazepine.

'I hope you don't mind me calling out of the blue,' I said, flashing my Law Society ID card at the man who answered the door. He was middle-aged, thick around the middle, with a good head of sandy hair that matched the beard into which he was cramming a sandwich.

He took another look at my ID card. 'A lawyer?' he

71

chomped, then stopped chewing. 'Are you from the Procurator Fiscal? Is this about the break-in? I thought it was all over and done with?'

'I'm not from the PF's office, and you're right, the break-in case is finished,' I said. 'There was just something I wanted to clear up.'

'Who is it, Reuben?' A woman's voice called from further inside the house. 'Is it the charity people?'

From somewhere behind me, a fluffy white dog came bounding down the garden path towards us in a state of frantic excitement. Ignoring me, it began jumping all over the man called Reuben.

'No, it's a man about work, Mrs Glowacki,' the man called back, crouching to give the dog a quick pat and then attempting in vain to shoo it away. 'Nothing for you today, Frosty. Come back tomorrow.' His efforts to get rid of the animal continued unsuccessfully until a woman, whom I took to be a neighbour, arrived on the scene, apologised, picked up the excitable bundle of fluff and carried it off in her arms.

'*Who* is it?' The woman's voice from inside called again.

Reuben sighed. 'It's just a man about work!'

'Tell him you're having lunch! And when the charity people get here, let them in.'

The man joined me outside, closing the door behind him and causing me to move off the doorstep onto a granite path that led down a river of pearl gravel to the roadway. 'I don't mean to be rude,' he said. 'It's Mrs Glowacki. She's ninety-one and every time anyone mentions the break-in she gets very upset.'

'I can understand that,' I said.

'Can you? If you're not from the Fiscal's office, I'm guessing you might be the lawyer for the man who broke in here. Cops said they'd got someone called McCann for it. I expect you're pretty pleased with yourself that he's getting off with it.'

Long ago, I'd stopped trying to explain to people that even criminal defence lawyers could find it within the darkness of their souls to sympathise with the victims of crime. 'I *was* his lawyer,' I said. 'He's dead now.' I thought that might cheer him up. It didn't. 'He was murdered. They've got someone for it.'

The man threw his head back and let out a moan. 'Oh, great. That's all we need. Now we're going to end up witnesses in a murder case.'

'I'll try my best to make sure that doesn't happen,' I said, graciously.

'Please do. For nights after the break-in Mrs Glowacki wouldn't sleep. She kept going on about the war and the Nazis. When she heard she might have to be a witness, it was all too much.'

'Are you her carer? Was it you who told the police nothing had been stolen?'

'Off the record?' he said. 'I really don't want this break-in thing to resurface.'

I told him there was no longer any record of house-breaking to be on. Nothing was reported stolen and the thief was now dead. There was more chance of the *Titanic* resurfacing.

'Good,' he said, 'because even the thought of having to go to court would be too much for Mrs Glowacki. It's what happens when you get old, I suppose – everything becomes a major worry. I didn't think it fair to put her through all that. Not for the sake of some property she'll never see again.'

'Then you've answered my question,' I said. 'I was

curious why someone would say nothing was stolen during a break-in, when I had good reason to believe there had been. That's all. When Mrs Glowacki gave a statement to the police, did they not tell her she could be excused attendance at court? Uncontroversial evidence is often agreed.'

'*Would* you have agreed it?' he asked.

The problem with agreeing the evidence of a civilian witness is that you are, in effect, agreeing to what is set down in their police statement. From experience, I knew that police officers tended to note down what they would like a witness to say, rather than what the witness actually did say.

'See what I mean,' he said, after I'd given him a smile so watery you could have floated a ship. 'Anyway, you say it's all over, so that's good. Though it would have been nice for Mrs Glowacki to get her property back. Your client helped himself to a lot of stuff. Items belonging to her husband who died just over a year ago. Mr G was a great guy. I used to take him down to the pub every Thursday night, and come over sometimes to watch the football with him.'

'Are you related?'

He laughed. 'I worked for Mr G for nearly thirty years, from when I left school at sixteen, and never once called him by his first name. He never asked me to. He was that kind of man. Demanded respect and deserved it. I took over running the business when he took ill and retired. I own it now. Well, half of it. Mrs G is a sleeping partner and likes to be kept up to date with how business is doing. We're not related, but I'm all the family she's got. She's in poor health and you'll have worked out that her hearing isn't great.'

'Her vocal cords seem fine,' I said.

He grunted good-naturedly. 'And she'd be a lot less deaf if she put her hearing aids in, but she thinks hearing aids are for old people.'

'What exactly was taken?' I asked. 'Off the record.'

'Your client broke in through the window of what was Mr G's study, where he kept some personal belongings. Nothing of huge value, just a few keepsakes.'

'Whisky?'

'He used to have quite a collection. He drank most of it. No point keeping it for someone else to enjoy after you've gone.'

'He could have left it to his wife, or to you.'

'Mrs G doesn't drink, and *whisky*? I hate the stuff.'

'It was valuable. You could have sold it.'

'You seem to know a lot about it.'

'Before you changed your mind on whether anything was stolen, I had some discussions with the Procurator Fiscal to see if he'd accept my client's plea of guilty to a lesser offence.'

'Why would he do that?'

'I was hoping to have my client return the property. The Crown prefers not to take matters to trial where possible. Even the most open and shut case can throw up evidential difficulties.'

'Like defence lawyers not agreeing evidence and the prosecution failing to bring scared, old ladies to court? I don't know how you people can live with yourselves, defending criminals.'

'Unfortunately, Mr ...'

'Berlow. Reuben Berlow.'

'Unfortunately, Mr Berlow, my clients don't come ready-labelled as criminals, and even those who should be, occasionally surprise me by being innocent.'

He took another bite of his sandwich. 'No offence,' he muttered through what looked like a tuna, mayonnaise and sweetcorn filling. 'I suppose you've got a job to do.' He glanced at his watch. 'And so do I.'

A charcoal Audi turned off the main road and up the long driveway, to park between mine and a small blue van. The curtains in a window of one of the distant houses twitched, and I saw a woman peer out, alongside her a small white furry face.

Two people alighted from the car and crunched their way across the gravel to the path, one male, one female, both smartly dressed, the man carrying an attaché case.

Reuben chewed some more, face twisting as though someone had slipped a slice of lemon into his sandwich. 'This'll be the people from the charity,' he said. 'Last time I checked, their CEO was taking home a six-figure salary. Look at the car they've come in. How much of Mrs Glowacki's money will make it to worthy causes, do you think?'

The new arrivals had lots of teeth and were putting them all on show as they approached. Reuben wiped crumbs from his beard, assembled what just about passed for a smile and pushed the door open for them.

They were met in the hallway by a sprightly old woman, face as wrinkly as a toe too long in the bath, her thin, incredibly black hair pulled tight and tied in a bun.

'Is it not time you were back at work, Reuben?' she told him rather than asked.

'On my way,' he said, as the door closed on us. 'And there you have it, Mr Munro. I hope that's solved the mystery for you. Wish I could say I was sorry about your client, but, if you live by the sword ...'

I could well understand his lack of sympathy, but

though Genghis McCann had been a thief and a junkie, he'd never, to my knowledge, raised a hand in anger towards anyone, far less a weapon. He'd left that sort of thing, if required, to his girlfriend.

The last morsel of sandwich disappeared into the beard. Reuben dusted his hands. 'Well, that's another fun-filled lunchtime over for me.' He opened the front door a crack, shouted a goodbye, and without waiting for a response, pulled a set of car keys from his pocket. We walked together to our vehicles. Reuben yanked open the door of the blue van, the Glowacki name and business address stencilled in gold on the side panels. I was climbing into my own car when I heard him call to me. 'If you have any idea at all what happened to the property, let me know, will you? It would really mean a lot to Mrs G. She might even let you keep the whisky as a reward.'

13

I didn't want the Glowacki whisky, which was just as well because I was pretty sure it had all been drunk. However, I did believe I knew where the other stolen belongings might be, plus I had Shannon Todd's alibi to check out.

It was my first visit to Davie Bell's place, though I knew he operated from a unit situated on land owned by my former landlord, frequent client, and full-time psycho, Jake Turpie. Bell's premises were built of breeze-block with a corrugated iron roof, orange with rust, and a solid wooden door that had once been painted green. The structure was surrounded by a ten-foot chain-link fence, the top of which was wrapped around with barbed wire. I'd been pacing the perimeter for ten minutes, trying to catch sight of the proprietor, when a pickup truck arrived in a cloud of dust and exhaust fumes. Jake Turpie jumped out and, hands stuffed into the pockets of an oil-stained boiler suit, sauntered over to me. 'Thought I recognised that old heap you drive.' That hadn't been quite how he'd described my 3 series when he'd sold it to me a couple of years before. "Classic and reliable" it had been then. So far, it hadn't let me down and I hadn't had to buy another. Maybe that's what annoyed him. Then again, Jake was never not annoyed, there were only varying degrees of annoyance. 'What are you wanting with Ding-Dong?' he asked, in his usual lovable way. 'Got some gear to sell him?'

'I just need a quick word with him about something. Is he in?'

'Soon find out,' Jake said. With a steel toecap, he dug up a boulder about the size of his fist from the rough track. He hefted it a couple of times to judge the weight and then hurled the stone up and over the barbed wire fence. After re-entering earth's atmosphere, the stone landed on the tin roof like a mortar-bomb, rattled its way down the slope until it bounced off the edge and onto something out of sight that, by the sound of things, had once been made of glass. It wasn't how they announced debutantes at the Queen Charlotte's Ball, but it did attract the requisite degree of attention. The door of the unit was thrown wide and our host charged out.

Davie Bell was a man whose idea of healthy eating was a bag of doughnuts with no jam in them, and the belly that protruded from beneath his grubby white T-Shirt was in a long-distance relationship with the top of his filthy jeans. By the angry look and open mouth, I could see he was ready to let fly a stream of expletives. That was, until he noticed the man at my side. It was all very well for Jake to be annoyed with people, but not for people to be annoyed with Jake. Fat Davie knew that. He also knew that while his facial features might not be to everyone's taste, appearing to be unhappy to see his landlord would put Jake to all the inconvenience of rearranging them. Davie's mouth closed, slowly transforming into a sickly smile. 'Good to see you, Jake. How's it going?' He unpadlocked the gate and let us in to a yard cluttered with old washing machines, sofas, mattresses, pallets of concrete slabs and reclaimed wood, a few rotting oak barrels and several crates of golf balls. 'What can I do you for?' he asked, pretending not to notice the smashed stack of double-glazed units propped against the side of his building, on which Jake's boulder-sized calling card had landed.

'We're here to ask you about Shannon Todd,' I said, hoping that aligning myself with Jake would put me in a better bargaining position.

'Who's she?' Jake asked, not helping.

'You'll have heard that Genghis McCann was killed the other night?' Fat Davie could muster only a shrug in reply, so I continued. 'It was on Tuesday. His girlfriend's in the frame for it and she says she was here at the time, trying to sell you stuff.'

The fat man grimaced and looked heavenwards at a sun that had decided breaking through the banks of cloud just wasn't worth the effort. He rubbed a few of his chins and shook his head. 'It's hard to remember that far back. I'd have to think about it.'

Ostensibly, Davie Bell was in the business of clearing houses. He had contracts with various private landlords, property developers and small-time business men who, whenever they needed a house or industrial unit cleared, gave him a shout. There was no fee for this service; instead, Davie kept the old furniture and any other unwanted moveables or equipment, which he then sold on. Davie's main occupation was as a receiver of stolen goods. No stranger to the Sheriff Court, for a fat man he'd managed to squeeze out of a lot of tight situations. When he wasn't being charged with possession of stolen property, Davie was often called by the Crown as a witness, especially in housebreaking cases, in the hope that he'd testify as to just who had brought him certain stolen items. His poor memory was legendary, but I was asking him about something that had happened three days ago, not to recall *The Thirty-nine Steps*.

I tried a different approach. 'What did you tell the cops?'

'Cops?' Jake pointed a finger in Davie's round face. 'You'd better not be bringing the polis here. I've warned you about that.'

Davie showed Jake the palms of his hands. 'I don't know what he's talking about, Jake. The cops haven't been anywhere near me.'

I wasn't enormously surprised that the police hadn't bothered to check into Shannon's alibi yet. They'd assume it was a lie and that Davie would be hopelessly lacking in credibility, even if he did give evidence in support of my client's defence.

'She tried to sell you some whisky. Ring any bells?' Not so much as a tinkle, apparently.

The whole thing was absolutely none of Jake's business, but he stared down at a steel toecap he was tapping on the ground impatiently, as though we were all guilty of wasting his valuable time. I thought I'd try and harness some of his simmering malevolence.

'The property was stolen from an old woman,' I said, reinforcing that with, 'who was ninety-one. What kind of a man takes property stolen from a ninety-one-year-old woman? What do you think, Jake?'

Jake looked up from his steel toecap tapping. 'Ninety . . . ?'

'Hold, on a minute,' Davie said. 'Is this about wee Shannon Todd? I think I do remember her being here.' He wiped sweat from his top lip, cleared his throat and croaked a laugh. 'She never said anything about an old woman, though. Honest, Jake.'

'What time was she here?' I asked.

'I locked up at the back of eight on Tuesday, and I

dropped her off at her pal's house, so she must have come here about half-seven, quarter to eight.'

'What happened to the stuff?' I asked.

'I never took anything off her. All she had was a bottle of whisky she'd already opened. I got some stuff from her junkie boyfriend the day before. It's still inside,' he said, jerking a thumb at the dilapidated unit. 'But, mind, I'm saying none of this in court.'

'All you might need to do is confirm the times you saw Shannon,' I told him. 'You don't need to say what about. Just that you were discussing business, she was here between about seven-thirty and ten past eight, and then you dropped her off at her pal's. Where was that, by the way?'

He gave me an address on the other side of town that would have taken at least another ten or fifteen minutes to get to by car. That was nearly an hour accounted for altogether.

'Are those times okay?' Davie asked Jake in a tone that suggested, if they weren't, other times could be made available.

I told him his times would have to do. Although Yasmin Ashmat had been helpful, the forensic pathologist had been unable to give me an accurate time of death. There were various calculations still to be carried out.

'Was there anything else, Jake?' Davie asked. 'Or can I get back to work?'

'Hold on,' I said. 'If you've still got the stuff, give it to me, and I'll take it back to the old lady. She's very upset about losing it. She's ninety—'

Horrified, Davie took a step back. 'I know, I know, you said how old she was, but I never knew whose stuff it was. I had to pay, twen … fifty quid for that gear. I've already texted photos of the stuff to my regulars.'

Jake frowned. 'The woman's ninety what?'

'Okay, tell you what I'll do,' Davie said, with a tight, little laugh. 'Thirty quid and it's yours, Robbie. That's fair. Come on, Jake. I'm trying to run a business here, and I've already got someone interested in buying the stuff.'

Jake wasn't listening to him. He turned to me, puzzled. 'So what if she's ninety odds? What difference does that make?'

Davie looked at me. Like many before him, he'd fallen into the trap of believing that Jake Turpie possessed a single scrap of human decency.

Jake pushed his face into mine. 'Why should he give the stuff back? The man's got a living to make.' It was my turn to be pointed at. 'You'd better not be bringing the cops here, bawheid. Me and Davie are business men. We're not needing the mob snooping around.'

The sound of tyres on the rough track came as a welcome distraction. Not so for Fat Davie, I noticed. In fact, he grew even more nervous as a battered Peugeot hatchback pulled up at the open gate and a couple of tracksuit clad youths alighted. One went to the back of the vehicle and popped the boot, while the other came down to meet us. Davie's sweaty top lip was now in competition with his brow.

'I've brought those alloys I telt you about,' the tracksuit said. 'It's okay, I never saw that fanny you told us to watch out for ...' The tracksuit looked from me to Jake and held his gaze there. By his change of expression, I assumed the description he'd been given of the fanny to watch out for fitted precisely the man standing beside me.

The first set of alloy rims clanged as they emerged from the boot of the car and were dropped onto the track.

'What did I tell you about dealing in parts for motors,

Fatty?' Jake asked, before Davie could stutter an excuse. 'I thought I told you that was never to happen again? You do the junk. *I* do the car parts.'

The tracksuit swaggered over to us, gallus and all ready with an explanation. The young man might have been a fast thinker, good on his feet, but neither his brain nor his feet were anywhere near as fast as Jake's left hook.

Jake stepped over the now prone, track-suited figure and took Davie by the front of his T-shirt. 'Help that other laddie put the alloys on the back of my pickup.' The fat man's frantic nodding and flapping jowls indicated his readiness to do as he was told. Jake pulled him closer, flecks of spittle spraying Davie's face. 'And then give that poor old woman her stuff back.'

14

Carrier bags. As a subject of great legal importance, they don't come up much during law lectures at university, but carrier bags, and especially the people who bring them to appointments, are one of the first things they warn you about in practice.

My five o'clock appointment arrived with one such bag crammed full of paperwork. He wanted to apply for the restoration of his driving licence. He'd been disqualified for life when in his twenties, after a string of motoring offences. Now, ten years later, approaching forty and a self-employed joiner, the ability to drive would be of great benefit to his business as well as his private life. From the bag he removed stacks of crumpled letters of thanks he'd received from various satisfied customers.

'I'll look at these later,' I said, pushing the thank you letters back into the carrier bag. Of more relevance than his joinery skills and happy customers, was the amount of time that had elapsed since the disqualification, and his lack of further offending. Those factors would decide whether a petition to the court to have his licence restored was likely to be looked upon favourably. Unless, that is, he was unlucky enough to have his application called before Sheriff Albert Brechin – a judge not inclined to give second chances.

'But what are the odds?' he asked.

'Reasonable,' I said. 'We can whack in a petition and fix a date for a hearing. The cops will come and speak to you and do a background report. After that, it's a case of me persuading the court that it would be in the interests of justice to let you drive again. How will you be paying?' A man with his own joinery business surely wouldn't qualify for legal aid.

'Paying for what?'

'For me to act on your behalf,' I said, in case he'd forgotten why he and his carrier bag were taking up office space at five o'clock on a Friday, with the weekend beckoning and my secretary already out of her blocks and away.

'No, that's okay,' he said. 'I'm not looking to hire a lawyer. I'm just after some advice.'

There were so many responses that sprang to mind. So few for which I wouldn't be arrested.

'That wouldn't work,' I said.

'No, it would,' he smiled, only too happy to explain the niceties to stupid old me. 'It's just legal stuff. If you tell me what I have to do and how to go about it, I can do it myself.'

I was going to suggest I order in a pile of wood, a hammer and some nails and have him come round to my place one evening to talk me through fitting a new kitchen. Instead, I told him to put his reasons down on a piece of paper and hand them into the Sheriff Clerk's office. It would save all the bother of having a legally qualified person draft a complicated legal document tailored to his particular circumstances. 'You'll need to pay the court dues for lodging the petition and serve it on the PF, but after that, a court date will be fixed and it'll just be a matter of persuading the Sheriff to grant your application,' I said, steering him towards the door. 'It's only legal stuff.'

'Will there be other people in the court?' he asked, as we walked downstairs to the front door. 'It's just that I'm not all that good on public speaking.'

I put his mind at ease. 'Don't worry, it'll just be you, the Sheriff, the clerk, a bar officer, a Procurator Fiscal – who'll try and talk the Sheriff out of granting your petition – a few solicitors, maybe some newspaper people, social workers, cops and, of course, the general public.' I opened the door and showed him onto the High Street where I shook him by his now sweaty hand. 'And when you speak to the Sheriff Clerk,' I said, with a wink, 'ask for your case to be set down for Sheriff Brechin's court.'

The phone was ringing when I returned to my office. 'Robbie, old boy. Hoped I might catch you before you disappeared off for the weekend.'

It took me a moment or two to recognise the owner of the jovial voice on the other end of the line. 'Professor Bradley, is that you?'

'Robbie, please. How long have we known each other? It's Edward, and I've been sitting here thinking how rude I was to you yesterday. After all, you only wanted a little information.' He sighed. 'It's just that I'd had such a busy morning, and when you're having to babysit people . . . well, you know how it is. You've a daughter.'

He was right, I did have a daughter. But she was a seven-year-old schoolgirl, not a twenty-eight-year-old, fully qualified, forensic pathologist. In other words, she wasn't Dr Yasmin Ashmat, because she, I strongly suspected, was the reason for the phone call. When, in his long career, had Prof B ever apologised to me or to anyone else for that matter? No, Yasmin had told him about Oscar Bowman's case, and this was him trying to muscle her out of the deal.

'I understand perfectly,' I said. I couldn't tell him what I'd learned from Yasmin without landing her in trouble, but even though she'd given me the cause of death, I still didn't have a timing, which would be all important when it came to establishing Shannon Todd's alibi. 'I'll get the information I want all in due course as you said. It's not as if my client's going anywhere, and they won't start the trial without letting me see your report.'

'Yes . . .' the professor agreed. 'It's been dictated and out for typing. Maybe I could give you a heads-up on a few things though: cause of death for instance.'

'I'm more interested in the time of death,' I said.

There was a short pause, during which I thought I could hear the professor's teeth grinding. If the Crown had made him aware of my client's position, he'd know that by telling me the time of death it would greatly assist in preparing an alibi defence if, as he no doubt believed, I was intent on concocting one.

'It's not that easy to assess,' he said at last. 'We know McCann was alive at around noon on the Tuesday, because he got out of jail and spoke to a few people when he got off the bus. He was found about six-thirty the following morning, wasn't he?' He had been. The average junkie is an early riser. A member of the dawn brigade, up and about and looking for their breakfast fix, had walked into Genghis's house on spec and found him lying in a pool of blood in the kitchen. 'That's an eighteen-hour window I'm having to work with.'

'Oh, well, if you can't help . . .'

'No, no, I can make an educated guess. It helps when you have my level of experience in relation to muscle behaviour and that type of thing. Let me check my notes ... Yes, I see that livor was well established when I was called out at eight o'clock, with no suggestion the body had been moved. Rigor was poorly developed in some of the larger muscle groups, so by my way of thinking, that would put time of death certainly no earlier than midnight. Temperature wise, the house was a reasonable eighteen degrees Celsius. The body was down to around twenty-five degrees when I came on the scene, so on a rough 1.5° loss per hour, I'd say we were looking at midnight or an hour or two after. Does that help?'

'Not really,' I said.

'Oh, then, if you like, I'll run some more tests and we can discuss them later.' He laughed, which was when I knew for certain something was wrong. 'You know, after all our years working together, that I'm always at your beck and call.'

'Thanks. I'll take you up on that,' I said.

'When?' the professor asked, almost before I'd got the words out.

'Sometime before the trial, when everything is a little clearer.'

'And by *the trial* you mean ...'

'The murder trial. The one we're talking about.'

'Oh, not the ...'

'No, not Oscar Bowman's trial, the high publicity trial in which I have instructed your colleague, the one you babysit, as my expert witness. Don't try and pretend this isn't what you phoning to apologise is really all about.'

'That's an outrageous accusation.'

To answer the professor's earlier question, I had known him for nearly fifteen years, and during that whole time I'd never known him to be deliberately helpful to any defence case. The only reason I tried to instruct him whenever possible was so the Crown wouldn't, and because, with a reputation such as his, any point favourable to the defence that I did manage to drag out of him, was usually enough on which to hang a reasonable doubt.

'Listen,' I said. 'I've instructed Yasmin and I'm not going back on my word. She's explained everything to me. All about myo ...'

'Myoclonus? This snooker fellow, has he health problems? Any early signs of dementia, Parkinson's, epilepsy, brain tumour?'

Not that I knew of.

'What about drug or alcohol withdrawal?'

'Definitely not.'

'In which case, it's my opinion this theory you and the pipsqueak are hatching is complete nonsense.'

'Then it's just as well no one's asking for your opinion,' I said. 'I'll give you a shout when I need more information on my murder case. Meanwhile, I look forward to receiving your report.'

'Oh, you'll have my report, all right,' he said. 'In fact, I'll tell my secretary to make it high priority. Right after everything else she has to type.'

15

It's a great feeling. That moment when you awake thinking it's time to get up and go to work, and then realise it's Saturday morning and you don't have to. It's a feeling of serenity, peacefulness and pure relaxation that's difficult to shatter. But a seven-year-old child dive-bombing your serene, peaceful and relaxed abdomen will give it a go.

'Mum wants to speak you,' Tina yelled in my ear, pushing her face against mine and recoiling from the jagginess of my unshaven jaw. She rolled onto the side that Joanna had vacated, stood up and started bouncing around. 'She's in the kitchen! She wants to speak to you and then you've to take me to dance class because gramps is playing golf and she has to stay home with the baby in her tummy.'

Clothed and in my right mind, I found Joanna sitting at the kitchen table with her iPad in front of her. She stopped spooning Ovaltine granules into her mouth when I came into the room and shoved the jar at me. 'Take it away before I eat any more,' she said, as if her Ovaltine addiction was down to me.

I screwed the lid back on. 'Was there anything else?' I asked, having returned the jar to the kitchen cupboard.

'Yes.' Joanna swivelled the tablet to face me. 'They didn't even have the decency to send me a letter.'

I sat down and pulled the iPad towards me. The email

was from the HR department of the Crown Office and Procurator Fiscal Service, who were sorry to advise Joanna that her contract with them would not be renewed.

'They can't do that,' I said. 'Not while you're pregnant.'

She picked up her teaspoon and licked it. 'They can. My contract finishes in a month's time. I'm going to be paid full salary up to the end of it. There's nothing I can do. I've not been employed two years yet. My previous tenure was broken when I left to work with you and so doesn't count. They also say it's down to restructuring of the organisation due to the fall in prosecutions, and that there's a last-in-first-out policy in place. They'll consider me for a further contract should a need arise in the future.'

I read the email to the end. She was right. They'd really nailed down all the corners of her dismissal. I still didn't understand. 'How can they possibly be letting you go? Are they crazy? Name a better trial depute than you. There isn't one. Still, if that's how it's going to be, you'll just have to come and work for ... I mean, *with* me. Probably for the best with the new baby. We can be flexible.'

'Grace Mary won't like it. You know what she thinks about husbands and wives working together,' Joanna said.

I pushed the iPad back across the table to her. 'Let's remember that Grace Mary's my secretary and not the boss.'

Joanna tried to cover up a laugh with the clearing of her throat and by muttering something about Ovaltine sticking in it.

'Okay,' I said, 'let's *pretend,* just for a moment, that Grace Mary isn't the boss. She's not always right – no, stop looking at me like that, she isn't. You and I worked for years together—'

'Before we were an item,' Joanna rightly pointed out.

'And there was no problem then—'

'Because you were my employer and always got your own way. Sending me off to do no-hoper trials all the time, and you know the kind of hours I had to put in. Are you telling me it's going to be different this time?'

I'd always thought Joanna and I to be the perfect match. I believed I was right about everything; she knew I wasn't. This time, I had to agree with her. I had scarcely enough business to keep myself going, far less take on a partner. 'There's plenty of time to assess our options,' I said. 'For the next few months, you're going to be busy enough being a mum.'

Joanna put a hand on my arm. 'Our credit card is maxed, Robbie. All the stuff I've bought for the baby ... I couldn't help myself.'

I went over and put an arm around her. 'We'll manage. Business is already picking up, and I'm thinking of ditching legal aid cases altogether. Grace Mary keeps going on about it. She calls it working smart, not hard.'

'Take on only private cases? What happened to Robbie Munro, man of the people?'

'He's now Robbie Munro, man with a wife and soon-to-be two kids, none of which he can afford to keep on legal aid rates.'

'Still ... only private work – you could have stayed at Caldwell & Craig and—'

'And I'd never have met you.' I kissed her worried face. 'Look on the bright side. This Bowman case will be worth a few quid, and it's just what I need to boost my reputation.'

'That's if he doesn't sack you first,' Joanna said.

'He's not going to sack me. He's dead against an

adjournment, and there's no time between now and the trial for him to start instructing a new solicitor.'

'No adjournment?' Joanna went over and took the jar of Ovaltine down from the cupboard. 'You can't possibly prepare for a case like that in a week. Have you even had a proper look at the evidence yet?'

It was true. Other than having brought home the DVDs Peter Falconer had given to me and watching them a few times with my dinner on my knee and Tina jumping around in front of the TV, there hadn't been a huge amount of preparatory work done.

'I haven't seen *all* the evidence,' I conceded. 'I've seen most of the video clips, though. What more can there be to see? Some statements from a series of has-beens or never-wazzers saying that Bowman's misses were deliberate?' Once I'd found out who exactly was on the Crown witness list, I'd spent a couple of hours researching YouTube to find clips of their sporting bloopers, as well as footballers missing open goals, track runners tripping up, baseball players bumping into each other ... perhaps I'd just play the jury Dire Straits' "Walk of Life" video and sit down. 'He might be a famous sportsperson, Jo, but Oscar Bowman is a human being – even if he tries to give the opposite impression. He's fallible like the rest of us. He pots some, he misses some. Who never makes a mistake? There's your reasonable doubt right there.'

'Robbie, I've heard the commentators. They don't describe him as human, they describe him as a machine.'

'Don't worry. If that doesn't work, I've got an ace up my sleeve,' I said.

'And what might that be?'

'It's not a what, it's a who. Dr Yasmin Ashmat will give evidence to say that Bowman's misses could be down to muscle twitching due to pressure. Myo ... something.'

'Myoclonus?'

My wife never ceased to amaze me. 'You've heard of it?'

'Yes, involuntary muscle twitches and spasms. It's one of the things they tell you to watch out for when you're pregnant. Especially in the later stages. Abdominal myoclonus is sometimes mistaken for contractions or kicks but can be symptoms of something more serious.'

'You haven't had them, have you?'

'No, thankfully, but unless Oscar Bowman's in the family way, why has he got them?'

'I'm not completely unprepared,' I said.

'Don't tell me. You've been googling?'

'It's a legitimate form of research and from it, I have discovered that Myo-whatsit can be brought on by stress or even nothing at all. Eye-twitching, hiccoughs, they're all forms of it and can strike at any time,' I said.

'Except,' Joanna countered, 'Bowman only suffers from it during certain frames of snooker where there are thousands of pounds bet against him winning?'

Tina marched into the kitchen wearing a pair of multi-coloured dance joggers and a starry T-shirt that was on the wrong way round. She demanded to know what was for breakfast.

I ruffled Joanna's hair. 'You're sacked from the Fiscal Service. If you're going to work for me—'

'With you.'

'I'm going to need less criticism and more support. Or maybe, seeing as how you know so much about muscle twitching, you should do the trial. You could really play on the sympathies of the jury. I'm not saying your waters would have to break during the closing speech, but, if you could see to it that they do, I'm sure it would help.'

Joanna levered herself to her feet using the back of the chair. 'It's not funny, Robbie,' she said, whisking off Tina's T-shirt, birling it the right way and pulling her arms through. 'We've no money, and the one case that might bring us in some extra cash, as well as build up your reputation, you're not taking at all seriously. You can't just waltz into the courtroom, show the jury a funny video, let them hear the opinion of an inexperienced doctor and expect to win.'

'But I can do that,' I said, 'because dance is in my blood.' And bringing the conversation to an end, I took Tina's hands in mine and together we waltzed out of the kitchen.

16

Monday and Tuesday, I spent watching footage of snooker matches, catching up with paperwork and battling with the Scottish Legal Aid Board. Wednesday, I was trying to find my files for court when Grace Mary came into my room for her daily update on the Munro foetus. I told her that apart from the fact that, rather than awaiting normal delivery, he or she seemed intent on kicking their way out of Joanna, everything was fine.

Grace Mary located in ten seconds some files I'd spent the last ten minutes hunting for and handed them over. 'I forgot to ask. How did your late Friday afternoon appointment go?'

'It didn't,' I said. 'Another client not in need of any actual legal assistance – only a spot of free advice. How about you vet these time-wasters more closely before they have me spending Friday afternoons listening to them? If they're not eligible for legal aid, ask for money up front. Ever been to the dentist? They keep you strapped in the chair with the drill buzzing until they've emptied your pockets. You need to stop being so soft.'

'I'm soft? You're the one who insists on doing legal aid work. I've told you before. If you don't want to waste time, start picking and choosing the cases you do. Find more cases like that snooker one. Do less for more. It's called—'

'I know. I know. Working smart. But what happens to people who can't afford a lawyer?'

'Why's that your problem? What are you running here – a charity?'

'Okay,' I said. 'For a trial period, unless it's one of my regulars, new clients are going to have to dig deep and pay private fees.'

'Does that include your six o'clock appointment?'

'When? Tonight?'

'Yes, tonight. Don't make a face. It's Wednesday. You moan if I give you a Friday afternoon appointment because it's the weekend, and you moan if you have to see someone late on a Monday because it's too soon after the weekend. So, I've made you a late Wednesday appointment. Sorry if I've ruined two weekends for you.'

It was true. Lately, I had stopped putting the hours in when really I should have been working more. The problem was the general lack of business and the morale-sapping legal aid fees.

'And what are you going to do about this thing?' she asked, giving the large cardboard box at the side of my desk a prod with her toe. It was the stuff I'd got from Davie Bell. I'd meant to deliver it to its rightful owner by now but had never got around to it. 'What's in it, anyway?' She opened the box and rummaged through an assortment of whisky collectables: hip flasks, quaichs, Glencairn glasses, a crystal water jug and decanter in a satin-lined presentation box, polished oak stave glass holders, various porcelain ornaments, including Johnnie Walker's walking man and the Black and White Scotty dogs, a grimy oil painting of three codgers drinking out of wide-brimmed glass goblets, a framed print of Easter Elchies House and umpteen single malt miniatures and various other odds and ends. After a quick look at the contents, she closed it again. 'Get this box of junk shifted or I'll end up tripping over it and breaking my neck.'

Up until then, I hadn't realised that was an option.

Grace Mary dropped the big black diary on the desk. 'This appointment tonight. He says he's an old client of yours from your Glasgow days with Caldwell & Craig. For some reason, he speaks very highly of you. I don't suppose you'll remember him after this length of time.'

But my secretary was underestimating the Robbie Munro powers of recollection. Somewhat suspect though they might be when it came to less important matters, such as the law and procedure, for clients who liked to pay for legal services handsomely and in cash? Well, those were the sort of clients who I found stuck most in my mind.

I recognised Elliot Holliday's face the moment he walked through the door, even if it was fifteen years older and looking a lot less worried. It was one of those faces that was hard to forget. A mass of dark hair, now greying at the temples, heavily-lidded eyes, a slight hook to his nose, thin lips and cleft chin. Even as a fully paid-up member of the heterosexual male club, I had to admit he was one handsome devil.

'Remember me?' he asked.

I did. Very clearly. How could I have forgotten him, or the when and why we'd first met?

The when was during my legal traineeship. After the years of hard toil at law school – drinking, lounging about and chasing girls can take its toll on the young male student – like every other would-be solicitor, I'd had to find myself a two-year traineeship. Mine was spent in the wood-panelled offices of Caldwell & Craig. The venerable old Glasgow law firm had decided that the one arrow missing from its quiver of services was a solicitor prepared to soil his hands in the grimy business of criminal law. And so started a career with Caldwell & Craig that lasted as long as it took the other partners to realise that if crime meant legal aid, and it usually did, then crime didn't pay.

The why was slightly more difficult to explain. Generally speaking, Caldwell & Craig's newest recruit had not been allowed anywhere near matters of civil law, but late one Friday afternoon, with most of the partners long gone and the support staff under starter's orders, my immediate superior, Maggie Sinclair, was happy to make an exception in exchange for a flying start on the weekend.

'I think he's some kind of a travelling salesman,' she'd said, in the tone of one who suspects the man in the waiting room, drinking the complimentary coffee, might be a cholera carrier. 'See what he wants and then get rid of him.' To sweeten the deal, Maggie had offered me the use of her office, a large room filled with law books, period furniture and works of art. My own office was a lot smaller, and mostly filled by a broken photocopier the firm hadn't worked out how to dispose of yet. Maggie's chair was padded and comfortable. It swivelled and reclined. Like her desk, all teak and tooled green leather, it had come from Sotheby's. My desk and chair had come from IKEA with assembly instructions someone hadn't read properly. I'd jumped at the chance to pretend to be a real lawyer.

'Tell me why you're here, Mr Holliday.' The young Robbie Munro reclined in his boss's big black chair and stared out of a rain spattered window at the bustle of the Merchant City.

'I've had a curse put on me. I want you to take it off,' wasn't the answer I'd been expecting. I took a moment to mull it over . . . Nope, I'd skipped a fair few law lectures in my time, but still, I was reasonably sure curse removal hadn't been part of the University of Edinburgh's law curriculum. I mulled some more, and then with pursed lips and a sage nod of the head, came back with a considered, 'Eh?'

It transpired that Maggie's suspicions had been correct. My client did indeed do a lot of travelling: going house-to-house buying unwanted items, and then selling the property from a second-hand shop on the Great Western Road. His problems had started when he'd been visiting a travellers' site and become over friendly in a caravan with a seventeen-year-old girl whose grandmother had arrived unexpectedly to put an abrupt interruptus to the ongoing coitus, in a manner only unexpectedly-arriving grandmothers can.

'She cursed me. She said that all my luck would be bad luck, and I'd die a bloody death.'

I asked him to wait and went through to speak to Maggie who was putting her coat on while trying her best not to be spoken to.

'Tell him you need money up front to get started,' was my superior's take on things once I'd summarised the client's predicament. 'Quote a ridiculous fee. That'll get rid of him. Oh, and another thing . . .' Buttoning up her raincoat, she marched to the door with me following, hoping she might spill a few more pearls of wisdom on the way. 'The air freshener is in the bottom right drawer of my desk.' And, with that parting advice, she disappeared off for the weekend.

I returned to find my client waiting patiently. He looked

to be in his late twenties or early thirties, smartly dressed in a checked suit with a felt collar. At the time, my salary had netted me just under one thousand pounds a month. I thought two thousand pounds a ridiculous enough fee and was busy explaining the prohibitive cost of curse removal court actions when he lifted a carrier bag from the floor and began pulling out rolls of twenty-pound notes, each bound by a single, red rubber band.

'Seems fair enough,' he said, placing four of them on the desk. 'Let me know if you need more.'

And so, having transferred the worried expression from his face to mine, Elliot Holliday left, leaving me armed with wads of cash, the promise of more, and no idea as to how to go about earning it. After a weekend's careful thought and a search through Gloag & Henderson on the Law of Scotland, which had carelessly omitted a chapter on curse law, first thing Monday morning I'd raised an interdict action against Granny, preventing her from approaching, molesting or verbally abusing my client, making threats or invoking curses. This last part of the crave was viewed askance by the Sheriff at the first calling, but since interim orders were made on a balance of convenience, and there being no prejudice to Granny were she to be temporarily stopped from throwing curses about, the interdict was granted pending a Proof several months hence. It was the hence part I was worried about, for while my manoeuvres might, at least for the time being, prevent Granny issuing further curses on pain of a contempt of court charge, I had no idea what my next step in litigation should be to have the curse withdrawn or how anyone could prove it had been withdrawn. Was there a ceremony involving black cats or something? That was when good fortune struck. Fortune, of course, being a relative thing. Good luck for one person is often bad luck for another. One person's gain, another's loss. One person's curse removal, another person's freak accident at the Appleby Fair. A horse had bolted, knocked Granny over and killed her outright. I was undeserving of any credit, if indeed credit was due, but my client thought otherwise. On hearing the news, he returned and paid me another two thousand in cash. I'd thought the initial payment sufficient fee for Caldwell & Craig, especially given my employer's reluctance to take on the case, and so accepted the second instalment as a gift and put it towards a deposit on my first flat.

Fifteen years on, Elliot Holliday was still the man I remembered, even if today he didn't have a carrier bag with him. He reached inside his jacket and produced a wallet that would have been classed as excess luggage by a budget airline. 'You did the business for me the last time,' he said. 'I need your help again.'

17

'He offered you *how* much?' Joanna asked after I returned from dropping Tina off at her Wednesday night dance class.

My daughter had swapped football for dancing, which I thought a shame and my dad a tragedy, because she'd been something of a star at the fun-four-a-sides. Poise-wise, she had inherited none of her Uncle Malky's genes. Big galoot though he was, on the pitch my brother had great balance, sailing through matches, effortlessly changing direction, sending opponents the wrong way. Tina could scarcely walk along a pavement without falling off, but with the ball at her feet she could charge through the opposition and smash in the goals, much in the same way as she charged about our house smashing ornaments.

The first time I'd taken Tina to the dance studio, I'd been interested to see how she'd fare in her new pastime. It hadn't taken long to realise that my daughter was never going to pass the Bolshoi auditions, though grape-treading was a definite career option. So, leaving the little girls in their tutus and leotards, I returned home to where our spare bedroom was being transformed into a nursery. The electricity was off at the mains and Joanna was shining a torch while holding the legs of the stepladder on which my dad was perched, as he secured a new light-fitting to the ceiling. I wasn't permitted anywhere near electrical circuitry any more. Not since what had become known in the Munro household as the Great Christmas Blackout of 2018, when I'd almost fried myself with a set of tree lights.

'Two thousand pounds,' I repeated.

Joanna shone the torch in my face. 'For a box of odds and ends?'

'Shine that thing up here,' my dad called down to her.

'You can't take the money, obviously,' Joanna said, swinging the beam ceiling-ward.

I was wondering why it really was quite so obvious, when my dad clattered down the shoogly set of aluminium stepladders, walked to the light switch and turned it on with a confidence I could never muster after a DIY electrical job. If it was me, I'd have donned protective clothing, rubber-soled shoes and switched the light on with a broom handle.

'That's it,' he said with satisfaction as the room illuminated. 'What's next?'

Joanna took him by the arm. 'That's enough for tonight, Alex. Come through the room and have some of Robbie's birthday whisky. He can drop you off on the way back for Tina.'

'Joanna's right, by the way,' my dad said, sitting at the fire holding a glass of my whisky that had been poured by my wife's overgenerous hand. 'Bottom line, it's not yours to sell. It's stolen property. You'll have to take it back to the owner.'

'Okay,' I said. 'Let's take a moment, step back and break that statement down.'

Joanna hammered the cork back into the whisky bottle. Maybe one day I'd get a chance to sample my birthday present.

'There is nothing to break down,' she said.

'Hold on,' I told her. 'Even Sheriff Brechin lets me make legal submissions. He might ignore them, but—'

'Go on, then,' my dad said. 'You try and explain why keeping someone else's stolen property isn't theft.'

'That's precisely my point,' I replied. 'Was the property actually stolen?'

Joanna had definite views on that. 'Yes, it was. Your client broke in through a window and took it away. I'd say that makes it about as stolen as property gets.'

'What if the owner doesn't care or was happy to have the stuff removed?'

My dad had been listening in to my earlier conversation with Joanna far too carefully. 'I thought you said she wanted it back?'

'Let's stick to the legalities,' I said. 'Her carer told the PF there was nothing stolen.'

'But there was,' wife and father said in unison.

'Not in the eyes of the law.'

'But the property still exists. It must belong to someone,' Joanna said.

I had an answer for that too. 'Not necessarily. Not if we look at it as abandoned property. You don't think the bin men steal the rubbish in the wheelie bin every four weeks, do you?'

'Used to be every week,' my dad said.

Joanna tried to interrupt my flow, but I didn't give her a chance. 'The person who ended up with the gear is a man who clears houses for a living, and sells property the owners don't want. I had to pay him thirty quid for it. Which must mean I am now the rightful owner of this abandoned property.'

'Legally, all abandoned property belongs to the Crown,'

Joanna said. 'Even the rubbish in the wheelie bin.'

'Well, if you don't tell the Queen, I won't either,' I said.

My dad refuelled himself with a large sip of my whisky. 'What was your reason for buying the stuff?'

I hesitated.

Joanna was right in there. 'You bought it with the intention of returning it to the owner, didn't you?' That had been my plan, but I had no time to confirm or deny the position, because Joanna followed up with, 'You were all set to give the property back, and then someone offered you a lot of money, so now you're trying to weasel your way out of doing what you know is the right thing. Is that really the price of your principles – two thousand pounds?' She rubbed her bump, as though consoling her unborn child for having such a reprobate as a father. She looked at her watch. 'You'll need to go for Tina in ten minutes.'

My dad knocked back the rest of the whisky and looked around for the bottle. Ten minutes was plenty of time for the other half of his dram. 'Well?' he asked, as Joanna squeaked the cork from the bottle and poured him another. 'What are you going to do, Robbie?'

I was going to think about it, but Joanna had already thought about it for me. 'He's going to give it back, that's what he's going to do. Ask the real owner to reimburse you the thirty pounds if you must, Robbie, but give it back.' She came over and stared me in the eye.

'All right,' I said, 'I'll give it back.'

Joanna kept staring. 'Promise?'

'Why do I always have to promise everything? Isn't my word good enough?'

I heard my dad splutter into his whisky glass as I walked through to the kitchen to fetch my car keys.

On my return, Joanna and the bump were blocking the doorway. 'Are you going to promise or not?'

'Okay, okay,' I said, pecking her cheek and moving her to the side. 'I promise.'

Joanna stepped into my path again. ' . . .Not to sell the stolen property.'

I put up my right hand. 'Not to sell the stolen property.'

Which wasn't going to be easy, because I already had half the cash in my back pocket.

18

After last Friday's call, I hadn't expected to hear from Professor Bradley for quite some time, but he phoned first thing Thursday as I was preparing to leave for court and Shannon Todd's full committal hearing.

'Have you received the report yet?' he asked.

'The autopsy report on George McCann? I'm not expecting that for weeks. Is it even typed?'

'Not *that* report. The pipsqueak's report on the snooker player.'

As a matter of fact, I had. Yasmin had emailed it to me overnight. It was brief, but the contents extremely helpful and precisely along the lines I'd suggested to her.

'I might have. Why do you ask?'

'Because I've read it. It's waffle and incredibly vague,' he said, as though vague waffle wasn't what I looked for most when it came to evidence. It was lurking within the miasma of vagueness and waffle that reasonable doubts could be found.

'I'm a defence lawyer, give me ambiguity or give me something else,' I said.

It was one of my better lines, at least I thought so. The man on the other end of the phone gave it no acknowledgement other than an impatient clearing of his throat. 'Don't do this, Robbie. I know your game.'

What was he talking about? 'Look, Ed—'

'It's Professor Bradley to you.'

He really was taking my decision not to instruct him in the Bowman case badly. I had another go. 'Professor Bradley, I came to see you this time last week—'

'In order to try and obtain confidential information.'

'That's right,' I said. 'Information you have now provided me with, and which somehow no longer seems quite so confidential. I'm sorry, but as I've already told you – I've instructed Yasmin Ashmat on this one, and, from a quick look at her report, I'm glad I have. Perhaps if you hadn't refused to talk to me, I'd have asked for an opinion from you.'

'No, you wouldn't.'

'What makes you think that?' I said.

'Because you know I'd see this line of defence for what it is – a load of unmitigated tosh.'

'Yasmin doesn't seem to think so, and she's got nearly as many letters after her name as you. The jury will love her.'

'You're using that girl.'

'She's not a girl. She's a woman and, more importantly, a forensic pathologist who says that in her opinion, under times of extreme anxiety, it is possible that my client may have suffered involuntary muscle spasms.'

'In the bicep?'

'Could happen.'

'And this spasming bicep of his. It causes your client to miss shots he would otherwise pot with ease, does it?'

He was catching on fast.

'We're talking about professional snooker players. It only takes one bad miss to lose a frame,' I said.

'Yasmin hasn't given evidence before.'

'Then she'll be fresh and her natural self. A jury can

relate to that. The young doctor doing her best to tell it as it is.'

'But she's not telling it as it is. You've talked her into telling it as you'd like it to be. She'll be torn apart by the prosecution.'

'She'll cope.'

'You're not at all bothered, are you? Just because you don't care about your own reputation, there's no need to ruin hers.'

Things were getting a wee bit personal now. I did care about my reputation. It was a defence lawyer's reputation and little else that brought in business. 'I like to think my reputation is that I fight for my clients and win more often than I lose.'

The professor snorted. 'And at any cost to anybody who's not your client.'

It was nine-thirty. I'd be lucky to make it to court by ten. 'Sorry about the way things have turned out,' I said. 'I'll be sure to keep you in mind as an expert witness in my next media-sensational trial.'

'Robbie . . .'

'I've got to go.'

'What if I gave you some more confidential information on your murder case? Would that help change your mind?'

Had I not made myself clear? Other than send a plane to sky-write it over Edinburgh, how could I make myself any clearer? I tried again. 'Your colleague, Dr Yasmin Ashmat, has been sent a citation to attend court as an expert witness for the defence in the case against Oscar Bowman. I am not going to instruct you in this case. Get over it.'

'I don't want to be instructed by you, and I most

certainly do not wish to be a witness for the defence.'
The professor was sounding nearly as exasperated as I
was feeling.

'Then why are you phoning me?'

'So that you'll countermand Yasmin.'

'Why would I do that? I have her report lying on my
desk and, believe me, it's everything I dreamt it would
be.'

'What if I gave you information that might clear your
Todd woman of the murder? Would that make you
reconsider?'

He was a trier, I'd give him that much, but the fact
of the matter was that Oscar Bowman's case and that
of Shannon Todd were in no way related. Why should
helpful information on Shannon Todd's case cause me to
discard Yasmin Ashmat's helpful information on Oscar
Bowman's? Did the professor think I would pick one
client over the other? There was absolutely no chance of
me not calling Yasmin as a witness; however, he didn't
need to know that.

'Try me,' I said.

'The toxicology report on George McCann was negative for opiates or any other prescribed drugs, but there
was a substantial amount of alcohol in his system. And
that's not the interesting part.'

I hoped not. I already knew that Genghis and Shannon
had cracked open and consumed all but an inch of thirty-
two-year-old Brora single malt.

'Shannon Todd was apprehended at a friend's house
mid-morning, a couple of hours after McCann's body was
found.'

I really wished he'd spit it out. I was never going to
make it to court on time at this rate. 'So?'

'So, her blood alcohol reading was sky high; somewhere between level five and six.'

There are seven recognised levels of alcohol intoxication. Level one: sobriety; level two: euphoria; level three: excitement; level four: confusion; level five: stupor. According to the professor, Shannon Todd was somewhere between that and level six: coma, when taken into police custody and from there to hospital. The only level after that was seven: death.

The professor continued. 'On a count-back from her hospital-admission alcohol reading, there is no way she could have murdered anyone from around 10 p.m. onwards. She wouldn't have been able to walk or control her bodily functions, far less wield a knife. Do we have a deal? I can set all that out in a written opinion, and if it doesn't get your girl released sharpish, I'd be very much surprised.'

He really did think I'd ruin one client's chances in favour of another. Perhaps it was because for one client the downside was loss of face and occupation, while for the other it was loss of liberty, potentially for the rest of her life.

'You're right, that is very helpful information,' I said. 'And I'd be very grateful if you would set it down in an opinion, but I'm not selling one client down the river for the sake of another. You might not think much of my reputation, but I have some principles.'

'Last chance,' he said. 'Do you want my toxicology opinion or not?'

I'd obtain those toxicology results with or without his assistance. If need be, Yasmin Ashmat could opine on those too.

'Have you ever heard of attempting to defeat the ends

of justice?' I asked. 'Try and withhold that information and it'll be you needing a defence lawyer.'

'How dare you! I am simply trying to prevent you from making a fool of my colleague, and of yourself, by leading this spurious myoclonus defence. Do what I tell you for the sake of your own reputation, if not for Dr Ashmat's – whose head you have obviously turned.' The professor made his colleague sound like a character from a Jane Austen novel.

'Send me the opinion on the toxicology results for Shannon Todd,' I said. 'Don't worry, I'll make sure you're paid for it. But as for what defence I choose to lead on behalf of a client, leave me to decide that. Now I've court to get to, and I'm sure you've a body waiting to be cut up.'

'There's only one body I'd like to cut up right now . . .' he said, but before he could clarify further, I'd already put down the phone.

19

Word travels fast in the legal world. I'm sure it did in the days of quill pens, pink string and sealing wax just as much as it does now with the internet, cell phones and email. I'd only walked through the front door of the court when my phone buzzed. It was Fiona Faye.

'I thought I might have had a call from Grace Mary by now,' she said.

'Why, are you joining her bridge club?'

'Hugely droll as ever, Robbie. No, I'm referring to your snooker case.'

'Oh, that? I'm doing it myself.'

'You've heard who's prosecuting, have you?'

One of the alleged match-fixing incidents had taken place during the early rounds of the Scottish Masters competition at the Emirates Arena in Glasgow, and so Scotland, and Glasgow Sheriff Court in particular, had claimed jurisdiction.

'Some Weegie PF out to make a name for themselves, I suppose,' I said.

Fiona snorted a laugh. 'No, this prosecutor has got a name already. One you'll recognise. It's Cameron Crowe.'

Oh, great. Nosferatu in pinstripes. Cameron Crowe was someone blood-sucking parasites left alone out of professional courtesy.

'Are you sure you don't want to send me the brief?' Fiona asked.

'Why, would I want to do that? It's the Sheriff Court. I've done hundreds of sheriff and jury trials.'

'Not many with senior counsel on the other side, you haven't.'

'He's a man dressed up in mid-eighteenth-century clobber. So what?'

'So, you know how much Cameron likes to win, and how much he doesn't like you. That's what.'

'He's going to like me even less when I send him back to Crown Office having lost their most publicised case of the year.'

'And there was me thinking you might be just a tad worried.'

'Why, would I be? This is the Sheriff Court, Fiona. This is my turf. Crowe's the one who should be worried.'

'Well, I warn you. It might be your stamping ground, but it's not your usual type of case. You won't be able to bully-boy your way through these witnesses. Not when the whole Crown case is based on expert testimony. And, let's face it, you're not exactly an expert on . . . well . . . on anything.'

What was she talking about? Expert testimony? From ex-snooker players? Grown men who used to make a living out of playing a parlour game?

'There's a forensic accountant, a bookmaker and man from HMRC too,' she reminded me.

'Yeah, I'm sure the jury will have a lot of sympathy for the folk who have been ripping them off for years.'

'Well, it's nice to hear you sounding so very confident,' Fiona said. 'For a moment I forgot what an unyielding faith you had in your own abilities.'

Yes, I was confident. Why shouldn't I be? I had Dr Yasmin Ashmat all set to blind the jury with science. Hers was expert evidence not even some bean-counters and a bunch of sour-grapes, ex-snooker pros, could contradict.

'Just don't come running to me when it all goes horribly wrong,' she said and with that, cancelled the call, leaving me to the joys of the remand court.

Once the morning business had finished, the Sheriff left the bench for a coffee while the court was cleared to allow Shannon Todd's full committal hearing to call in private. That left just me and the Procurator Fiscal. Now was my chance to impart the toxicology news.

'You don't say?' I could tell by his failure to suppress a wide yawn, that Hugh Ogilvie was less than impressed when I relayed to him the gist of my conversation with Professor Bradley.

'You can't possibly commit my client for trial in face of this new and compelling evidence,' I said.

Ogilvie poured himself a plastic cup of water from the carafe on the table. 'And by *new and compelling*, you would be referring to the unverified medical opinion that your client was too drunk to murder her partner?' He took a sip of water from the flimsy cup and, careful not to spill any, set it down on the table again. 'If I believed everything you said about your clients I'd be out of a job and the prisons would be empty.'

'This information comes straight from Professor Bradley – the expert you instructed to perform the Crown post-mortem examination.'

'Well, you shouldn't have been speaking to him. He's my witness not yours.'

'You know fine well there's no such thing as Crown and defence witnesses, Hugh. There are only *witnesses*, and if the one you just happen to be paying decides he wants to speak to me, in the interests of justice, who am I not to hear him out?'

'Hear him out? You mean hear all the good bits and forget the rest. I'll consider the toxicology results when I'm ready,' Ogilvie said, as the door next to the bench opened and the Bar Officer brought the Sheriff on, 'but I'll take them from Professor Bradley, not from you.'

There were footsteps on the stairs leading to the dock and Shannon Todd appeared, handcuffed to a court security officer. The case called. After Ogilvie had asked for the accused to be committed for trial, the only live issue was where my client should spend the next few months awaiting trial. The short answer to that, despite my plea for bail, was prison.

Client and Sheriff were led off again; one to his chambers, the other to her cell. I was making to leave, when Ogilvie called me back. 'They tell me you've got the Oscar Bowman case.' Whoever had told him, Ogilvie seemed to be quite pleased at the news. 'You know who's prosecuting, I take it?' he said in a manner that suggested he hoped I didn't, and he could be first to tell me.

'Cameron Crowe, isn't it?' I replied, casual as you like.

Ogilvie's lips slithered into a smile. 'And coincidentally, when you were mentioning Professor Bradley earlier, Mr Crowe contacted me this morning to ask if I could serve this on you personally.' From his jacket pocket the PF produced an envelope and handed it to me. I ripped it open. Inside was a section 67 notice, advising the defence of a new witness to be added to the indictment in the case of *HMA v. Oscar Bowman*.

'They're calling Prof Bradley for the prosecution?' I said.

'So, it would seem. Mr Crowe says to tell you that he knows it's late intimation, but doesn't see a problem getting leave of the court since your own witness list wasn't lodged on time. Another thing Mr Crowe told me is that you're calling Yasmin Ashmat. I always thought she was the girl who typed the Professor's PM reports, but, apparently, she's a doctor too. Looks like you may be outgunned when it comes to medical expertise.'

Outgunned? Yasmin Ashmat was a water pistol compared to the flame-thrower that was Edward Bradley, Regius Professor of the University of Edinburgh's School of Forensic Medicine.

Ogilvie took another sip and smacked his lips as though tasting finest champagne and not some dusty old court water. 'Cameron Crowe QC. Not every day you get senior counsel in the Sheriff Court. I hear tell that Crowe's tipped for Lord Advocate one day.' Ogilvie collected his bundle of case folders together, dropped them into a big red plastic box and laid a claw on my shoulder. 'Looks very much like you're outgunned on legal expertise too.'

20

I relocated my last appointment of that Thursday after-noon from the office to the Red Corner Bar. Joanna's friends had organised a shopping trip to buy baby clothes the next day, and I'd agreed to finish work early and look after Tina. Friday was the start of the fortnight-long October school holidays and she was getting out early. As a quid pro quo for being such a good husband and father, and since I had no chauffeuring duties lined up for that evening, I'd awarded myself a couple of pints before I went home, partly because I'd forgotten the taste of beer and partly because I thought alcohol might lubricate the bad news I was about to give to one particular client.

'But I've given you half the money,' Holliday said. We were standing at the bar. He wasn't thirsty. I was. 'That was the deal. We shook on it. I've got the rest of the money in my pocket, and you've got the stuff. What's the problem?'

Why had I mentioned it to Joanna? I should have known what she'd say. And then I'd gone and made her a promise. Conscience, it's a terrible thing.

'The problem is that the stuff's stolen,' I said.

Holliday glanced around the bar in case any of the patrons might be eavesdropping. He needn't have worried. In the Red Corner Bar patrons got strange looks if they weren't discussing criminal activity. He took hold of my arm, preventing me from lifting the beer glass to my mouth. 'Not here. Somewhere private.'

Brendan the barman came over and took a wide sweep of the counter with a damp rag. 'Your friend not drinking, Robbie?' he asked.

'I'm fine, thanks,' Holliday said. He slid a twenty across at Brendan. 'But Mr Munro will have another. Keep the change.'

Brendan reached for the money, but not before I'd slapped my hand down on it. 'You couldn't clear the pool room for us, could you, Brendan?' I asked.

Brendan poured my second pint. I hadn't sipped the head of it by the time he'd frogmarched a squad of under-agers out of the small side room that housed a battle-scarred pool table and an array of broken cues that were better classed as offensive weapons than items of sports equipment.

'How's this for private?' I asked, racking up the spots and stripes.

'I'm not here to play games,' Holliday said. 'I'm here to talk about a piece of serious business.'

I spotted the white and with the one intact stick, sent it crashing into the pack, scattering pool balls everywhere apart from into the pockets. 'You're certainly talking serious money for a cardboard box full of junk.' I held out to him the envelope of cash he'd given me a few days before.

'I don't want the money.' He snatched the cue from me. With barely a glance at the table, he slotted a long diagonal ten-ball, coming off the side cushion perfectly in line for the twelve into the centre bag. That was followed by the thirteen and nine before, on his next shot, the cue ball was deflected off target by a rip in the felt. He handed me back the cue. 'I want what we agreed.'

'It's the painting, isn't it?' I said, scraping blue chalk onto a cue-tip so wide I could have balanced my drink on it.

'What makes you say that?' he asked.

'It has to be. Even if whisky collectables are going up in price, I could buy all the rest of the stuff tomorrow at a car boot sale and still have change of fifty quid. There's nothing remarkable about any of it. The only thing I can't put a price on is the painting. I don't know much about art, but I can tell it's an original oil on canvas and it's old. What makes you think it's worth giving me two grand for?'

I lined up the three-ball and managed to ram it into a corner pocket before sending the white up the table and snookering myself behind the eleven.

'I'm an antiques dealer. It's my job to assess the price of things, buy them, sell them and, hopefully, make a profit more often than not,' he said.

'Well . . .' I attempted a tricky two cushion escape shot that was narrowly out by a foot. 'I've had time to think things over. The stuff isn't mine to sell.'

Holliday took the cue from me. 'I thought we'd already had this discussion. You said the owner had disclaimed it, told the police it hadn't been stolen. You said you'd bought it from someone else, and that made you the legal owner. What's changed?' Without another word, Holliday sunk the fifteen and the eleven, before missing a cut on the final black.

'Where did you learn to play like that?' I asked. Having potted the two, I found myself tight against the baulk cushion and could only try and play safe.

'I was in the Marines. There was a lot of hurry up and wait. I did most of mine around a pool table in the mess.'

'You weren't in the Forces when I first met you, back, when was it? Fourteen, fifteen years ago?'

'No, I was medically discharged a couple of years before then. I used my compensation money to set up my own business. I've always been interested in art and antiques. I started out door-to-door. Everything's cash. With a good eye, there's money to be made and not much tax to pay.'

'And there's money to be made on a grotty old painting of three men having a drink? You must think so or you wouldn't be so ready to part with two grand.'

'That's right,' he said. 'The operative word being *think*. I don't know for sure. The antiques business is always a gamble. I could make a profit, or I could end up with a loss. Either way, you'll be two thousand pounds richer.'

I handed him the pool cue. 'I'm sorry. The owner, the real owner, only told the cops it hadn't been stolen to save herself from having to go to court. I sort of agreed that I'd try and get the stuff back.'

Holliday eyed up his next shot. My positioning of the cue ball hadn't been quite as safe as I'd thought and he snicked the eight-ball into the middle from an impossibly tight angle. He threw the cue onto the table. 'So, what you're really saying is that you've suddenly had an attack of conscience?'

The man needed to calm down slightly.

'You've already admitted it's a gamble,' I said. 'The painting could very well turn out to be worthless. How did you even hear about it? For that matter, how did you know I had it?' It had been a minor source of concern to me that the antiques dealer had learned so easily of my possession of stolen goods.

Holliday didn't answer. He began pacing the small

123

room, staring at the cracked lino. After another pull from my pint, I asked him again.

This time he waved the question away. 'I'm in a WhatsApp group. It's like Gumtree,' he said, still walking up and down. 'There's new stuff comes on every day. If you see anything good, you need to act fast. I phoned the number and was told it was already gone. I had to PayPal the guy fifty quid for your name.'

I put my hand in my pocket. I didn't have fifty pounds on me, but I had a twenty somewhere, and, anyway, I'd already lashed out thirty pounds for the stuff. It seemed the only person making a profit from the box of second-hand junk was Ding-Dong Davie Bell.

Before I could extract the crumpled note, Holliday stopped pacing and looked up at me. 'Three thousand,' he said. 'Four . . . Final offer, five grand. Keep the thousand you have already. I'll give you another grand right now and the rest tomorrow. How does your conscience like the sound of that?'

I drank some more beer in the hope it would keep my conscience quiet. Five grand for a filthy old painting? Genghis and Shannon had drunk the rare whisky. I could tell the old dear that I'd got the rest of her stuff back but that the painting had gone too. Why wouldn't she be happy enough with that? I studied the expression on Holliday's face. It was hard to describe. Earnest, I suppose. The man seemed to be a straight-shooter, even if his living was buying things from people so he could sell them on at a profit. I hated to disappoint him. 'Look, once I've given the stuff back, I'll tell you who the owner is. Maybe she'll sell the painting to you. You might get it for a lot less than you've offered me.'

'And what if she doesn't want to sell?'

I took another long drink of beer and made a point of looking at the clock on the wall that had stopped sometime around the Millennium. A taxi would have me home in ten minutes.

'So that's it? You're going back on our deal?' Holliday said, when he realised I'd finished talking about it. 'The deal we shook hands on? Your conscience is okay with that, is it?'

'In the circumstances, I think it's the lesser of two evils,' I said. 'I hope there are no hard feelings.' He backed away from my proffered hand as though it were contagious.

'Don't be like that,' I said. But it looked as though he very much intended to be like that. For a moment, I thought he might even take a swing at me.

'I'm going to make you another offer,' he said to my back as I headed for the bar. Another offer? I really wished he wouldn't. If it was ten thousand, I had a feeling my conscience was going to be taking a taxi home by itself.

'I'll give you nothing up front. But I'll give you half.'

I turned. 'Half of what?'

'Half of whatever I make on the painting.'

'For that to be worth my while, it would mean you'd have to sell the painting for over ten thousand since you've already offered me five,' I said.

'Is it a deal?' he asked. This time it was his hand that was held out.

I laughed. He was a hard man to say no to, but what option did I have? I couldn't tell Joanna I'd sold the stuff; not after promising not to. And, anyway, the stuff wasn't mine. It had been my original intention to give the old lady her dead husband's property back. That was why I'd gone to see Davie Bell and forked out thirty quid for it. Now I wished I hadn't bothered.

I stared down at his hand and instead of shaking it, shook my head. 'I just can't do it. I don't care if the painting is worth ten thousand pounds, even twenty—'

'One million.'

'One . . . ?' It was a big figure to get my head around. Once I'd packed away all the zeros, I looked him in the eye. His gaze was steadfast, trustworthy. He was a man who, I knew from experience, paid his debts. 'One million? What? Pounds?'

He nodded.

'That would make my share . . . ?' I knew what half of one million was, I just wanted to hear him say it.

Holliday smiled and said slowly. 'Five, hundred, thousand, pounds.'

I waited for my pulse to come down to the low hundreds, wiped some sweat that had gathered across my brow and then grabbed hold of his hand like I was cast adrift and he was winch-man on a Sea King helicopter. 'Tell me more.' I lifted my pint glass and gulped down what was left. 'But first, I'm going to need more beer.'

21

Sleeping's not easy when you've just been told you're about to become a half-millionaire. I even tried counting fifty-pound notes, but nothing could get me to nod off. Around five o'clock, I got up without waking Joanna, went down to the kitchen and drank coffee. Thinking about what I would do with the money was hugely entertaining, but the trouble was that every time I imagined a new sports car, I saw the old lady from "Machseh" in the driver's seat. I couldn't steal her money. Could I? Why not? Was it really stealing? She was the one who'd changed her mind, saying it hadn't been stolen. And who was it who'd traced the stuff and splashed out thirty quid to get it back from fat Davie Bell? Me. If I hadn't gone to all that bother, she would never have had a chance of seeing any of her property again. *Her property*. That was the problem. There was no getting away from that. I knew it was hers, just as I knew Genghis McCann had stolen it, and just as I knew the story about it not having been stolen had only been a ruse to avoid the old lady attending court as a witness. Why had I shaken hands with Holliday – again? Was I going to have to go back on the same deal a second time? The answer, after much reflection, was a horrible yes. My only hope was that I might be able to talk the old lady into paying a reward. It wouldn't be half a million pounds, but it might be substantial enough to keep both me and Holliday happy. I could only ask.

Like most parents whose children own a dog, I was allowed the privilege of feeding Tina's pet, paying the vet bills, taking it for walks and scooping its poops. That morning, I took Bouncer on a detour while, earlier than usual, we were out for his constitutional.

This time, there was no blue van outside "Machseh", and it took several rings before the lady of the house came to the door in a dressing gown, her thin, black hair poking from beneath a swirly-patterned silk headscarf. 'Can I help you?' she asked, tucking the ends under.

'Hello,' I said. 'I don't know if you remember me. I was here a week ago. I was talking to . . . Reuben . . . About the property that was stolen . . . You know . . . during the break-in?'

She shook her head. 'Why are you here?' she asked in a loud voice, as though I was the deaf one.

'I was here last week! I was speaking to Reuben!'

'Reuben's not here. He's at work.' She made to close the door.

I put out a hand to stop her. 'I'm a lawyer!' All of a sudden, I realised just how unlawyerly I must have looked to her, dressed in jeans and jumper and accompanied by a mutt on a leash.

She looked at me closely. 'A lawyer?'

I fumbled in vain for some form of identification and found none. 'I was the lawyer for the man who broke into your house!' I said, loudly, even though it didn't help explain my pitching up at her front door first thing on a Friday morning.

'Am I in trouble?'

I assured her she wasn't. She bent down and patted Bouncer lightly on the head with a frail, blue-veined hand. I thought she had a dirty mark or a bruise on the outside of her wrist, but on second glance it looked like a number – probably a telephone number to call if strange men came to the door. 'Nice dog,' she said. 'What kind is he?'

That was something we'd not quite worked out yet.

'What's his name?'

'Bouncer,' I said.

She straightened. 'My husband loved animals. Strange in his line of work, I suppose, but he especially liked dogs and they loved him. Maybe that wasn't so strange for the same reason. Wait there and I'll fetch Bouncer a treat.'

She disappeared for what seemed to me a long time, before returning with a slice of roast beef. She tore it and tossed half to Bouncer. As she did, I saw her look over my shoulder, and I turned to see the curtains of the house across the way twitch. I wondered, had the treat-fetching been an excuse to call a neighbour and ask for an eye to be kept on the strange man and his dog?

Mrs Glowacki held out the other piece of meat, and I told Bouncer to sit.

'Reuben was telling me that the property stolen belonged to your late husband and how anxious you were to have it returned!' I said, loud enough to hail a passing ship, and in an attempt to steer the conversation back on course. 'I wanted to speak to you about a possible reward.'

She threw the meat to Bouncer, her wrinkled old face changing from a smile to a scowl in less time than it took the dog to devour the morsel.

'So that's what this is about?' she said. Reaching out, she placed a hand on my chest and shoved.

It didn't have much effect, but out of politeness I took a step backwards down onto the path. I cupped a hand to my mouth and yelled, 'I don't think you understand!'

The old lady thought she understood perfectly well. 'Your crook client stole my husband's property and now you expect me to pay money to get it back?'

A small woman wrapped in a dressing gown appeared on the lawn of the house opposite. She didn't say anything, just left me in no doubt that she was watching. The fluffy white dog I recognised from my previous visit, jumped playfully around her slippered feet.

I put on my best smile and tried to speak as slowly, clearly and loudly as I could. 'I'm not here to cheat you, Mrs Glowacki. I'm here to tell you that the painting is valuable. Very valuable. All I want—'

She pushed the door more firmly this time. If I hadn't jumped up and jammed my foot in the gap it would have closed completely.

'Just listen to me for one moment!' I called through the three inches of space available. 'It's not what you think. I'm not trying to—'

'Oy!' The small woman and fluffy white dog had been joined by a much larger and less playful looking man in bare feet, trousers and a half-buttoned shirt.

'It's all right,' I called to them.

'*No, it's not*!' Mrs Glowacki screeched.

The dog came bounding over and, ignoring Bouncer, tried to squeeze through the gap in the door.

'Please listen,' I said, removing my foot as the dog climbed over it and inside. I put a hand around the edge of the door to prevent it from closing. 'You don't understand. I'm not—'

Pulling the door back six inches, Mrs Glowacki

slammed it as hard as she could, and I had to wrench my hand away or it would have been crushed. 'Keep the junk for all I care!' she yelled through the letterbox at me. 'Just go away and never come back!'

22

They say the sea is a cruel mistress. She was only a slightly tetchy girlfriend when, later that Friday morning, my daughter and I caught the Gourock to Dunoon Ferry.

'Wait until Mum hears I was in a big ship on the sea.' The more I'd sworn Tina to secrecy, the more she seemed intent on squealing to the boss about our trip out west.

'Let's not tell Mum,' I said. 'She might be worried, and the baby wouldn't like that.'

Tina's little face looked up at me. We were standing on the top deck and looking over the railings of the small Western Ferries vessel that carried our car and nine others on the twenty-minute trip from one bank of the Firth of Clyde to the other. No one else had bothered to get out of their vehicles. My daughter had already enquired as to the prospects of going for a swim once we'd reached the other side, as she did whenever we came in sight of a shoreline. For Tina, no trip to the seaside was complete without a dip in the briny, as I knew from many a Munro day out to the beach at St Andrews where I was often to be found knee deep in the freezing waters of the North Sea, ensuring my daughter didn't drown, usually while Joanna waved encouragingly from further up the beach, wrapped in a fleece and sipping something hot from a flask.

'If I tell Mum, will it hurt the baby?' Tina asked. Her bottom lip trembled a little. 'Will the baby die?'

'No, of course not—'

'But you said—'

'Look, a seagull. Over there!'

When Tina turned to look, I began the descent of the metal stairs to the car deck. The questions continued as we started the car journey from Dunoon to the top of Loch Striven and down the Kyles of Bute to our destination. Tina fell asleep through part of the trip. A lot of people do when I tune into Radio 4. She woke when the reception deteriorated into white noise.

'Are we there yet?'

We were. Tighnabruaich. A town that was saving up to buy a horse. A town where they collected the internet from a well with a bucket, a mobile phone signal was science fiction and the tearoom on the main street was imaginatively called The Tearoom. We parked outside and went in. The interior was small with only a few tables. The walls and serving counter were wood planks painted blue, white and brown and the tablecloths pink with white polka dots. The whole place was fresh and clean and I felt like I'd shrunk and stepped into a dollhouse.

The only unoccupied table of the five available had two rickety kitchen chairs on one side and on the other a window seat strewn with cushions of different materials, patterns and colours. Tina clambered onto it and looked out across the narrow street to where an Aunt Sally sat on a public bench clad in a red dress, frilly white apron and green striped stockings. Asking questions about it kept my daughter amused until our guest arrived.

Bridget Goodsir's was another face I hadn't seen in a long time. And what a face it was: heavily powdered, with way too much mascara and red lipstick and much of it covered by an enormous pair of pink spectacles with lenses that gave her saucer eyes. But it wasn't Bridget's face that had most caught Tina's attention.

'Your clothes are funny.' And my daughter was right about that. They were. A long shapeless frock of crushed velvet, patterned with a cat motif, was set off by a felt hat, brim turned up, a sprig of dried heather sticking from the band and wisps of grey hair making a bid for freedom from under it.

'I'd look even funnier if I was wearing what you've got on, honey,' Bridget said, while at the same time trying to attract the attention of the waitress. I'd had to give Joanna the impression I was taking Tina to school that morning, which was why she was in her little black and white uniform with a black and gold tie. 'Come back to me when you're eighty-two, and I'll give you a free fashion appraisal.'

Tina turned to me. 'What's a appraisal?'

'It's why we're here,' I told her.

'I take it you've come all this way to collect the favour I owe you?' Bridget said, after she'd asked for a pot of tea and a Tunnock's teacake, and I'd ordered a coffee and a fried haggis roll for myself, and a glass of orange juice and an Empire biscuit for Tina.

Bridget Goodsir was not a household name and throughout a long career in crime, she'd liked to keep it that way. She was an artist, if one without, by her own admission, a creative bone in her body. But she could copy. Give her paintbrush, oils and canvas, and she could knock you up a Renoir that most experts couldn't tell from the original. That had been her problem: most hadn't; one or two had. Years ago, Bridget had sold a work, purportedly by Claude Monet, to a drug-dealer looking to launder some cash. At auction, it was discovered to be a forgery.

Bridget had been prosecuted for art fraud. It was one of my last cases while at Caldwell & Craig. Bridget had been in her early seventies at the time, and I'd managed to win the case without evidence being led. After several meetings with the prosecution, they were eventually persuaded that it was not in the public interest to prosecute an elderly woman, especially one who'd duped a money-launderer. Bridget paid what was left of the money she received to the Crown, and that, along with a medical report from a friendly doctor to the effect that her eyesight was so poor she would never paint again, had swung it for the defence. I had never felt Bridget beholden to me. She'd been a client and I'd done my best. It was she who had said at the time that she owed me a favour. Now I was calling it in.

I unslung Tina's schoolbag from the back of the chair, loosened the buckles and slid it across the table. Carefully, Bridget removed the small painting, still housed in its scabby gilt frame.

'I can do paintings better than that,' Tina said. 'I can do houses and I can do boats and I've done Bouncer and I've done a horse once, except Dad thought it was a ice-lolly.'

'My daughter dabbles in the abstract,' I explained to Bridget, who, having held the painting up to the light and flipped it over a few times, was now running the thick lenses of her spectacles across the canvas, one inch from the surface.

By the time our refreshments arrived, she'd seen enough. She replaced the painting in the satchel and poured milk from a tiny jug into a china cup that didn't match the saucer. 'I assume you know the story?'

I did. Holliday had told me. In 1624, or thereabouts, Rembrandt Harmenszoon van Rijn, whilst still a teen-ager, had created five paintings, each depicting one of the five senses. Until recently there had been only three in captivity: Hearing, Sight and Touch. Then, in 2015, Smell was found in the basement of a house in New Jersey. Originally valued at a few hundred dollars, when its provenance was realised, it sold for over $800,000. One of the five remained at large: Taste. I wanted to know if it was in my daughter's schoolbag. It wasn't that I didn't trust Holliday; I had no reason not to. He'd always kept his word to me, something I had so far failed to do with him. In the end, we'd reached an understanding. I'd ascertain the worth of the painting and then, if I decided to go in with him, we'd share the profits fifty-fifty.

Bridget sipped her tea. I thought her hand was a little shaky now. 'Where did you get it?' she asked.

'I'm here on behalf of a third party,' I half-lied.

'A very trusting third party,' she said.

Reaching for her biscuit, Tina knocked over her glass of orange juice. Bridget soaked up what she could with a little white paper napkin until the waitress took care of the rest with a damp cloth.

'How sure are you about the painting?' I asked Bridget after the waitress had gone to fetch Tina a replacement drink.

'It's filthy and in need of a lot of restoration work,' she replied, 'but then so would you if you'd been in someone's attic or basement for the last four hundred and fifty years. It has Rembrandt's monogram. Everything about it seems kosher ... But you must remember, this is a painting no one has seen before: no one living at any rate. It would be a great subject to forge, and it's highly coincidental that it appears now, so soon after the last one was discovered. Almost as though someone has been biding their time. It's the final piece of the jigsaw. The last of the five senses. With this, the whole is worth more than the sum of the parts.'

We sat drinking in silence for a moment or two. Silence, if you ignored my munching into a fried haggis roll and Tina's commentary on why she thought a Smartie to be a better choice of centre piece for an Empire biscuit than a jelly-tot.

'This third party . . . Anyone I know?' Bridget asked.

I smiled at her through a mouthful of haggis roll.

'I didn't think you'd tell me,' she said. 'You don't need to. Only three types of people possess paintings like this. Rich people and lucky people are the first two. I don't know how many rich or lucky people you know, Robbie, but I'll guess they're out-weighed by the third type.'

'Who's that then?'

'The bad people.' Bridget drained the last of her cup and poured another. 'Twenty thousand. That's how much it will cost you to know for certain.'

'Twenty thousand pounds?' I said. 'I could take it to an auction house for a free valuation.'

'You could if your client is rich or lucky. But you won't.' Bridget removed the foil from her teacake. 'You won't because you're here with me, which means there's something dodgy going on.'

Her eyesight might have been failing, but her mind was at the top of its game.

'Bruni van der Ham's your man,' she said. 'He worked in New York for the Leiden Collection for years. There's no one knows Dutch art better than he does.'

'But twenty grand . . .'

'It's the same money whether it's real or fake. It's a lot to gamble, but I say it's a risk worth taking. Twenty thousand is less than two percent of what the picture could be worth.'

'And this . . .'

'Van der Ham.'

'There will be no questions asked?' I said.

Shaking her head so that the flap of her felt hat fluttered, Bridget bit into the teacake, smearing white mallow across her crimson lips. 'He knows to keep his mouth shut. Bruni will put you on to the right sort of auction house too, if you ask him nicely, though he'll want a larger cut.'

'Still, twenty thousand pounds for a valuation, win or lose. Why so much?' I asked.

'Because,' she said, looking around for a napkin on which to wipe the stickiness from her lipstick. 'Ten thousand of it is for me.'

'What about the favour you owed me?'

'You've just had it,' she replied. 'The appraisal was free. The ten grand is for *me* to keep my mouth shut.'

23

When we returned to civilisation I gave Tina her tea, so that by the time Joanna had returned from her day out I'd already packed our daughter off to dance class.

On the pretext of having a lot of work to do for the big trial starting on Monday, but mainly to avoid my daughter recounting tales of Tighnabruaich, sailing ships and strange old ladies, I'd arranged for her to stay the night at my dad's. I'd already phoned Holliday with the news and, in the spare hour before I had to collect Tina, we met at Sandy's cafe. It was seven o'clock. Sandy was looking to close up and welcomed our arrival like a bout of listeria.

'Quit moaning. We're only wanting a couple of coffees. We'll be out of here in ten minutes,' I said, and he went off to the kitchen, mumbling to himself in a language he probably thought was Italian.

I joined Holliday at one of the deserted tables. 'What did I tell you?' he said smugly.

'Not so fast,' I replied. 'My expert *thinks* it's genuine, but she's not one hundred per cent certain. She says to be sure, we need to speak to an expert in Dutch art. A guy called Van der Ham. He's in Holland working at some museum or other. The one where they have the *Girl with the Pearl Earring*.'

'The Mauritshuis,' Holliday said. 'They've quite a

few Rembrandts as well as Vermeer. My favourite is the *Goldfinch* by Fabritius. He was pupil to Rembrandt and master to Vermeer. Got the best of both worlds. I think it's the simplicity of the painting that gives it such an ethereal quality, and—'

'Yeah, well, anyway, like I said on the phone, it's twenty grand for his expert assessment, with no questions asked. He can even handle the sale if we want.'

'Sounds good to me,' Holliday said, as we took receipt of two of the fastest coffees ever prepared.

I took a drink. It was lukewarm.

'But twenty grand . . .' I said.

'We're in this fifty-fifty,' Holliday said. 'If you want out, my offer of five thousand still stands. You can walk away.'

'No, I'm still in.'

He reached across and slapped a hand on my shoulder. 'We make a good team. Just tell me when you need the rest of the money.'

'It's a lot of money to trust me with,' I said. 'Ten thousand in cash and a million-pound painting.'

'You haven't let me down before. You did the business the last time.'

'Are you talking about the curse?' I said. 'You *must* know I had nothing to do with that old woman's death. How could I?'

He shrugged. 'That old witch told me all my luck would be bad luck and that I'd die a bloody death. I asked you to remove the curse and all I know is that, right now, my luck couldn't be any better.' He downed his coffee in a oner. 'And far from being dead, I'm pretty bloody pleased with life.'

Which was more than I could say a couple of hours later,

after a run-out at Malky's regular Friday night five-a-side match. The school holidays were to blame for a shortage of players, as some of the usual squad were away with their families, so I'd been given a surprise call-up. Even more of a surprise was Kim's presence. She had a game the next day and charging around with a group of forty-year-old men, the lateness of whose tackles could be timed with an hourglass, was, I thought, a sure way to pick up an injury. Half an hour into the game, I was the subject of several hefty challenges. The opposing team, reluctant to tackle Kim, seemed intent on taking it out on me. With a dead leg and a sore knee, I saw out the second half of the game in goal, a duty I usually did my best to avoid. With the opposing team bulleting footballs at you from point blank range, a goalkeeper in a five-a-side match has to be the sort of person who'd be unflustered facing a firing squad. The only thing missing was a cigarette and a blindfold. Needless to say, my tendency to occasionally throw myself out of the line of fire, rather than into it, met with some criticism from my teammates, but I had more important things on my mind. In the changing rooms before the game, I'd sounded Malky out about a loan. Joanna and I had just over five thousand in savings and I needed the same again to meet my half of the bargain.

'Five thousand? What's it for?' Malky asked, lacing up a trainer.

'It's an investment. I can't give you the full details, it's sort of confidential,' I said.

'So, the deal is I give you five thousand pounds and a month later you give me six thousand back? What's the catch?'

I felt obliged to tell him the catch was he wouldn't necessarily get anything back.

141

'So, it's really more of a gamble?' he said. 'After the week I've had at the bookies, I'm placing no more bets. I mean, how can Scotland ship three goals against Kazakhstan? And what about the World Match Play golf? Out of the five players I had each way, not one of them made the cut. And then,' he said, lacing up the other shoe, 'on Saturday night the champ goes and gets himself TKO'd when I had a ton on him at four-to-five on. I mean to say . . . ?'

'Never mind, Malky. The Ashes start next week,' said one of his pals, who was strapping on a knee support. 'It's going to be close, but you can still get good odds on the series going to a final game.'

'No thanks. Not for me,' Malky said. 'I don't know anything about cricket.' He stood up. 'Sorry, Robbie, if you want the money so badly, you'll need to go for a bank loan.'

I'd already considered that, but taking out a personal loan would have been difficult. Joanna would have noticed and started asking questions for which I wouldn't have the right answers. I could have secured a loan over my business premises, if it wasn't for the fact that my current rent-free status was the only reason I was staying afloat. And yet, I had to have that five grand.

'Okay,' I'd said, as we all trotted out onto the pitch. 'How about I *guarantee* you get six thousand back?' Why not? The Bowman case would bring that in easily.

A snort followed by a, 'That'll be right,' had been Malky's take on this latest improved offer, and there was no talking him round.

Kim was waiting for me at the end of the game and walked with me as I limped towards the changing rooms. 'Great save on that penalty kick.'

'Some would say it was what my face was made for,' I said, and she laughed.

She paused at the door to the female locker room. 'I overheard you talking to Malky . . . something about a loan.'

'Do you think you could work on him for me?' I asked. 'Get him to change his mind?'

She smiled. 'Unlikely. He's very stubborn. You know that. No, I was thinking I might take up your offer. What was it? Five thousand now, six thousand back, when . . . ?'

'End of the month,' I said.

'Guaranteed?'

I put my hand on my heart. 'Of course, guaranteed. That goes without saying.'

She thought about it. 'Okay.' She untied the string that had been holding the hair out of her eyes and shook out long blonde locks across her slim shoulders. 'How would you like the money paid?'

'Quickly,' I said, 'and in cash. Preferably euros.'

24

Glasgow Sheriff Court was busy enough on any given Monday, let alone when the UK's top snooker player was about to stand trial on charges of match-fixing.

Having arrived early, suffered an agents' room coffee, sorted my papers and climbed into my gown, I went down to the main foyer. At nine-thirty precisely, Oscar Bowman swept through the front doors, dressed in a white suit that, today, was set off by a black shirt and pink tie. He was in the company of a small entourage that included his close-protection officer and Peter Falconer. They, in turn, were stalked by packs of journalists, well-wishers and autograph hunters.

When it comes to privacy, like most Sheriff Courts around Scotland, there was none, so I had to take my client, minus all the hangers-on, through the solicitor's entrance to Court 5, while the public doors remained locked.

'Right,' I said. 'The case is down to start at ten. I'll confirm your plea of not guilty and the clerk will ballot the jurors. There will be fifteen of them.'

'How long does jury selection take?' Bowman asked.

I had the feeling he'd watched too many American legal dramas.

'About five minutes,' I told him. 'We have to take who we get. You've no right to object to anyone unless you have good reason, which is extremely unlikely because we're only given names and addresses, no other information.'

Bowman glanced around. The only other person present was a clerk who was busy folding pieces of paper with the names of potential jurors and dropping them into a large glass bowl. Bowman reached into his top pocket, removed a tin of mints and popped one into his mouth. 'I won't be taking the stand,' he said, matter of factly.

'It's true, there is no obligation on you to give evidence,' I said, 'but we should discuss whether it's a good idea once we see how things pan out. If you do give evidence, it won't be until after the close of the Crown case in a few days, so there's plenty of time.'

'I'm not giving evidence,' he said. 'Take that as a given before we start.'

I shrugged. Putting your client into the witness box was always a gamble. Many experienced lawyers believed the height of the defence case coincided with the last Crown witness. Not calling your client had two benefits: firstly, it prevented them from saying something stupid and ruining all the work you'd done during cross-examination, and, secondly, you could always try and sell the jury the line that the prosecution case was so woefully inadequate, the accused wasn't going to even bother acknowledging the absurdity of it.

There were also good reasons for taking the opposing view. For instance, if an accused badly wanted to give evidence, you really had to let them, otherwise it would all be your fault if things went wrong. The main reason, though, was that a jury might actually be interested in hearing what the accused had to say. There were two sides to every story. Many a seemingly unsinkable Crown case had been fatally holed by the man in the dock looking the jury in the eye and telling the ladies and gentlemen he wasn't guilty. Unfortunately, it was impossible to know what jury members were thinking, or even if they were thinking. Whether I'd recommend Bowman testify was a tactical decision, and most likely a last resort.

We'd only been present in the courtroom for a couple of minutes, but already it had become the place to be, with a series of unusually diligent clerks, cops and bar officers dropping by to make sure everything was going smoothly, and just happening to catch a glimpse of the man of the moment at the same time.

I told Bowman to sit in one of the pull-down seats at the side of the court that were reserved for social workers and the press. That way when his name was called, he could slip into the dock without any fuss and minimum embarrassment. Not that he seemed the slightest embarrassed.

At five to ten, the erect figure of Cameron Crowe QC emerged through a side door. Dressed in a black silk gown, his dark hair slicked back under an ivory horsehair wig, he floated into a seat in the well of the court and was joined a few moments later by a female PF depute who was there to note evidence. The six fraud charges on the original petition had been cut back to three when the final indictment was served, another charge of being involved in organised crime having been deleted due to evidential difficulties. I was sure it had been Crowe's decision to cut back on the number of charges. That was his style: short, sharp and straight for the carotid. Don't give the jury too much evidence. It only confused them. Hit them with the highlights and demand a conviction before the defence had a chance to muddle things up and pull down a curtain of reasonable doubt. After all, what did it matter if Bowman was convicted on six or sixty crimes? Everyone knew that a single conviction on one of the remaining match-fixing charges would be enough to ruin the young man's unsullied reputation and destroy his career.

'How long is this charade going to last?' Bowman asked, looking up at me.

'I don't see the Crown evidence taking more than two or three days,' I said. 'It's just a case of them showing video clips and calling some former professional players to give their opinion. After that, there's a bookmaker to say some unusually large bets were placed on certain inexplicably close matches that you were expected to win comfortably, and some other witnesses to say how unlikely that was unless pre-planned.' In addition, there would be one or two police witnesses speaking to Bowman's arrest and charge, but most of the uncontroversial items had already been agreed by way of joint minute between the Crown and one my client's many previous lawyers.

The main doors to the court opened and spectators stampeded, jostling for position as they sought out the best seats. As I was about to make my way to the front of the court, Bowman grabbed the sleeve of my gown and tugged.

'I'm expecting to be found not guilty,' he said, through a toothy smile for his public.

'I'm going to do my best to see that you are,' I replied.

He pulled harder so that I had to stoop to his level. Not letting me go, he hissed at me. 'You will not try. You will succeed, or else—'

I don't know what the "or else" was, because I wrenched myself free to take up a seat opposite the prosecution team. I had only laid out my papers on the table when the sheriff was led on to the bench and, along with the rest of those present, I stood while she took her seat.

Sheriff Lorraine Arrol, like so many before her, was a refugee from the Faculty of Advocates. I'd come across her on a number of occasions and had the usual run-ins we defence lawyers tend to have with sheriffs. All in all, I'd found her to be reasonable, if slightly out of touch with the average accused person: not realising, for instance, when it came to imposing fines, four hundred pounds was benefit money for the month, not just the price of a half-decent spa day.

'Mr Crowe,' the sheriff said with a smile to her fellow Faculty member, 'so nice to see you again.' Turning to her left, and, for some reason, no longer smiling, she stared down at me. 'And, of course, Mr Munro.'

I didn't know the significance of the "of course" or the accompanying sigh, but I smiled up at her nonetheless. Not that she noticed for she was already directing her gaze straight down.

'Call the diet please, Sheriff Clerk,' she said, and without further ado the case was called, whereupon Bowman rose gracefully from his seat and strode forward to the dock amidst murmurs from the gathered ranks.

The charges were read, the pleas of not guilty confirmed, and a jury of eight men and seven women was empanelled without any difficulty.

There are no opening speeches in Scotland, apart from the one in which the judge tells the jury there are no opening speeches, and so, after a short break to allow the jurors to divest themselves of coats and jackets, the first witness was called. I recognised him straightaway, as did everyone else in the crowded courtroom. Steve Perry, a former professional snooker player, was now a coach and pundit whose plump smiley face could be found on the sort of TV shows populated by D-list celebrities. He had lots of hair, a close-cropped beard and eyes embedded somewhere beneath his brow that, when he blinked, looked like two flies trying to escape a batch of bread dough. He was twice the man he'd been when playing professionally, and the mother-of-pearl buttons on his mustard waistcoat threatened to ping off and do someone an injury.

Duly sworn-in by the sheriff, Perry rhymed off his qualifications – there was no award for modesty among them – and was then led through video footage showing a series of misses by my client. At some of the clips, the witness frowned as though disappointed. At others, he smirked. At the final shot, a straight blue into a centre pocket that rattled in the jaws before bouncing out again, he laughed disdainfully.

It was perfect timing for Crowe. 'What do you find so funny, Mr Perry?' he asked, innocent as a cat in a canary cage.

Still smiling, the witness replied. 'That last clip. To believe a player the calibre of the accused could miss a pot like that . . .' He stared down at the ledge of the witness box and shook his head. 'It's . . . it's unthinkable. He could have potted that, and the others you've shown me, with his eyes closed.' He looked up again, no longer smiling. He raised a hand, pointing a finger that shook with anger. 'That man,' he said, unable to bring himself to name or, indeed, look at the person in the dock, 'is a disgrace to our sport. In my book, he is nothing but a cheat.'

The Sheriff interrupted. 'That's enough,' she said, turning to the jury box. 'Ladies and gentlemen, please remember that it's not what's in Mr Perry's book that counts, but what's in yours at the end of the trial. I can assure you we have a lot more evidence to hear before you can consider a verdict.' She glanced down to her right. 'Anything further, Mr Crowe?'

It had been the prosecutor's first meaningful question, but like the slash of a femoral artery, it was enough. With a polite thank you to the witness, a nod to her ladyship and flap of his silk gown, Crowe once more took his seat at the table.

It was my turn.

25

'Mr Perry, do you consider yourself to be a snooker expert?'

I saw Crowe twitch as though about to object. He'd already led the witness's credentials and had the sheriff certify him an expert, thus able to give opinion evidence. He settled himself when the witness answered right away.

'I do. And others too.'

'Yes,' I said, 'but I wasn't asking about your mum and dad.'

There were a few sniggers from the public benches. One or two of the jurors looked shocked. Fortunately, they were outnumbered by the smilers. Crowe jumped to his feet.

The Sheriff held out the flat of her hand to him to signal she had this under control.

'So soon, Mr Munro?' she said. 'I had hoped you might at least wait for your second question before you started insulting the witness. You'll stop it now, understand?'

I took the reprimand. I'd expected it. Indeed, had intended it. A jury trial is seldom won by a fatal blow from the defence, it's more often a thousand cuts through which the Crown case exsanguinates. That one quip had produced, I hoped, some important results. As well as an attack on the witness's pomposity, it had caused the Sheriff to rebuke me. Now it looked like she was anti the defence and if there is one thing a Scottish jury likes, it's an underdog. They were probably already wondering why the prosecution guy had on a wig and I didn't, but, and more importantly, if Perry's suffused chubby face was anything to go by, it had annoyed him, and when cross-examining a witness, that's exactly how you want them.

'How many world snooker titles do you hold, Mr Perry?' I asked.

The witness stared straight at me. 'I reached the quarter-finals in two thousand and the semis the year after.'

'I see. So, none then. What was your best ever world-ranking?'

'I reached number ten in two thousand and one.'

I walked over and leaned an arm on the edge of the dock and cocked my head at Bowman. 'My client was number one for eight years running until this allegation was made. He's won the snooker world championship six times, and yet you, who has never even played in a world title final, seem able to explain where he's gone wrong. How is that?'

'I coach several top-ranking players.'

'Any of them won a world title?'

'Not yet.'

'But they might if Mr Bowman is out of the way, is that correct? What's your cut if they do?'

'Mr Munro, I've already warned you,' the Sheriff said.

Meantime, if there was a Richter scale for anger, Perry was verging on San Francisco 1906. His knuckles whitened on the sides of the witness box. 'Are you suggesting I would commit perjury to put a fellow professional out of business in order that I can benefit?'

It was nice of him to summarise exactly what I was suggesting. It saved me the trouble.

'I'm not suggesting anything,' I said, with a sideways glance at the jury. 'I'm only asking questions. Questions you don't seem to be answering. Let me ask you another. First of all, take a look, if you will, at defence label one.' I signalled to the bar officer and he replaced the Crown's DVD with my own.

The YouTube logo came on momentarily, followed by the headline, "UK Sporting Disasters vol. 12".

'I think yours is coming up any moment now,' I said, as a series of sporting blunders, in football, rugby and cricket played on the screens all around the courtroom, until we came to the section on snooker. 'Ah, here you are.' Using the remote control, I paused the clip, showing a much thinner version of the witness lining up a long shot to a red that was hanging over a corner pocket. 'Recognise yourself?'

Perry looked to the jury, patted his waistcoat and smiled. 'That was many dinners ago.'

'This is you playing the final frame in the World Championship semi-final match, isn't it?'

'It is.'

'The one you lost.'

He didn't reply. I resumed play and the courtroom watched as the cue ball struck the red and went in-off into the pocket.

'I'm not an expert like you,' I said, 'but that shot looked harder to miss, and yet you seemed to manage.'

'A question please, if you don't mind, Mr Munro,' the sheriff said.

'Are you a cheat?' I asked, once the screens went black again.

'How dare you!'

'Did you mean to miss that shot?'

'Of course not.'

'And yet you did. Isn't that what you'd term as an unthinkable miss?'

Perry didn't answer until the Sheriff prompted him to do so.

'No, it isn't unthinkable,' he said at last. 'In fact, there's hardly a day goes by when I don't think about it and what could have been.'

I had to keep going on the same tack, but realised I'd have to be very careful in case Perry attracted a sympathy vote.

'If I brought a snooker table into court and gave you that shot over again, you'd sink it without any problem, wouldn't you?'

'I would.'

'Blindfolded?'

Perry didn't answer. He didn't need to. I'd made my point.

'It was all down to pressure, wasn't it?' I said.

'It played a part.'

'Like the golfer who knocks in six-foot putts all day long on the practice green, and goes on to miss a three-footer for the Open?'

'I don't comment on other sports,' Perry said, dryly. 'Only snooker.'

'They call it the yips in golf. Do they have a different name for it in snooker?'

'No, we call it the yips too.'

'It's a slang term for an involuntary muscle twitch, isn't it? Ever heard of myoclonus? It's a medical term.'

'I'm a former professional snooker player, not a doctor,' Perry replied.

'That's right,' I said, looking at the jury as I returned to my seat. 'You're not. Perhaps it would be best if we asked someone who was qualified to give a proper expert opinion.'

26

The evidence of Steve Perry was followed by the reading of a joint minute of admissions agreeing the provenance of the video footage shown to the jury. After that, a couple of cops gave evidence about my client's arrest and charge and his no comment interview. It was all formal stuff, filler material, because the next Crown witness had been delayed in transit, and it was enough to take us to near enough one o'clock and lunchtime.

Peter Falconer slapped me on the back as I left court. 'Oscar thinks you're doing a great job!' My client's close-protection officer had already whisked him through the crowds and away. 'He may not show it, but I can tell he's dead chuffed at how things are going. Malky was right about you.'

Peter seemed to catch sight of something out of the corner of his eye. With another hefty slap on the back he hurried off.

'Where's Pete going?'

I turned around to see the something, or, rather, the someone who I thought might have caused the big man's hasty departure. It was Kim.

'He's not answering my calls and I was hoping to have a word with him,' she said. 'Doesn't matter, though. I really came to see you.' She opened the bag she was carrying to reveal a white envelope. 'That's five thousand pounds in

Euros. You can have it when I've seen exactly what I'm investing in.'

'You're looking at it,' I said. 'You're investing in me. You give me the five thousand and I'll give you back six before the end of the month. That's all you need to know.'

'And if you don't give me the six thousand, what then? What actual guarantee do I have?'

'I'm a solicitor. My word is my bond. I can't go about not settling my debts. If you want something in writing from me, just say so.'

Kim thought about that and then said, 'Does Joanna know about this arrangement?'

'No, and she doesn't need to.'

'Why not, if it's such a certainty?'

'It's not a certainty for me. It's a certainty for you. I'm putting five thousand of my own money in. I might lose out, I guarantee you'll definitely be one thousand pounds better off.'

Kim screwed up her face. 'That's what I can't understand. If you don't have the extra five thousand you need now, why, if whatever you're up to goes pear-shaped, would you have six thousand to give me later?'

'It's a minor cash flow difficulty. That's all.' I jerked a thumb back at the door to Court 5. 'I'm in the middle of the trial for Oscar Bowman. It's going quite well, though I say so myself. Once it's over and he's paid my fee, the six thousand to pay you back won't be a problem.'

Kim closed her bag. 'Let's say whatever you're up to does go wrong. You're down five thousand pounds that Joanna knows nothing about and owing me another six. You've a wife off work, a daughter to keep in ballet pumps and another child on the way. Somehow I think you might have other priorities.'

'I always pay my debts,' I said.

'The ones you can't weasel out of – or so your brother says. No, I'll give you the money, but on one condition. I want to know how it's being spent. Show me this deal is genuine and that way I can trust you with my money.'

Trust *me*? Could I trust *her*? I really didn't want the whole world knowing about the painting – especially the parts of the world that contained the rightful owner or, even worse, my wife. I needed Kim's money. Why I needed it was none of her business. She didn't need to know the truth, not the whole truth. She was giving me half the money. For that I was prepared to tell her half the truth. 'Of course you can trust me,' I said, reaching for her bag.

She pulled it away. 'No money until I know exactly what I'm risking it on.'

Some people were *so* suspicious.

'Okay,' I said. 'I'll give you a call after I've finished in court. There's someone I'd like you to meet.'

27

The next witness for the prosecution was a small man with a large moustache, and enough fuzz protruding from his ears that he could have combed it over his bald head and given himself a centre parting.

Crowe began leading his evidence in chief. 'You are Mr Charles Fitzsimmons?'

He was. He was also sixty-three years old and employed by the National Association of Bookmakers or NAB for short.

'And what is the purpose of NAB?' Crowe enquired.

'NAB exists to raise the status and prestige of bookmaking, to safeguard the rights and interests of its members and to give practical help and advice to the membership, both directly and through the affiliated area associations.'

The sheriff stepped in to assist the jury. 'You're a watchdog organisation?'

Fitzsimmons turned to the bench. 'That's partly our function,' he said stiffly. 'Hence my appearance here today.'

Crowe spent some time taking the witness through three tournaments in which Bowman had participated, highlighting that, in each, he'd lost the first three frames against unseeded opposition. To compound matters, there had been an unusual amount of betting activity surrounding each of those lost frames.

'What were the odds at which these bets were placed?' Crowe asked, drawing his questioning to a close.

The man from NAB was directed to a Crown production that set out the figures in table form, and which was put up on the TV monitors for all to see, if not understand.

'Take the Scottish Imperial Tournament for instance,' he said. 'Mr Bowman was world champion and favourite to win the competition. The odds on him failing to make it through the first round were 100/1.'

'Which means . . . ?' Crowe asked, turning his attention to a jury, many of whom looked like they knew how to fill out a betting slip okay.

'It means that in order to win one hundred pounds, a person would only have to wager one pound.'

'And the bookmaking industry,' Crowe said, his gaze still directed at the jury. 'It's not a charitable cause?'

The witness smiled. 'We do our best to promote certain chosen good causes, but no, when it comes to gambling it is strictly business.'

'What were the odds of the accused losing a single frame in the first round of the tournament?'

'The first round was best of seven frames. For Mr Bowman to win four frames to zero, was four to five on.'

'Which means?'

'In order to win four pounds, a person would require to wager five.'

'How about losing a particular frame?'

'For each frame in the first-round match, the odds were three to one against Mr Bowman losing.'

'How many did he lose?'

'Two. The first two. In fact, as you know, he lost the first two frames in the first round of the three tournaments I've been asked about.'

159

'Correct me if I'm wrong,' Crowe said, knowing he was one hundred per cent correct, 'but if a person were to have placed a bet on the accused losing the first two frames at three to one against, that would amount to . . . ?'

'Nine to one,' the witness replied.

'And that means?'

'It means a wager of one pound would win nine pounds.'

'And to wager that same pound on him losing the first two frames in each of the three tournaments?'

'Then you're taking about odds of nine, times nine, times nine to one.'

'I don't have a calculator,' Crowe said.

'It comes out at odds of seven hundred and twenty-nine to one.'

'And did anyone place such a daring bet?'

Several people had, via the internet from the Far East and Las Vegas, in three consecutive tournaments.

'And when that came to your attention at the National Association of Bookmakers, did you think it strange?'

It was a leading question, but to object would only let the jury think I was bothered by the witness's evidence, an impression I was doing my best to dispel by doodling, yawning a lot and pouring myself glasses of water.

The witness smiled. 'They say lightning doesn't strike in the same place twice. When it strikes three times, you start to wonder if someone is working a switch.'

Crowe began to walk back to his chair, the sleeve of his gown rubbing against the back of my neck as he did. When he reached his side of the table, he paused before sitting. 'How much money did your members lose in total on such bets?'

'Over one and a half million pounds,' the witness replied.

'Thank you,' Crowe said, taking his seat. 'Wait where

you are. If I know Mr Munro, he'll have one or two questions for you.'

'Do you, Mr Munro?' the sheriff asked.

I did. 'Mr Fitzsimmons, is it your evidence that for a punter to win a bet where the odds are nine to one against, is unusual?'

'It's nine times more unusual than the usual. That's what nine to one means.'

Crowe made a show of covering his mouth and sniggering into it. What was of rather more concern was that some of the jurors also found the reply amusing.

I ploughed on regardless. 'Do you ever buy a national lottery ticket?'

'Never.'

'Why not?'

'The odds against winning.'

'What are they?'

'Around forty-five million to one.'

'That's a lot more than nine to one, or even seven hundred and twenty-nine to one, isn't it?'

The witness was forced to agree.

'And yet, even gambling at those astronomically high odds, some lucky people still win the lottery, don't they?' Again, the witness had to agree.

'So, it seems that the unexpected does happen occasionally?'

'It does.'

'In fact, it happens most weeks.' I said. I could tell the witness was about to butt in with some facts, so I didn't give him the chance. 'Was it the National Association of Bookmakers who brought these lucky people who won on my client losing some snooker frames to the attention of the authorities?'

'It was.'

'No professional snooker players sounded the alarm?'

'No.'

'Not, for instance, Mr Perry, who has already given evidence today. He didn't come forward and tell you he'd noticed something funny going on with the standard of my client's play?'

'No, it was the pattern of betting and the amount of the losses sustained that alerted our association.'

'And does your association ever complain to the authorities when punters lose large sums of money, or is it just when their members have to pay out?'

It was a question I hoped would bring the jury onto my side. I didn't need to wait for an answer.

'Thank you, Mr Fitzsimmons,' I said, and sat down.

Crowe levitated to his feet to re-examine. 'Mr Fitzsimmons, how many lottery tickets are bought each week?'

'At least fifteen million,' said the witness. 'Sometimes as many as forty million.'

'How does that affect the chances of somebody winning?'

'It means that while the odds of a particular person winning remain the same, the odds of someone, some-where, winning are quite high.'

'Less than seven hundred and twenty-nine to one?'

'A lot less.'

'Less than nine to one?'

'Again, yes, if enough people buy a ticket.'

'How many people placed bets on Mr Bowman losing two frames in the first round of each competition? Forty million, fifteen million? Perhaps only seven hundred and twenty-nine?'

162

'Six,' the witness replied, smugly.

Crowe returned to his seat and from there said, 'Six extremely lucky people, as Mr Munro would see things. Do you agree?'

'No,' the witness said. 'I don't think luck had anything to do with it at all.'

28

There was a final witness before close of play: a forensic accountant whose view on things was even more incriminatory than that of the man from NAB. I didn't ask any questions. All I could do was feign lack of interest and hope the jury would get bored, forget or not fully understand the significance of the evidence led.

After court, I made straight for Holliday's antiques shop on Great Western Road.

'How is this going to work, exactly?' he asked, when I'd told him to expect a visit from Kim within the next half hour, and the reason for it.

'It's simple. You just show her a painting—'

'I don't have it. You do.'

'Not *the* painting. Any old painting is fine. No one would believe the actual painting was worth anything anyway. Tell her we're buying it for twenty thousand and it's a dead cert that we'll make a profit.'

The bell above the door tinkled and Kim walked in much earlier than arranged. I gave her a wave. 'Kim, this is Mr Holliday. He's the man I told you about earlier.'

The two of them shook hands. My phone buzzed. It was Peter Falconer. Having fought his way through the crowds, Peter was now sitting in the suite of a city centre hotel along with our mutual client who was demanding a post-mortem on the day's proceedings.

'Got to go,' I told Kim. 'Mr Holliday will explain everything. Once you're happy, give him the money.'

When I arrived at the hotel, there was a maid with a trolley clearing the complimentary minibar of alcohol, coffee and tea, all beverages classified by the Mormon Church as "strong drink" and therefore not fit to be in the presence of my client. It had all been paid for and it seemed a shame to let it go to waste, so I pocketed a couple of whisky miniatures before joining Bowman and Peter in the sitting room.

For someone who, according to his agent, thought I was doing a great job, the snooker player was managing to conceal his delight. 'Was that the best you could do?'

'Yeah,' Peter said, 'what was all that nonsense about the national lottery? That really didn't help much.'

Bowman threw two mint breath-fresheners into his mouth, one after the other, and crunched them.

'Is it too late to change lawyers?' he asked Peter.

The big man seemed to be giving the question some thought.

'Of course it's too late,' I said. 'In case you haven't noticed, we've just had the first day of evidence. You can't tell the sheriff you don't like the way things are going and is there any chance we could start again.'

Bowman stood up and paced the room.

'All the same, I thought Robbie dealt very well with Steve Perry,' Peter said, sticking up for me at last. 'And as for the statistician guy, I don't suppose he could do much about him. The figures don't lie.'

Bowman came over and looked down at Peter. The only time anyone could ever do that was when the big man was sitting. 'Whose side are you on?'

'I'm on your side, of course,' Peter said. 'We're all on

your side. It's not just your career that will be affected by conviction. So will mine, and I'm sure Robbie would like to be paid for his efforts.'

'Whoah,' I said, launching to my feet. My client's close-protection officer's body tensed. Parts of mine loosened. 'What do you mean? The deal is I get paid win or lose.'

Bowman looked at me as though there should be people with a big net and a van out looking for me. 'Who gets paid for losing?'

Lawyers, was the obvious answer, but before I could give it, Peter was off his seat and standing between myself and Bowman. He put an arm around my shoulder and led me a few steps away. 'The deal is that this is a no win no fee case,' he said in a hushed voice. 'Malky said you'd be fine with that.'

Malky. Typical. He'd recommended me for the job to curry favour with big Peter on behalf of his girlfriend. If he only stood to gain if I won the case, why shouldn't that apply to me too would be his way of thinking.

'Why do you think you're Oscar's fifth solicitor?' Peter hissed in my ear.

It was a question that had puzzled me. Now it was purely rhetorical. I answered it anyway. 'I'm guessing because no one was crazy enough to take on this stinker of a case unless they were certain to get paid.'

Peter had a more diplomatic way of putting that. 'Oscar doesn't think anyone without a vested interest in a successful outcome will try hard enough.' He turned to his client. 'Isn't that right, Oscar?'

Bowman crunched noisily on another mint. 'Like I say. Who gets paid for losing?'

'See?' Peter said, smiling, as though all was now made perfectly clear. 'Oscar only wants winners to do

166

business for him.' Still grinning he gave me another one of his friendly thumps on the back. At this rate, any fee I managed to secure would be spent on chiropractors. 'And that's what you are. A winner. Right, Robbie?'

As pep talks went, I felt like the boxer, a mile behind on points, being assured by his cornerman that all he needed to do to take the belt home was KO the champ in the last.

I was about to tell Peter that Bowman's suggestion of finding a new lawyer wasn't such a bad idea after all, when my phone buzzed. A text message from Joanna. "The baby's coming!"

29

I arrived home in a state of panic to a scene of tranquillity. Joanna was lying along the couch cuddling Tina, Bouncer snoring by their side. From the tone of my wife's text, I'd half expected there to be another, much younger member of the Munro family present by now.

'False alarm,' she said, sitting up. 'I thought I was having contractions, but it was Braxton Hicks.'

'Who's he?'

'Were you even listening at the antenatal seminar? Braxton Hicks. Cramps in my womb.'

'Have I got a womb?' Tina asked.

Leaving my wife to field that question, I went through to the kitchen to find my dad at the table doing a newspaper crossword.

'Finally show up, did you?' he asked. 'Your wife could have had triplets by the time it's taken you to come home.'

'I was in Glasgow. If you bothered to read that newspaper and not just do the puzzles, you'd know that I'm in the middle of a very important trial right now.'

He jotted down an answer. 'Oh, aye. The snooker cheat. American, isn't he? Never liked him. Too flash. All those white suits. What do they call him? Bowman the showman. Doesn't smoke, gamble, drink or chase women? Not to be trusted if you ask me. And what's his hair doing? All over his face. If it was down to me, I'd save everyone the bother and throw him out of the game and into jail.'

'That's why it's not down to you,' I said, filling the kettle. 'I'm hoping the people it *is* down to have old-fashioned ideas about the presumption of innocence.'

A snort was my old man's response to the concept of due process and the right to a fair trial. 'Any news on Kim?' he asked.

What had she been saying? 'What kind of news?'

'Malky says she's looking for a new contract and having trouble. It's top secret.'

'Is that why you're telling everyone?'

'I'm only telling you because Malky said you were helping him out on it.' He patted the chair beside him. 'Come on, make us a cup of tea, sit down and tell me all about it.'

So, I did. I told him how Malky had got me lumbered with a no win no fee criminal trial which had about as much chance of success as Tina's two left feet performing *The Nutcracker* at the Royal Opera House come Christmas.

'Why would he do that?'

'Because, if by some miracle I do win, Malky thinks Kim's agent will owe him a huge favour—'

'And that favour would be pulling the strings to get her a new contract?' My dad took a slurp of tea. 'You'd better win, then.'

'Whatever happened to throw him out of the game and into the jail?'

The next crossword clue so caught my dad's attention that he was unable to answer me. My phone buzzed with another text message. It was from Jake Turpie. Like most of Jake's communications, whatever format they came in, it was short, to the point, unwelcome and impossible to ignore: "*Get down here.*"

30

The area surrounding Davie Bell's barbed-wire compound was cordoned off with blue and white police tape. A couple of uniforms were patrolling the perimeter. I met Jake as he was walking back up the track towards his own yard. 'What's happened?' I asked him.

'Ding-Dong's dead,' he said.

'Dead? How?'

'Killed. The cops wanted to see him about something, couldn't get an answer and asked me if I'd seen him. I came down here with them and brought a pair of bolt-cutters. They went in and found him. That's when I sent you a text. But you're too late. I've already given a statement.'

For Jake to say anything to the cops during an interview was highly unusual. He must really have been innocent.

'What did you tell them?'

'That I never saw anything. There's always folk coming and going down here.'

'They didn't suggest that you might have ... you know—'

'Killed him? Why would I do that? He was better at paying his rent than you used to be, and I never killed you, did I?'

'Yeah, thanks for that,' I said. 'Do you know how he died?'

'The cops I was speaking to said it was messy. The place

is stinking. Ding-Dong must have been lying in there for ages.'

'When was the last time you saw him?'

'That time you were here.'

That had been about ten days before, when I'd bought Mrs Glowacki's property from him. No, not *her* property. I had to stop thinking like that. It was mine. She'd said so herself.

The small matter of a violent death on his land having taken up enough of Jake's precious time, he stomped off back up the track to his yard, leaving me standing, the subject of suspicious glances from the cops on guard duty. I was about to leave when I spied a familiarly tiny figure dressed in a white paper suit coming out of the breeze-block building, iPad under her arm and ripping off a pair of blue nitrile gloves.

I waited until she'd disposed of the rest of her protective gear into a plastic basket inside the cordoned-off area and put on a coat that had been folded inside a black canvas holdall.

'Don't bother asking me a whole lot of questions,' Yasmin said, as I slid from the shadows and into her path.

I gave her a nudge. 'Oh, go on. Just a couple. Is it Davie Bell?'

'Big man, six feet and around twenty stone. Sound like him?'

'Very. I'm told he was murdered?'

'That would be my considered opinion,' she said.

'Lots of blood, I heard.'

'There usually is, if someone jams a knife between someone else's legs and slices the thigh to the bone.'

'Not unlike another recent murder,' I said.

'You think that what's-his-name McCann was

murdered now, do you?' Yasmin said. 'What happened to him accidentally rolling onto a broken whisky bottle?'

'Any sign of a weapon?' I asked, rising above her sarcasm.

'None.'

'Time of death?'

'Sorry, Robbie. I've told you all I'm going to tell you. I've been called out to confirm life extinguished and make some notes that I've already emailed to Prof Bradley. He might fill you in on the details after the PM if you ask him nicely.'

The chances of that happening were fatter than the late Davie Bell.

'Prof B and I are not exactly on speaking terms at the moment,' I said.

'Because of the Oscar Bowman case? I wanted to speak to you about that.'

'No time like the present,' I said. 'I take it you know that Prof B is less than enamoured by your myoclonus theory.'

We came to a Fiat 500, brilliant red under the arc lights, and stopped. Yasmin took a key from the front pouch of her bag and stared at it for a moment. 'That's the thing, Robbie. It's not really my theory, is it? It's more like yours.'

I took hold of her shoulders and squared her up to me. 'You're not going back on our deal, are you? What about your written opinion?'

'I may have over-expressed a few things in all the excitement,' she said, fiddling with the car key.

'But you're giving evidence on it the day after tomorrow,' I said. 'I've lodged the report in court.'

'Then perhaps you'd better unlodge it because I'm no longer prepared to stand by my opinion.'

Yasmin pulled away from me and pointed her key at the car. The lights flashed orange. I stepped in front of the driver's door. 'Don't be like that, Yasmin. Let's talk this over sensibly.'

'I'm not sure if that's possible with you, Robbie. You're not interested in sensible. All you want is for everyone to see things your way.' What was she talking about? Didn't everyone want people to see things their way? Why should I be any different? 'Well, I'm sorry,' she said, 'but I won't perjure myself—'

'Hold on a minute,' I said. 'Let's not forget whose signature is at the bottom of that opinion, or the size of your fee note.'

'I don't want a fee. Yes, I signed the opinion, but you practically dictated what went in it. I should never have gone along with your suggestion. You talked me into it. You turned my head.'

Turned her head? Where had I heard that expression before? Professor Bradley was behind Yasmin's sudden change of mind.

'Influencing a witness can amount to an attempt to defeat the ends of justice,' I said.

'Well, why did you do it?' she asked.

'I'm not talking about me. I'm talking about your boss. He's—'

'Exactly. He's my boss. And he's a witness.' Yasmin shoved me aside and yanked open the car door. 'How silly would I look standing in the witness box, trying to contradict his evidence? Can you imagine the kind of cross-examination I'd be subjected to?'

Unfortunately, I could. Cameron Crowe would have a whale of a time. '*You've been specialising in forensic pathology for how long, Miss Ashmat? A whole year?*

Who was your mentor? Professor Bradley, you say. And what was the name of the textbook you studied from when at University? Oh, I see, Professor Bradley wrote that too.'

'Don't make me do this, Robbie. If I'm forced to give evidence, it won't end well for your client.' Yasmin threw her holdall over onto the passenger seat, climbed in and lowered the window. 'It's nothing personal.'

Of course it wasn't. Accusing me of trying to fabricate evidence wasn't personal.

'You do understand, don't you, Robbie?'

The only thing I understood was at least I now had Shannon Todd's defence all but sorted. Leaving the toxicology evidence aside, another large, very large, reasonable doubt would soon be on its way to the City Morgue.

Without another word, Yasmin raised the window, started the engine, and I watched as the little car pulled away, headlight beams swinging across the rough track as it bumped down to the main road taking Oscar Bowman's hopes of an acquittal with it.

31

Next morning, I phoned Professor Bradley while I was on the train bound for Glasgow Queen Street.

'I suppose I should be glad you've come to your senses at last,' he said.

'On one condition. Actually, on two conditions. Well, sort of a joint condition.'

'You want my toxicology report on your murder charge woman,' Bradley said. 'I've got that.'

'Yes, and I don't want any ambiguity about the findings,' I said. Forensic experts were great at producing reports that concluded with lines like, "*I remain not entirely unconvinced that these findings are not without insignificance,*" and then charging a whopping fee for a report that took no one anywhere. 'I want it made quite clear that Shannon Todd was not in any fit condition to have committed the murder of George McCann during the time frame we discussed.'

'All right, all right, I've got that. What else?'

I was going full belt and braces. 'I want a report on last night's murder too.'

'I don't know anything about last night's murder. I've not carried out the autopsy yet.'

'Yasmin has sent you her notes. All I want you to do is take a look at them and set out something in writing to

175

say that, in your opinion, it looks like the same MO as in George McCann's case.'

I thought that would be plenty. A report from the Crown pathologist to say that Shannon Todd would have been too drunk to kill her partner, supported by an exactly similar murder committed while she was remanded in custody, would surely be enough to persuade the Prosecution to free my client from prison.

Professor Bradley grunted. 'And that's all? I give you that, and you agree not to call Yasmin as a witness?'

'Yes.'

I could hear a throaty grumble of approval.

'But I want it today,' I said. 'This morning.'

'This morning!'

I saw no reason why my client should spend another day in prison for a crime she patently didn't commit. 'Yes, this morning. You don't need to write lengthy reports,' I told him. 'A two-paragraph letter will do. Mark it for the attention of the Lord Advocate and email it to the Sheriff Clerk at Glasgow. I'll collect it when I get there. That gives you half an hour.'

I hung up before he could argue. He didn't call back, which I took as a good sign.

'What are you looking so pleased about?' Cameron Crowe wanted to know. He was sitting in the well of the court poring over the statement of his next witness.

I laid Professor Bradley's opinion, hot off the Sheriff Clerk's printer, down on the table in front of him. 'I've a proposition to make you.'

Crowe lifted the two-page letter and glanced at it. 'HMA against Shannon Todd? Who's she?'

'She's my client. She's remanded in custody alleged to

176

have murdered her boyfriend. In my view, there wasn't enough evidence to have her committed for trial in the first place.'

Crowe tossed the letter aside. 'So, why was she?'

'Because your colleagues at Crown Office couldn't think of anybody else to prosecute for it. But, as you can see . . .' I picked up the letter and waved it in his face. 'Your own pathologist says it couldn't have been her and I don't think they let her out of jail to commit this latest identical murder.'

'And so you'd like her released?'

'Yes please.'

'Then contact Hugh Ogilvie. He's the Procurator Fiscal through your way.'

Hugh Ogilvie couldn't make up his mind which tinned fish he preferred. He'd take an age to make a decision on Shannon's release or delay it even further out of spite.

'You know Ogilvie will only seek Crown counsel's advice on this,' I said. 'You *are* Crown counsel. I'm cutting out the middle man.' I pulled my mobile phone from my pocket. 'Give him a call and tell him to contact the prison with a PF release.'

Crowe's hand made no move towards the phone. He leaned back in his seat. 'I hear a demand. I don't hear a proposition.'

I put the phone down on the table and nudged it towards him. 'Do this and I'll undertake not to call Dr Yasmin Ashmat as a witness.'

'And why would you do that?'

'Make the call.'

He sat forward and pushed the phone back at me. 'I don't believe you. Why would you throw away the only straw the defence has to clutch at? I hope you're not bartering one client's interests for that of another?' he sneered. 'No, somehow I don't think you'd sell a rich, private client down the river to save this Todd woman who's probably on legal aid.'

'I do what's best for all my clients,' I said.

Crowe coughed up a laugh. 'Sure you do. Anyway, why should I care if you call this Dr Ashmat? She's Bradley's understudy and, in case you hadn't noticed, he's on my witness list.'

'Well now you won't have to call him.'

He hesitated.

I picked up the phone and dropped it back into my jacket pocket. 'Suit yourself. Just remember, this time next week, when we're still here arguing the toss over types of neurophysiological abnormalities, that it's me who's got the rich private client and you who's being paid by the state.'

He let me walk to the other side of the table and sit down before lifting the report again. I'd already had a quick word with Bowman. Very quick. He wasn't in a talkative mood. The court was closed and he was sitting in the dock awaiting the start of the second day's evidence. The doors opened to the public and spectators began to file in. As we stood for the sheriff to be led onto the bench, Crowe was still reading Professor Bradley's letter.

'All right,' he said across the table to me as we sat down again. 'You give an undertaking not to call your doctor, and I'll make the call at mid-morning break. Deal?'

I stuck up a thumb. 'Deal.'

32

George Dalling was friendly, polite, understated and painfully honest – everything you didn't want in a witness. A household name in the nineties, no one could don evening wear like Gentleman George. He'd probably been born wearing a bow tie and matching silk cummerbund. Former BBC sports personality of the year and ex-fashion model, he also did a lot of charity work about which others, but never he, boasted. The four times world champion was led sycophantically through his evidence by Cameron Crowe, and come mid-morning break, Dalling had viewed all the footage of Bowman's alleged deliberate misses. By lunchtime I didn't have a defence case, I had a basket case.

There is a school of thought that says you should never cross-examine an obviously truthful witness because the jury will only end up hearing his or her evidence twice. The Robbie Munro school of thought, though less well subscribed to, is that it's worth the risk because it only takes one hole to sink a battleship.

'Do you know the meaning of the term ring-rust, Mr Dalling?' Was my first question when the court resumed after lunch. The witness had returned to the stand looking just as calm, fresh and downright pleasant as he had during his morning's evidence. 'It's used mainly in boxing, I believe,' Dalling said, 'but I suppose it could be applied

179

to other sports. Even snooker,' he added, helpfully. He was like that, helpful. It made him dangerous.

'And just so the ladies and gentlemen of the jury understand, would you agree that an example of ring-rust in snooker would be when someone practised for hours on end, as I'm sure professional snooker players must do, but once in actual competition they took a little time to get going properly.'

'That's an excellent way of putting it,' the witness said with a smile.

So far so good. 'You'd agree, then, that in the early rounds a player might not be at his best?' I said, pressing home the point.

'Yes, players tend to improve as they progress through a tournament. They have to.'

'Because . . .' I suggested, 'you meet a better standard of player in the later rounds, and you don't get away with the occasional poor shot or lost frame?'

'Exactly.'

'And in addition to ring-rust, is it possible that in the early rounds a top player facing lesser opposition might become slightly careless and over confident?'

Again, Dalling was happy to concur. 'It shouldn't happen, but it frequently does.'

In hindsight, that was when I should have sat down. The art of cross-examination is like heaping your plate at a buffet. You need to know when to stop or else that last sausage roll will topple off the pile and end up on the floor. But my next question was too tempting a morsel.

'Ring-rust, overconfidence, these could both have caused my client to underperform in the early rounds of certain competitions, wouldn't you agree?'

It was a leading question, permissible during

cross-examination, and a torpedo that could sink the Crown case or backfire and send my client to the bottom.

The PF depute sitting next to Crowe, squirmed in her seat. The QC himself sat rigid. The Sheriff lifted her pen and poised it over her notebook. Fifteen pairs of eyes in the jury box were fixed on the witness.

Dalling thought carefully, his face a mixture of conflicting emotions. 'I'd like to say yes . . .'

Why didn't he, then? That way my client could continue entertaining snooker fans everywhere, the Mormon Church could remain proud of him and, even better, I could get paid. But, in my experience, no one who started a sentence with the words, *I'd like to say yes,* ever went on to actually say yes, no matter how much they might have liked to.

'Thank you, Mr Dalling,' I said, 'I have no more questions for you.' I was about-turning and striding back to my seat when the sheriff called to me, 'Mr Munro, I really think you should wait until the witness has finished answering the question.'

'Hasn't he finished?' I asked. 'I thought I heard him agree with me.'

Crowe was on his feet. 'I'm happy to clear this up in re-examination, M'Lady.' He approached the witness box. Standing only a few feet from the witness, he looked him straight in the eye. 'Well, Mr Dalling . . .' Crowe began, in a dry, grating voice that sounded like someone sandpapering the defence's coffin. 'Do you truly believe the spectacularly poor play you've been shown today was caused by either ring-rust or overconfidence on the part of the accused?'

Dalling smiled grimly. 'When Oscar first came over from the States, he was scarcely more than a boy. I watched him play in the final of the UK Junior Masters. It was the best of fifteen frames. He won eight-nil, and with three century-breaks. When I went to congratulate him afterwards, he asked me for advice. I gave him some tips and told him that in a few years I'd be looking to him for advice – I was right. The man is the finest snooker player of his generation. He has won more world championships than me and will go on to break the record if given the chance. He is the most consummate professional I have ever had the privilege to meet. To answer your question honestly . . .' I, for one, really, really wished he wouldn't. Dalling turned to look at the man in the dock, who, head bowed, couldn't hold his gaze. 'No, I don't believe that those misses could be down to either ring-rust or overconfidence. Oscar is too good. He's simply the best.'

As on the previous day, my client was bundled through the awaiting crowds and whisked off to his hotel straight after court, without a glance, far less a word of instruction, in my direction. Today, Peter didn't go with him. He was waiting for me in the lobby, a lighthouse of a man amidst the sea of people churning around us.

'I'm worried,' he said.

'You should be,' I replied, making my way towards the stairwell that would take me to the agents' room.

Peter pulled me back by the shoulder. 'This is serious, Robbie. You have to win – for all our sakes.'

'Don't I know it,' I said.

'Is that a dig at the no win no fee arrangement?'

'The arrangement that no one bothered to arrange with me?' I said. 'Yes, it is.'

Peter shook his head. 'Malky was supposed to tell you. He said you'd jump at the chance of such a high-profile case. The publicity alone must be worth thousands in advertising to you.'

'Yeah, I can see my name up in lights: Robbie Munro – the cheats' lawyer.'

'So, you're not trying? Is that it?'

'Of course, I'm trying. It's just that it would be nice to know that I was being paid for trying.'

Peter snorted. 'It's like that old cartoon, isn't it? Two farmers fighting over a cow, one pulling it one way by the horns, the other pulling it the other way by the tail, and a lawyer underneath milking it. The no win no fee deal was Oscar's idea. It was meant to incentivise you. He's a winner—'

'When he wants to be,' I said. 'I don't suppose losing those frames did him any harm financially.'

Peter grabbed me. 'You can't talk like that here. The journos are crawling over this story like Spiderman on a New York skyscraper.'

I was beginning to wonder about Big Peter's links with ex-bookie Al Quirk; his business partner, who I knew had faced match-fixing allegations back in the dim and distant.

'Okay,' I said. 'If your man is such a winner, how about he comes up with something I can use as a defence? You *are* expected to have one of those when pleading not guilty.'

Peter led me to a more secluded area. 'You need to understand, Robbie. Oscar is a hugely principled young man. He doesn't drink, smoke, sleep around and he won't lie. Not even to his lawyer, and definitely not to a jury.' He held my gaze, waiting, it would seem, for the fog to clear in my head.

'What you're saying is . . .'

Peter nodded, then hurriedly, 'I'm not saying he definitely is, but . . .'

'I don't care. I have lots of guilty clients. I don't mind if Oscar is guilty or not guilty, but if he wants acquitted he needs to give me a line of defence. I can keep taking pot shots at the Crown witnesses, but very soon the jury will expect to be presented with some kind of an explanation.'

Peter winced. 'It's not his fault. It's mine. The way Malky sold you to me, he made you sound like a magician.'

'Well, a magician needs something to pull out of the hat,' I said. 'Even my guiltiest clients can usually come up with some sort of a story.' My attempt to walk away was aborted by one of Peter's oversized hands.

'What if I promise you'll get paid?' he said. 'Whatever happens. If you lose the case, I guarantee I'll pay your fee.' Guarantees clients give you about money always come before a but. Peter's was no exception. 'But you have to promise me you will try everything you possibly can to get Oscar off this charge. I don't care what you do or how you do it, just make sure he walks out of here still able to play professional snooker.'

'I can't do anything without some input from Oscar,' I said.

'That's one thing I can't guarantee,' Peter said. The hand on my shoulder turned into the offer of a handshake. 'Do we have a deal?'

I took his hand. 'Deal,' I said, though with no instructions and no Yasmin to call as a witness, I was left without a plausible defence.

Peter agreed to have a talk with his client and, the big man's confidence in my magical powers seemingly restored, strode towards the front doors and out of the building.

Realising I'd left my notes of the day's evidence on the table in the court, I went back to find Cameron Crowe still there. Everyone else had left.

'I was going to call another snooker expert tomorrow,' he said, packing his wig into a black tin box that had his name in gold lacquer on the lid. 'However, I don't think that will be necessary now. Not after that last witness and your extremely helpful cross. Will you be putting your man in?'

'Nothing else for it,' I said.

Crowe smiled, showing his teeth like a ghoul in a restaurant who'd just been told warm corpse was on the menu. 'Oh, good.'

33

'I was hoping I might catch you,' were the last words I wanted to hear after a hard day's trialling, followed by screeds of paperwork while fending off Grace Mary's unrelenting commentary on the firm's perilous cash flow situation. Around nine o'clock, I locked the front door to my office and was all set for home. It had been dark for several hours. The High Street was still and cold and the mist stuck to my face like a damp cloth. 'I wonder if I could have a very quick word.'

Not only were they the last words I wanted to hear after a busy day, they came from the last person I wanted to hear them from. Reuben Berlow was bundled up against the rawness of the mid-October evening in a long black overcoat, collar turned up, and a tweed bunnet on his head. He slapped his arms against his sides. 'Would you mind if we stepped in out of the cold?'

I could hardly refuse. Undoubtedly, he was here about the not-so-missing property. Pretending to fumble around for my keys while I unlocked the door, gave me time to think up what I was going to say to him.

'You're lucky to find me still here,' I said, when we'd moved inside, the darkness of the close lit only by the yellow glow of an ancient sodium lamp on the far away wall at the foot of the internal stairs. 'I'm usually long gone by this time.'

'I'll not keep you,' Reuben said. 'I was just wondering if you'd had any luck locating Mrs Glowacki's property. She told me a strange man pretending to be a lawyer was at her door. I thought it might have been you.'

Strange and pretending to be a lawyer, and naturally he'd assumed it was me? Nice.

'That's right,' I said. 'She told me she didn't want her property back and that it was a load of old junk. She got pretty angry, so I left.'

I waited for him to say something, but he just kept on looking straight ahead. The man could have won a staring competition with a wall. I took a step forward, hoping he'd follow.

He didn't. 'Are you saying you know where Mrs Glowacki's property is?' He pushed up the brim of his bunnet, the better to continue staring. 'And you're not giving it back?'

'I'm not saying anything,' I said. 'You're not my client, it's not your property and Mrs Glowacki made it extremely clear that she wants nothing to do with me or the property that was or wasn't stolen and, on that basis, I don't really see what more I can do for you, or even what it's got to do with you.'

I could have been more diplomatic, but I was tired and hungry and not wanting to surrender half a million pounds. Mrs Glowacki had no children and was in her nineties. What was she going to do with that kind of money? With no one to inherit, it would all go to the Queen's and Lord Treasurer's Remembrancer, aka the government, which meant the money would either be spent on Gaelic road signs or the paintwork for a Trident missile. I tried unsuccessfully to usher him towards the door and back onto the street.

'If you have Mrs Glowacki's property, return it now,' Reuben said, simply and politely and with a sufficient hint of menace to make me wish I wasn't alone in a dark close with him.

'How about you go back to Mrs Glowacki and see what she's got to say on the matter?' I said. 'Have her contact me. I can't speak to you about property that might once have belonged to her, and regarding which you have already admitted perverting the course of justice by providing false information to the police.'

'I spoke to you off the record.'

'Well, I'm telling you on the record that the false information you gave the police led to a housebreaker being wrongly released from prison and ultimately to his death.' As legal bullshit went, it was top quality fertiliser.

When I tried again to direct him to the door, Reuben refused to budge. His normally friendly expression took on a look I hadn't seen before. I was wondering whether things were going to become physical when the door to the street opened.

'That you, Robbie?' A woman's voice. This time when I moved, Reuben stepped to the side to allow me past. 'What you doing?'

'Just locking up for the night,' I said.

Reuben moved closer so that our chests touched. He'd had something garlicky for lunch. 'I'll speak to Mrs Glowacki. And be back to see you,' he said. Then, without another word, he marched back down the close and onto the street.

'Who's that fud?' Shannon Todd asked. Her week or so in jail had worked better than a TV makeover. Her hair was silky, not greasy and her face fuller and positively glowing.

188

'Nobody. No, actually, he is somebody. He's some-body who wants the stuff that Genghis stole from that old woman's house, and thinks I've got it.'

'Genghis selt it to Davie Bell,' she said. 'He should go there and buy it back from him.'

She obviously hadn't heard the news of Ding-Dong Davie's demise. I didn't want to get into that right now.

'I see you got out okay,' I said, turning to lock the door once more. 'I only spoke to the AD this morning. I never thought he'd have you out on a PF release so soon.'

'That's the thing, Robbie,' she said, sheepishly. 'I'm just off the bus. I've got a money voucher, but nowhere to cash it. I've nothing to buy food or a powercard with. I'm starving, and my place will be freezing.'

'Shannon, we both know that if I give you money you'll spend it on drugs.'

She stepped back, outraged at the very suggestion that she, a veteran heroin addict, would sooner spend cash on smack than a nourishing meal and the electricity meter. 'I'm clean. I have been since Genghis got out.'

'What about while you've been inside?'

'Wi' Genghis deid, how can I afford jail prices?' It was true. Very little money changed hands in prison where drugs sell for way beyond the normal street value. Money handed in for prisoners was not made over to them in cash, but allocated to their spending accounts, and prison canteens didn't sell drugs. To score drugs inside, someone had to pay for them on the outside. 'I'm telling you, Robbie – this time I'm staying clean.'

If I had a score bag for every client who'd told me that, I could have bought my own poppy field.

'Go on, Robbie. Please. Just a tenner. I don't know what to do now Genghis is gone. I've no one.'

She was so pitiful, and yet she seemed determined and it was the best I'd seen her look in . . . ever.

'I've only got a twenty,' I said.

'I'll pay you back tomorrow. Honest I will. I owe you big time, Robbie. I've got a giro waiting for me too. I'll cash everything in the morn and come up to your office. I'll catch you at lunchtime. Swear to it on Genghis's grave, so I will.'

Genghis McCann wasn't in a grave. He was still in a drawer at the City Morgue beside fat Davie Bell. The twenty-pound note was scarcely out of my pocket than she'd snatched it from my grip and was gone.

34

'What are you two doing here?' I asked when I arrived home later that evening to find my dad and Malky taking up valuable couch space.

'I don't know about him,' my dad said, giving my brother a nudge, 'but I've just dropped Tina off after her dance class because you were too busy with your criminals, and now Joanna's asked me to stay for a cup of tea – which is what you should be drinking more of by the sound of things.'

I had no idea what he was talking about until Joanna came into the living room carrying one of my suit jackets; the one I'd worn the day before. Currently, I had two suits that were in decent enough condition to be pressed into action for court work. Because of the TV cameras that were lined up outside court each morning, Joanna had suggested I wear the suits on alternate days, as well as a different tie to give the impression of an extensive wardrobe. Not that anyone was interested in me. Not when the man in the white suit was strutting his stuff.

Tina padded through from the kitchen having eaten her supper and was immediately sent off to brush her teeth.

Joanna held the jacket out in front of her at arm's length. 'I want to know the truth – are you a secret drinker?'

'What are you talking about?' I said.

'You heard.' I thought I had. 'Are you a secret drinker?'

191

'A secret drinker?' I said. 'I can't even be a public drinker because I'm either driving Tina about the place or—'

'Not tonight you weren't,' my dad chipped in.

'Okay, not tonight, but I usually am, and I'm also on permanent stand-by for baby Munro, and I'm in the middle of an extremely important trial. What's brought this on?' As if I didn't know. Joanna was a walking hormone cocktail. I put an arm around her.

'I found a stash of whisky,' she said, wriggling free.

'You mean there's whisky in the house that my dad hasn't drunk already?'

'I mean these.' Joanna plunged her hand into the pocket of the jacket and pulled out the two miniatures I had rescued from Bowman's hotel suite the day before. 'They were in your jacket.'

I went over, took the whisky miniatures from her, put them back into the jacket pocket, laid the jacket over the back of a chair and gave her a cuddle and a kiss. 'No, I am not a secret drinker. Those were a present from my client. He's a Mormon and doesn't drink alcohol. Now would you stop worrying about things and sit down?' I led her over to an armchair and lowered her into it. Tina came back so I picked her up and she gave me a toothpasty kiss.

'Anyway . . .' Malky said. I'd almost forgotten he was there. Come to think of it, why *was* my brother there? It was Tuesday. I never saw him on a Tuesday. I tried not to see anyone on a Tuesday. It was too near Monday. 'I'll tell you why I'm here. It's about Kim.'

My dad looked worried.

'You've not dumped her, have you, Malky?' Joanna said.

Tina squirmed, and I let her down. She went over to

Malky. 'I like Kim. She's pretty and she can run fast.'

Malky lifted my daughter onto his knee. 'Not fast enough,' he said, 'because I'm going to catch her.' He looked around at us. 'I just wanted to tell you all . . .' He was having difficulty expressing himself. That was unusual. People understanding what he was expressing was usually the problem. 'I think Kim's the one.'

'The one what?' I thought it pertinent to ask.

'*The* one,' he said. 'The one for me.'

Tina was quicker than the rest of us. 'You're going to marry Kim!' she squealed.

My dad reached over and pinched his elder son's cheek. 'That's great news.'

'Hold on,' I said. 'You've only been going out with her a few weeks.'

'You only officially went out with me for a few weeks before you proposed,' Joanna reminded me. 'Are you saying it was a mistake?'

'If it was, it was the best mistake of my life,' I said. I might not always ask the right questions, but I knew the right answers.

'When did you arrive at this realisation?' Joanna asked my brother.

'I think it was Saturday night,' Malky replied. 'Robbie's a man, he'll understand. We were out for a drink in Glasgow at a cocktail bar. And you know how Kim's talked me into doing Sober October?' I did, although I had a feeling my brother would follow it up with Can't Remember November.

'Well, when we went up to the bar, I asked for a Coke and straightaway Kim said she'd have a glass of white wine.'

'Impressive,' I said.

Joanna didn't understand. 'Why does that make her your soulmate?'

Malky shook his head, sadly. 'Explain things to your wife, Robbie.'

In football terms, that was called a blue light or hospital pass. Still, I gave it a bash. 'You see . . .' I said, coming over and taking Joanna's hands in mine in a gesture of affection, but also because there was less chance of her hitting me that way. 'Think what happens when we go out.'

'I'm not sure I can remember that far back,' she said. 'The pilot light in the boiler goes out more than us these days.'

I continued. 'I go up to the bar, take a quick look at the beers and ask for a pint of something.'

'So?'

'So . . . you have to find a seat, take off your coat, have the cocktail list brought to you, check the individual ingredients of each, ask the barman about a few of them and, eventually, once you've selected the one that takes the longest to make, I have to go over and bring it to you.'

'What's wrong with that?' Joanna asked.

'I'm not saying it's wrong. And it's not just you. It's . . . well, it's generally what women do.'

'And it's very annoying,' Malky added.

'Joanna's a woman,' my dad pointed out, unnecessarily from my point of view. 'Everyone knows they have problems making up their minds about things. It's how they're made. What do you expect Joanna to do? Shout a round up by herself and fetch her own drink? Don't be crazy. That's a man's job.'

I could tell my wife was having trouble knowing whether to side with my dad's well-intentioned, sexist remark, or remove one of her hands from mine and give him a slap with it. Instead, she turned on Malky. 'Is drink all you ever think about?'

'You're the person falsely accusing my brother of being an alcoholic,' he said.

But Joanna wasn't going to let herself be side-tracked by reason. 'Are you really trying to tell us Kim's drink-ordering decisiveness has made you realise that you want to spend the rest of your life with her?'

'Of course not. That's just a "for instance". There are other reasons. I just . . .' Malky coughed and patted Tina's head. 'Can't go into detail right now. Let's just say she's highly flexible and . . . amenable. You know . . . In bed.'

'Tina, go and brush your teeth,' I said.

'I've already brushed them.'

'Then brush them again.'

Tina trudged off to the bathroom and Malky continued. 'I'm thinking about asking her to move in with me when we get back from Leuven.'

'From where?' Joanna asked.

'Leuven. It's not far from Brussels. Scotland ladies are playing Belgium,' Malky said. 'Kim's captain. It's on Thursday night, eight o'clock kick-off. I'm going over with the team.'

'We should all go,' I said.

Joanna pointed to her bump in case I'd forgotten.

'Then I'll take Tina,' I said. 'Give you some peace. My trial should finish tomorrow.'

For once, my dad agreed with a suggestion of mine. 'It'll be good for the bairn to see the lassies playing football. Good role models for her.'

'You'll be all right alone for one night, won't you?' I said.

Joanna looked at the bump in case it had any contrary views on the matter. 'I suppose so. I'm not due for another fortnight. But where's the money coming from for this?'

I sat down on the arm of her chair. 'Just you relax and look after our baby. Let me worry about the money.'

35

Thoughts of my upcoming Belgium/Holland trip and my confrontation with Reuben, prevented me from having the best night's sleep possible. I woke early and tried to focus my mind on the coming day's court proceedings. At six o'clock, I phoned Peter Falconer to ask if I could have a pre-trial consultation with our client.

'You could, but I don't see the point,' he said, yawning down the line at me.

'The point, Peter, is that I don't care what he says, Oscar is going into the witness box today and he'd better have something to say. Hopefully something that includes a defence. Have you had a word with him about that?'

'Not yet, but I'll try. What kind of a defence were you thinking of?'

'Making up the defence isn't really my job, Peter,' I said. 'Oscar is supposed to tell me why he's not guilty, not the other way around. I need him to give me something I can put to the jury. Was he possessed by demons? Did his evil twin abduct him and take his place at the snooker table? The jury will expect to hear an explanation for those outrageous misses.'

Peter's lack of response was discouraging if not unexpected and, while making up defences might not be my job, I wasn't too proud to offer suggestions. 'Was he nervous or overconfident, maybe not feeling well?'

197

'I've told you, Robbie. The boy's got deeply held beliefs. He won't go into the witness box and lie.'

'But he doesn't mind ripping-off some bookies. That's okay, is it?'

'Gambling's a sin. Maybe ripping off sinners evens things out with the Big Man up there. How should I know? I'm not religious. Anyway, I don't know if he's guilty or not. He's confided in me about as much as he has with you. All I know is that he's dead against giving evidence, and I can only assume the reason is he doesn't want to take the oath and lie.'

'Does he have to?'

'Go into the witness box? I thought you said—'

'No, does he have to lie?' I said.

'What do you mean?'

'I meant plan A. Pressure.'

Peter thought about that. 'Snooker's certainly a high-pressure sport,' he said at last. 'You need to concentrate on every single shot. One slip-up can lose you a match.'

'And it must be tough getting to the top,' I said. 'Even harder staying there. Oscar's only human, and—'

'His nerves got the better of him? He got a bit twitchy sometimes?'

'Exactly.'

'You think that's the truth?'

I didn't know, but I hoped it was close enough for Peter to persuade Bowman to testify.

I cancelled the call, put on my suit-of-the-day and caught the next train. What would Crowe do, I wondered? Would he leave things as they were and close the Crown case? There was another ex-professional snooker player on the Crown witness list. Would he bother to call him? I might have made a few minor dents in Steve Perry's evidence, but I hadn't even scratched the diamond-coated veneer on George Dalling's account of things. Many a prosecutor would have called every witness on the indictment, boring the jury, and allowing the defence to nibble here and there at their credibility and reliability, undermining the Crown case. That wasn't Crowe's style. He was a man who thought no one ever lost a case by underestimating the attention span of the average juror. Don't give them too much to think about, was his motto. Give them a quick slap in the face with the best evidence you've got and demand a conviction. Knowing Crowe, he'd finish with Gentleman George's testimony still ringing in the jury's ears and close the Crown case at that. So, since I'd promised not to call Yasmin, I'd have to decide whether to go straight to speeches or risk putting Bowman in the witness box, not knowing what he might say.

I took the seat opposite Crowe in the well of the deserted courtroom around the back of nine. 'Still thinking about putting your client in?' he asked. 'Difficult isn't it – thinking?'

'What about you?' I asked.

'Just one more witness and then I'll close,' he said.

So, I'd been wrong. Crowe was going to blunt the sharpness of George Dalling's evidence by firing in another ex-player who, unlike Gentleman George, was not worthy to chalk my client's cue.

My path was now clear. I'd studied the CVs of all the so-called expert witnesses. Mike Smith was the third of a trio of ex-snooker pros on the Crown list, and the least successful. What right did he have to criticise my client, the man no less than Gentleman George Dalling had described as the best snooker player of his generation?

Crowe stared across the table at me. 'What are you looking so pleased about?'

I was looking pleased because Crowe had clearly lost his mind. I was already looking forward to my cross-examination of Smith. After I'd humiliated him sufficiently, I'd put my client in and ask him all about myoclonus. All I needed to do was spin things out so that I could give Bowman the heads-up during mid-morning break. I knew Crowe would cry foul-play, but I'd promised not to call Yasmin as a witness. I'd never said anything about not leading evidence from the accused or about the pressure induced muscle twitches that gave him the snooker yips.

I read over Mike Smith's statement. It was very short, as short as his list of sporting accomplishments. After that I went in search of a cup of coffee and my client.

'What do you know about Mike Smith?' I asked, once I'd smuggled Bowman and his agent into the courtroom for privacy, making sure we were out of Crowe's earshot.

'He's held a grudge against Oscar for years,' Peter answered on behalf our mutual client. 'Everyone knows that. Four years ago, Oscar held his own invitational tournament in Dubai, sponsored by a big oil company. The top prize was half a million, but everyone received a hundred grand just for showing up. Oscar didn't invite Mike. When he asked why, Oscar told him because it was a masters' event, not amateur night. Mike really didn't like that.'

Excellent. It was just the sort of sour grapes I wanted, and I couldn't wait to give the jury a bunch of them.

I was still smiling quietly to myself when the jury was brought on and the sheriff enquired of Crowe if the Prosecution was leading more evidence.

Crowe stood, his silk gown swirling about him like a cloud of black smoke. As he addressed the bench, his eyes never left me. 'Just one, M'Lady,' he said. 'The final witness for the Crown is Professor Edward Bradley.'

36

The sheriff saw no need for prosecution counsel to wade through all of Professor Bradley's professional qualifications; the court closed at four o'clock. Instead, she took it upon herself to advise the jury that the final witness for the Crown was Scotland's leading forensic pathologist, and the man who quite literally wrote the book on forensic medicine. She smiled down at the prosecution side of the table. 'That do you, Mr Crowe?'

It would do Mr Crowe very nicely, his delight expressed by an almost imperceptible creasing at the corners of his mouth and a slight tilt of the head.

'Can you tell us what myoclonus is, Professor?' he asked, cutting straight to it.

Professor Bradley rubbed his chin thoughtfully, as though the question had come from left field. I was pretty sure he and Crowe had already met and cultivated the answer.

'Myoclonus is an involuntary twitching of a muscle or a group of muscles.'

'Can you give an example that might help the ladies and gentlemen of the jury better understand that?'

Professor Bradley could. 'Occasionally, when falling asleep, one's arm or leg might jerk.'

'Any other examples?'

'Plenty.' Bradley turned again to a jury that was beginning to look worryingly interested. 'Sometimes a person's eyelid might twitch for no reason. Or, we've all had the hiccoughs, which are caused by an involuntary twitching of the diaphragm.' There were a few blank stares. 'That's the large sheet of muscle separating the thorax from the abdomen.' Still blank. 'Separating the chest cavity from the belly.'

'Thank you, Professor,' Crowe said. 'Now, if you wouldn't mind, I'd like to show you video footage of some snooker matches . . .'

'Will you be long with this witness, Mr Munro?' The sheriff asked, after Cameron Crowe had sat down. The Advocate Depute had kept Professor Bradley in the witness box until eleven-fifteen, around about which time there was normally an interval in the proceedings for refreshments.

'Not very,' I said.

'In which case, I think we'll dispense with a coffee break today. This is Mr Crowe's last witness, and I'm sure Professor Bradley will have important matters to attend to. Perhaps we'll stop early for lunch.'

There were a few grunts of disappointment from those jury members who were not Latter Day saints and had been looking forward to a mid-morning caffeine shot. In the face of some irritable looks, I began.

'Professor Bradley, you often give evidence in important cases, like murder trials, don't you?'

'I do.'

'You're called upon to use your expertise to give a considered opinion on such matters as how a person died and the timing of their death?'

'Amongst other things, that's correct.'

'And before you provide such an opinion, you carry out a post-mortem examination. Is that also correct?'

'It is.'

'Professor, in your evidence-in-chief, you seemed to rule out myoclonus as a possible explanation for my client's snooker errors. How can you be so sure?'

'I can't be,' Bradley said, straight-faced. 'Perhaps your client gets the hiccoughs a lot, or maybe he was nodding off to sleep when he was playing those particular shots.' There was laughter from the public gallery and scowls turned to smiles in the jury box.

'There are other more serious causes, though, aren't there,' I came back with. 'Causes that aren't funny.'

Professor Bradley conceded there were.

'Such as?' I asked.

'Such as multiple sclerosis, Parkinson's disease, Alzheimer's disease. Then there's Gaucher's disease, subacute sclerosing panencephalitis, Creutzfeldt–Jakob disease, serotonin toxicity and some cases of Huntington's disease.'

'Anything else?' I asked, giving the jury what I hoped was a, *not-so-funny-now-is-it?* look.

Professor Bradley thought for a moment. 'It can occur in some forms of epilepsy, one occasionally finds it in intracranial hypotension, and it can also be a symptom of severe alcohol withdrawal, or of suddenly coming off certain drugs, prescribed or otherwise . . . would you like me to go on?'

That wouldn't be necessary.

'Not all the conditions you have mentioned manifest themselves overnight, do they?' I said.

'No, they don't.'

'And have you personally carried out an examination

of my client to establish whether he suffers from any of the ailments you've mentioned?'

'No . . .'

'Have you even been asked to carry out a medical examination of the accused?'

'Again, no . . .'

'So, unlike the normal type of evidence you give in these courts, your evidence of the accused's state of health at the time he played the shots you've been shown is based on no first-hand knowledge at all?'

'That's true . . . But—'

'Thank you,' I said and sat down.

It wasn't much, but it wasn't going to get any better. I walked back to my seat. The procedure in the Scots adversarial court system is for the side calling a witness to lead evidence first, followed by cross-examination by the opponent. After that, the witness can be re-examined by the original side, but *only* on points raised in cross-examination. Simply put, re-examination was a chance to patch up any damage inflicted on a witness during cross, with no further comeback permitted from the other side.

Crowe began his re-examination with, 'Those video clips you've been shown, Professor. They were from tournaments, the earliest of which was nearly two years ago. If the accused was suffering from one of the conditions you've mentioned, do you think he'd be aware of such an illness by now?'

'Most likely,' Bradley said. 'The accused's reputation goes before him. As a Mormon, and a man not inclined to strong drink or even the drug caffeine, I think we can rule out alcohol and drug withdrawal as a cause. As for the others, I am sure he would be aware of them by now, as would his doctor.'

'I see there is a Dr Yasmin Ashmat on the defence witness list,' the sheriff said from on high. 'Is she the accused's doctor?'

'I understand Mr Munro is no longer intent on calling Dr Ashmat, M'Lady,' Crowe said. He was so many steps ahead of me that, when he looked back over his shoulder, I must have seemed like a dot on the horizon.

'Is that correct, Mr Munro? You are leading no medical evidence?' I confirmed the position and the sheriff replied with raised eyebrows, a glance at the jury and a simple, 'Oh.'

The prosecutor thanked Professor Bradley and, before taking his seat, advised the court that he was closing the Crown case.

It was not yet noon when the Sheriff decided to break to allow the defence time to martial itself, decreeing the court should reconvene at two o'clock.

'How's the thinking going?' Crowe enquired as the courtroom slowly emptied. 'Will you be calling your client?'

'I suppose.' What else was there for it? I was as interested as everyone else to hear what he had to say.

I took off my black gown and hung it over a chair. Of all the cases to be given in full glare of the media spotlight, I had to get the one with the mystery defence. I took the stairs to the agents' room. I was a day early for Curry Thursday, which meant I'd have to settle for a roll on square sausage for lunch. I stuffed a hand in my jacket pockets, searching for change, and brought out the whisky miniatures I'd helped myself to from Bowman's minibar. Tempting. For one minute, I thought about drinking them, but only for one minute because, two minutes later, I was outside the building and on the phone to Grace Mary. 'Has Shannon Todd been into the office today?'

205

'No. Why?'

'I loaned her twenty pounds last night. She said she was going to come back today to repay it.' I heard a snort and could picture the derisive look on my secretary's face. 'If she comes to the office—'

'You really think she's going to pay you back? How gullible are you?'

My plan to secure an acquittal for Oscar Bowman was a long enough shot without having to rely on the word of a junkie. Still, Shannon had promised, and I didn't know why, but I'd believed her. She was now my only hope.

'If you do happen to see her, tell her she can keep the money.'

'What?'

'Yes, tell her to keep the twenty, give her another twenty for the train to Glasgow, and say that if she meets me outside the Sheriff Court before one forty-five, there'll be another twenty waiting for her here.'

37

Oscar Bowman arrived at court at one fifty-five in the company of Peter and his close-protection officer. As usual there was a welcoming committee waiting to catch a glimpse of the great man, as well as others queuing to pass through security, all blocking my client's route to the door.

I fought my way through the crowd and took his protection officer aside for a moment to tell her there was a possibility the trial could end today and that if it did, whatever the verdict, the commotion would be considerable and she might want to think about approaching the police to see if a rear exit could be made available for our client to leave by.

She thanked me for the advice, but said that Bowman's instructions were that he wasn't going to hide. He was going to walk in and out of the front door with his head held high no matter what. With that she pushed her way through the mass of people in the entrance way, re-joined her charge and together they passed through the security gate.

There was just time for one last brief meeting before the trial recommenced. I told Bowman his only chance was to give evidence and put on a good performance. 'But,' I said, 'I need to know what you are going to say when you're asked why it was you missed those easy shots. That's what this is all about.'

Bowman looked at me. He said nothing until he'd reached into the breast pocket of his white suit, removed a small tin and popped a mint into his mouth. 'Peter says he's already explained it to you. It was all down to pressure.'

'Pressure.' I said. 'That's your defence?'

I was only making sure, but he seemed to think I was making fun of him.

'Yeah, pressure. How about you bring a snooker table in here? Have the jury try to make those *easy* shots I missed. I get one not guilty vote for every miss, one guilty vote for every pot. Do that and I'll walk out of here a free man.' It was a nice idea. One that might have worked in the movies. But this wasn't Hollywood. This was Glasgow Sheriff Court and the men and women on the jury weren't multi-millionaire snooker players who practised eight hours a day.

'If you're going to say you were nervous and feeling under pressure, you'll be cross-examined about that. Try not to be quite so . . .'

'Quite so, what?' he asked.

'Quite so . . . you,' I said. 'The witness box is not the place for arrogance. Let the prosecutor come across as the bad guy. If your defence is that you buckled under pressure, don't undermine that by coming across all bolshie. Let the jury see that you're human.'

Bowman poked my chest with a finger. 'You wanted to know my defence, and I've given it to you. If you don't like it, but you want to get paid . . .' Clearly Peter hadn't told him that my fees were being covered by the big man in the event of a guilty verdict. 'Then you'll take what I give you in the witness box and use it.' With that, another poke in the chest and a crunch of a mint, he walked into the dock and took his seat.

'Mr Munro, are you ready to begin the defence case?' her ladyship asked, once the court had reconvened.

I informed her I was all set and that I'd be calling the accused to give evidence. Bowman was led from the dock to the witness box. He raised his right hand and chose to affirm.

'I don't think we need to lead the formalities, Mr Munro,' the Sheriff said. 'I'm sure everyone here is well aware of your client's name and occupation, and he needn't reveal his address in open court.'

There was general murmuring around the courtroom as I walked to the edge of the jury box where I waited for silence before asking my first question.

'You're a Mormon, aren't you, Mr Bowman?' I said, across the width of the courtroom.

'That's correct,' he replied.

'And upon which do you place the greater importance: your career as a professional snooker player or your faith?'

'My faith, of course,' Bowman replied without hesitation.

'And can we take it that cheating or telling lies would not fit in with your faith?'

'Of course not.'

'Then could you please tell the ladies and gentlemen of the jury, in all honesty, why it was you missed those so-called easy shots we've watched over the course of this trial?'

The silence of a few moments earlier was shattered by a buzz of excitement. The Sheriff Clerk called order, the buzz turned into a low hum and then silence once more as everyone awaited the answer.

Bowman cleared his throat. His hand reached for the

tin of mints in the breast pocket of his jacket, paused and then fell to his side. He squared his shoulders, cleared his throat looked straight at me and said, 'Pressure.'

'Thank you,' I said, walked back to my seat and sat down.

38

It was a gamble. Cameron Crowe could choose not to cross-examine and go straight to the jury with his closing remarks. In which case, in my own speech, I'd make a big deal out of the fact my client's evidence had gone unchallenged. If the Crown wasn't challenging Bowman's reason – why should the ladies and gentlemen of the jury?

Crowe looked at me across the table, not so quick to rise to his feet on this occasion. I needed him to cross-examine. There were more questions I wanted to ask my client without the Crown having a chance to put those answers to the test. That could only be done in re-examination and re-examination was only permitted if there had been cross-examination in the first place.

'Mr Crowe?' the sheriff enquired. 'Do you have any questions for the witness?'

Crowe picked up a sheaf of papers, shuffled it, tapped the ends on the table and placed the bundle to the side.

'Mr Crowe?' The sheriff asked again.

By now the courtroom was a hubbub.

'Quiet!' the Sheriff Clerk called out. The noise gradually subsided until all that could be heard was the legs of Cameron Crowe's chair scraping against the floor.

'If it please your ladyship,' he said, turning to face the witness. 'Mr Bowman, those various shots you missed, you maintain they were errors caused by pressure?'

Bowman nodded. 'I do.'

'Then I wonder if you could please have a look at a video clip from Crown label number 3.'

We all waited for the bar officer to locate the relevant DVD and place it in the machine. At Crowe's instruction, it was fast-forwarded to a point near the end. I hadn't watched that far. It had only taken me a few views of the earlier shots to get the flavour of things.

'Could you describe what we are watching?' Crowe asked.

Bowman could. It was the final frame of a World Championship match some years earlier. On the big screen, the unmistakable white-clad figure of Oscar Bowman lined up a long-shot into a corner pocket. As the cue was pulled back, Crowe asked for the clip to be paused.

'We're looking at the shot that might win or lose you a third World title, am I right?' Crowe asked.

Bowman agreed that he was indeed correct.

'Can you think of a greater pressure shot than that?' The witness couldn't. 'What advice would you give a player in a similar position?'

The witness had to be encouraged by the sheriff to answer.

'I'd recommend they play safe,' he said.

Crowe nodded to the bar office, the clip recommenced and Bowman, along with the rest of the packed courtroom, watched as the red ball was slammed home before coming off three cushions and back into perfect position for the black ball into the opposite corner.

'I believe you have a professional moniker, a nick-name?'

'That's right.'

'Which is?'

Bowman allowed himself a little smile. 'It's Oscar "The Showman" Bowman.'

'And tell me, what is it you carry in the breast pocket of your jacket?'

'Mints.'

'Let me see.'

Before I could object, Bowman had produced the tin of mints. 'What does it say on the lid?' Crowe asked.

'It says, Oh So Cool Cue-ball Mints.'

Crowe came closer, took the tin of mints and studied it. 'There is a caricature on the lid, isn't there?' There was – of Bowman, bent over a snooker table. 'Because you have another nickname, don't you?' he asked. 'Other than Bowman the Showman, don't they call you Bowman the Snowman?'

'I've heard it mentioned,' Bowman replied. 'I don't really pay all that much attention.'

'Why do they think they call you that?'

'Perhaps it's to do with the white suits I wear.'

Crowe carved out a smile, shook the tin, tucked it back into Bowman's top pocket and patted it. 'Or perhaps it's because of your renowned coolness under pressure?' He could have finished his cross-examination there, but I'd gambled on Crowe wanting to hammer in what he thought to be the final nail in the defence coffin. 'Myoclonus . . .' he placed a finger along his top lip, stifling a smile. 'Do you have any of the illnesses or medical conditions that you heard Professor Bradley mention this morning?'

'Not so far as I am aware.'

'You're not prone to falling-asleep leg-jerks or hiccoughing fits brought on by the pressure of playing lesser opponents in the early rounds of snooker competitions?'

Bowman didn't answer. He didn't need to.

'Thank you so very much,' Crowe said, with huge mocking politeness and returned to his seat.

When I rose to re-examine, it was difficult to assess who was staring at me with the most hatred, the witness himself or big Peter Falconer in the front row of the public gallery.

'Myoclonus. Had you heard that word before today?' I asked Bowman.

'No.'

'But you now understand what it is?'

'It's something to do with muscle twitching.'

'We've heard it can be brought on by a lot of different medical conditions. You heard Professor Bradley tell us some of them?'

'I did.'

'And you told Mr Crowe just now that you don't suffer from any of them. Is that correct?'

'Yes, it is.'

'Then let me ask you again and this time, if you don't mind, answer honestly.'

'Is Mr Munro suggesting his client is a liar?' Crowe asked the sheriff.

'I think we're about to find out,' she replied.

The noise level in the court had increased again. The sheriff told her clerk to ask for quiet. 'And tell that man in the front row to sit down or I'll have him removed.'

I glanced over to where Peter Falconer was slowly lowering his six-foot-nine frame back into a seat.

After that short interruption, I repeated my question. 'Well, Mr Bowman, were you suffering from any of the medical conditions mentioned when you missed the shots we've been shown over the past day or so?'

Bowman flashed a puzzled expression from me to his

now seated agent and back to me. 'Not to my knowledge, no.'

'Before a competition, are professional snooker players drug tested?'

'They are, and quite rightly,' Bowman said.

'And is alcohol, once prevalent in the game, now considered a performance enhancing drug?'

'It is.' Bowman was no longer puzzled, he was downright confused. I was pleased about that.

'So, a professional snooker player who was addicted to alcohol would be wise to stop a day or so before a tournament for fear of a positive test?'

'He'd be wiser not to touch alcohol at all,' Bowman said.

'The first few days of alcohol withdrawal are the worst, would you agree?' I asked.

'I'll take your word for it,' Bowman answered.

'It's your word the jury is more interested in,' I said.

'Then how would I know? I've never suffered from alcohol withdrawal.'

'But if you had, is that something you'd be prepared to lie about?'

'That's a ridiculous question,' Bowman said.

'I'll decide how ridiculous Mr Munro's questions are, not you,' the Sheriff told him.

Bowman heaved a sigh. 'No, I wouldn't lie about it.'

'But if you were to admit that you were suffering from myoclonus brought on by alcohol withdrawal, it would damage your standing in the Mormon community, would it not?'

'Of course.'

'While a conviction for cheating would only damage your snooker career.'

Bowman looked about for help. There was none. 'This is not ridiculous,' he said, 'this is downright crazy.'

I ploughed on. 'Do you remember, earlier in your evidence, you told us that you place a greater importance on your faith than your career.'

'That's true. But I do not have a drink problem.'

I walked over and removed the tin of mints from his top pocket. 'You eat a lot of these in the course of a day, don't you?'

'I only endorse products I actually use.'

'And I'll bet they'd be good for concealing the smell of alcohol on your breath.'

The witness and Cameron Crowe were in competition to look the most indignant. Crowe was first to express his indignation by leaping to his feet. 'What Mr Munro would or would not bet on is not the issue here.'

The sheriff was going to interject, but my next question was already out. 'Do you have a mini-bar in your hotel suite, Mr Bowman.'

'Doesn't every hotel suite?'

'Then answer me, yes or no? Right now, is there any alcohol left in it?'

'You know I had—'

'Just, yes or no, please.'

'No.'

Crowe who had been lowering himself into his seat, stood up again, then thought better of it, sharp enough to know further attempts to object would only make the jury think he was trying to cover up something.

'Would you kindly put your hand in your jacket pockets?' I asked the witness.

Crowe did object this time. 'What the accused has in his jacket pockets is of no relevance, M'Lady.'

216

'You didn't seem to think so during cross-examination, Mr Crowe,' she replied.

'Do I have to do this?' Bowman asked.

There are few things annoy a sheriff more than a witness who asks questions instead of answering them. 'Perhaps if you did, we might find out why Mr Munro is asking you to.'

Highly disgruntled, Bowman shoved first his right and then his left hand into the side pockets of his jacket. As he did so his face beamed bright red from beneath his blonde quiff.

'Place what is in your pockets on the ledge in front of you, please,' I said.

Bowman didn't so much as twitch a muscle.

'Do it now,' the sheriff ordered.

Slowly, and simultaneously, Bowman pulled out a whisky miniature from the right pocket and one from the left. He set them down in front of him. 'These are not mine,' he said. Then again, straight at the jury. 'I do not have a drink problem.' And again, louder, this time looking around the courtroom. 'I do not have a drink problem!'

Turning from the witness box, I looked up at the bench. 'Thank you, M'Lady. I have no more questions for the witness.'

39

With my tickets booked for the flight to Belgium the next day, I'd hoped we'd might get things wrapped up that Wednesday afternoon. The sheriff didn't agree. With closing speeches and her own charge to the jury still to come, she thought it better to send the ladies and gentlemen home early with instructions to return fresh at nine-thirty the following morning.

The jury speech is a lawyer's chance to put a spin on things, to eliminate the negatives and accentuate the positives of their case. Jury speeches vary in length. The following day, Crowe spoke for forty-five minutes with references to various video clips and the evidence of his snooker experts. I, like many defence lawyers, believed the longer I spoke, the guiltier the jury were likely to think my client. The famous defence advocate and Dean of the Faculty, Gordon Jackson QC, is said once to have approached the jury box, looked at the assembled men and women, shrugged his shoulders and resumed his seat. If that's true, my speech to the jury on behalf of Oscar Bowman was not the shortest in Scottish legal history, but it was the shortest in my legal history. Then again, it did take a while for me to get started, since my own words were prefaced by my client screaming at me from the dock that he didn't have a drink problem – which was like screaming that he didn't have a defence. And who in their right mind would do that? Only someone who'd rather be found guilty and lose their career, than admit to alcoholism and lose their religious reputation. When eventually he'd been silenced by the sheriff, I walked slowly over to the jury box.

'Everyone knows someone battling with an alcohol problem,' I said. This was Scotland. This was Glasgow. I felt I was on safe ground with that opening remark. 'We all know that half the battle—'

'I don't have a drink problem!' Bowman shrieked for the umpteenth time.

I gave the jury the sincerest look of sympathy I could fake. 'Is admitting that you have a problem in the first place.'

40

No-one turns down a free meal unless it's court food. Before lunch the jury returned a majority not proven verdict. I waited until the courtroom had cleared before slipping out as discreetly as Shannon Todd had slipped the miniatures of whisky into the pockets of Oscar Bowman's pristine white jacket.

There was no one waiting for me; not even my client, which was good. I thought it best to let things settle before contacting him again and, in any event, it would take some time for me to prepare a fee note that properly reflected the efforts that had secured the world snooker champion's future professional career.

It was cutting it fine, but there was one thing I had to do before grabbing my daughter and catching the four-twenty flight to Brussels. From the Sheriff Court I took a taxi to Elliot Holliday's shop on Great Western Road where I found him cutting up some cardboard boxes for recycling, while at the same time talking a customer through the history of a nineteenth century glass scent bottle. When he saw me come in, he excused himself and we went through to the back of the shop where, amongst other pieces of vintage furniture, stood a fine American style pool table, much larger than the one in the Red Corner Bar, with brass and leather corner protectors, proper net pockets and carved mahogany legs.

'No wonder you beat me at pool,' I said.

He folded the blade, slipped it into his pocket and gave the green felt a rap with his knuckles. 'Solid slate. It's not for sale. I've got to do something between customers. Still, your game should have improved a lot considering the company you've been keeping recently. I heard the result on the radio just now. You and your client were unavailable for comment.'

I resisted the urge to brag about my famous victory. Holliday wouldn't care. His more pressing concern, like mine, was to establish the authenticity of the painting now locked in my office safe. 'I'm going to Holland tomorrow,' I told him.

Without another word, he went over to a sideboard, pulled open one of the drawers and removed a thick envelope. He handed it to me. 'I've been expecting you. That's my nine to go with the thousand I've already given you and the five from Kim.'

'And if it turns out to be a fake?' I asked.

'You places your bet and you takes your chances. If you ask me, though, this is a racing certainty.'

I really hoped so. Even with the promise of Bowman's fee to come, I couldn't bear the thought of losing five thousand of my own and still having to pay Kim six thousand as I'd promised.

'And if it turns out to be genuine?' I asked.

'Let me deal with that side of things,' he said. 'Getting cheats off on dodgy defences is your job. Selling antiques is mine.'

I'd be glad to. I was still worried about any backlash if word got out that I'd fallen heir to a fortune courtesy of a painting one of my clients had stolen. Mrs Glowacki may have told me to keep her husband's stuff, but I doubted whether she'd have been of the same opinion if she hadn't been quite so angry, or if she'd known the painting's true value. And then there was Reuben to think about. If the sale went public and he recognised the painting, he was bound to blow the whistle on me.

'Let me know as soon as you have any news,' Holliday said, walking me to the door, past the customer who was still closely studying the enamel on the scent bottle. 'If it's good news, bring the item here straightaway.'

41

That evening, Scotland's women's team came back from two-one down at the interval to win three-two. In the recent past, I'd taken Tina to a few Linlithgow Rose matches, where she'd spent most of her time running back and forwards to the pie stand or asking how long there was to go. Not today. Today she'd sat, waving her saltire and cheering her little heart out. When Kim had clinched the game with a late double, I knew my daughter's career in dancing was over.

Early next morning, while Malky relaxed with Kim and the rest of the Scotland women's team at our hotel in Leuven, Tina and I took a two-hour train ride across the Belgian border to The Hague. For all the hefty admission price, the Mauritshuis wasn't a particularly large art gallery, exhibiting mainly seventeenth century Dutch and Flemish art. I soon discovered that a tour of paintings of men dressed in black and big beards, studies in oil of bowls of fruit, and pastoral landscapes, wasn't the best way to show a seven-year-old a good time. Although I had held out some hope for the more famous exhibits on display, my daughter wasn't greatly impressed by the Girl with the Pearl Earring, and as for The Goldfinch on the adjacent wall, frankly, Tina thought she could have done better. She would have done a parrot. Parrots had a lot more colours than a goldfinch that was hardly gold at all.

In all it took me an hour to drag Tina around the two hundred or so paintings, which was half as long as I'd been asked to wait while Bruno van der Ham carried out his examination of the alleged Rembrandt painting.

We'd met him on the north side of the Hofvijver Lake, opposite the Dutch Parliament complex. It was not far from the art gallery, but sufficiently so for van der Ham not to be seen with us; though what was so suspicious about a father and his seven-year-old daughter handing over a child's rucksack, I didn't know.

'I can't be too careful,' he said about our meeting place.

'I can't either,' I told him, when he advised he would be taking the painting away to run some tests.

He sighed, 'Mr . . .' Knowing my name wasn't part of the deal. Bridget Goodsir had arranged the rendezvous, all part of her share of the twenty thousand commission. 'Look at me.'

I did. He was a small man, wrapped in a large overcoat. About his neck he wore a green cashmere scarf, and on his head a black homburg. Age-wise he could have been seventy, he could have been eighty. 'Do you really think I am going to run away with your precious painting?'

It wasn't the running away I was worried about. It was the not coming back.

'Mr . . .' he tried again. I didn't assist. 'You are a man who has come a long way to see me with what my old friend thinks is a very valuable painting. People who come to see me with valuable paintings, and do not want me to know their names, are usually here on behalf of other people who will not only know my name, but where I live and when to visit me. So, please . . .' He held out his hand to receive the rucksack. 'Trust me.' I gave the rucksack to him. 'And my remuneration?'

'Half,' I said. 'The other half when you come back.'

He shook his head. 'While you can trust me, I cannot trust a man who does not give me his name.'

Reluctantly, I put the second of the two envelopes into which I had divided the money on top of the first and handed them over. Why not? The whole thing was one big gamble anyway.

After the art gallery, I bought a huge cone of chips, squirted generously with ketchup and mayonnaise, and together Tina and I wandered through the Binnenhof to the original meeting point, stopping to look at the lake in front of the parliament building, and watching the swans swimming between the red, green and yellow platforms that floated on the surface.

Having come a distant second in the chip-eating competition, I saw, right on time, the small man in the homburg heading our way, Tina's little pink rucksack tucked under his arm.

'It is what you think it is,' he said, as he approached.

I felt weak at the knees.

'How much do you think it would fetch?' I asked, as he handed it over.

'That very much depends on how you choose to sell it and to whom.'

'If I sold it to you?'

'Four hundred thousand Euros,' he said without a second's hesitation. He'd obviously been giving the matter some thought. All the same, it was a lot less than the million pounds Holliday had mentioned.

'What about the one in New York a few years ago?' I said. 'It went for nearly double that, didn't it?'

He gave the rucksack a poke with his finger. 'Your painting is in poor condition. It needs cleaned and restored. That would be a six-figure sum itself. Perhaps then you would receive double or even treble what I suggest, I don't deny it. But that would be on the open market. Is that a market that interests you? If so, I would be happy to provide you with my written confirmation that the piece is genuine. My word would be good enough for any legitimate auction house. If you would prefer not to go down that route, then my offer is a generous one.'

We shook hands. 'If I need further help,' I said, 'I know where to find you.'

42

Tina couldn't wait to tell her grandpa all about the football match when we arrived at his place fresh off the plane late that afternoon. We were joined later by Malky. He'd caught a different flight and was now all set for his Friday five-a-side match. I left my daughter with them so I could nip through to tell Holliday the good news. Before that, I thought I'd drop into the office to see how things were going. First, I went home to see Joanna. She was in the newly decorated bedroom, standing on a set of aluminium stepladders, putting up a pair of curtains.

'Have a nice time?' she asked, turning around.

The stepladders wobbled. I grabbed them. 'Get down here. What do you think you're doing climbing up ladders when you're going to have a baby in a few days?'

I took the curtain from her and helped her down.

'I just want everything to be ready,' she said.

I climbed up the ladders and hooked the curtain onto the rail. 'I don't see why you couldn't have waited for me. What if you'd fallen?'

'I'm pregnant, I'm not disabled,' she said. 'Come here.' She hugged me and gave me a kiss. 'I've been thinking . . .'

When wives say that, while hugging and kissing their husbands, it means one thing.

'Buy it,' I said.

'But you don't know what I was going to say.'

'Yes, I do. You're thinking of spending money and I'm saying go ahead.'

Joanna let go of me. 'What happened over there?'

'Over where?'

'In Belgium, of course.'

'Nothing. Just a football match. I think Tina's giving up dancing and going back to the fun-four-football, by the way.'

'Don't change the subject. Why are you so willing to let me spend money?'

'How much were you thinking of spending?'

'You know how we've got about five thousand in the bank for a rainy day?'

'Go on,' I said.

'I thought we could use it to put a small conservatory on the side of the house. Think how nice that would be for us to sit in with the kids during the summer? My dad's not all that busy right now. He could do it for practically nothing. Or, at least, not much more than the five thousand. He'd only want money for materials. It would be his gift to his new grandchild.' She had it all worked out.

The Winnie the Pooh clock on the wall told me it was four o'clock. I still had to check in at the office before heading through to Glasgow to see Holliday. There was a great deal to discuss. Did I trust him to hold onto the painting? Thus far, he had trusted me.

I gave my wife a kiss. 'Sounds great. Tell your dad to crack on with it.'

'Really?'

'Of course. Why are you looking at me like that?' Joanna didn't say anything, just kept eyeing me suspiciously. I kissed her again. 'Anyway, got to go.' I slapped my pocket. 'Don't worry, I've got my mobile. Try not to go rock-climbing or roller-blading while I'm away. I'll only be gone a couple of hours.'

At the office, Grace Mary was sitting in reception slogging over a hot cup of tea and a *People's Friend*.

'You've got a visitor,' she said flicking to an article on hand-knitted cushion covers. 'Kaye Mitchell has been sitting in your room for half an hour. I said she could wait. I knew you'd be back before five to check up on me.'

Kaye was editor of the local newspaper. I assumed she'd be after the inside story on the Oscar Bowman case. Nothing I could tell her about it wouldn't end up with me in trouble.

'Sorry, Kaye,' I said, marching into my room. 'I'm sworn to secrecy on the whole Bowman thing.'

Kaye took her feet off my desk, tore herself away from the case file she was reading and looked up at me. 'Who?'

'Oscar Bowman.'

'Oh, him? The alky snooker player? He's yesterday's news. I did try and find you for a quote, but you were off watching football somewhere, or so Grace Mary said. No, I'm here about your client George McCann. I've just been reading his file. Not much to it, is there?'

'That's probably because he's dead.'

'Which is all very well for him,' Kaye said, 'but it doesn't help me much. It's still a week 'til Halloween, and I have to fill the pages with something.'

'Kaye . . . There's no easy way of saying this. No, wait, there is. Stop reading my confidential files and get out of my office.'

There are people in this world who take offence at the slightest thing. People who want safe spaces and restrictions on freedom of speech. Then there are people like Kaye; people who never take offence at anything anyone says, no matter how much other people want them to.

'How low can you stoop?' Pretty low was the answer, some would say, but for a change, Kaye wasn't accusing me. 'Imagine breaking into the home of a Mengele twin,' she tutted, ignoring my invitation for her to leave.

'Who did that?'

'Your dead client.'

'The woman's name is Glowacki not Mengele,' I said.

Kaye sighed. 'I know what her name is. I'm talking about Dr Josef Mengele of Auschwitz. The Angel of Death.'

I pulled up the seat my clients usually sat on, and not for very long if I could help it. 'I have absolutely no idea what you're talking about, Kaye,' I said, but I did, or at least an idea was forming in my mind and I didn't like it one little bit.

Kaye sat up straight. 'Aurelia Glowacki used to be Aurelia Bienka a farmworker from eastern Poland. She was taken to Auschwitz-Birkenau, along with her mother, father, older brother and her twin sister Zara in October 1944.' From somewhere, I recalled numbers I thought had been written in pen on the old lady's wrist. Kaye continued. 'She and Zara were experimented on by Josef Mengele. She doesn't know what happened to the rest of her family. They were either worked to death or died in the gas chambers. They used to say the only way out of Auschwitz was up a chimney. Zara died. Eva survived. Do you not read the *Gazette* or something? I did a centre-page spread on her at the start of the year. She was seventeen years old when the Russians freed Auschwitz in January 1945. She wrote a book about her experience: *Hitler's Guinea Pigs*. It was a bestseller. She assigned the rights to the Drezner Foundation.'

'Who?'

'The Drezner Foundation. It's an organisation that funds a group of Jewish and other charities. After the war, Eva married a Polish Resistance fighter, Jakub Glowacki. They married and moved to the Netherlands, then came to live in Scotland sometime in the sixties and set up a business here. Mrs Glowacki is terminally ill, but she's tough. She had six months to live a year ago. No one knows why she's still alive. They say her husband died from the stress of thinking his wife was going to die. She's a remarkable woman. She's moving to a private hospice for her last few weeks or months or however long, courtesy of Drezner. In return, she's selling up and leaving everything, including her home to the charity. When I heard her house had been broken into, and you'd acted for the person responsible, I thought it would make a good follow-up story.' She shook her head at the very thought of it, smiling in disbelief. 'I mean just how despicable can one person be?'

I tried to smile back, but it wasn't easy; not when you knew you were about to steal from a Holocaust survivor. Who was the more despicable? Drugged-up Genghis McCann for stealing the painting or me for keeping it?

Kaye continued. 'Now I find the burglar is dead and, according to your file, never even stole anything.' She closed the file and tossed it to the side. 'What else have you got? My readers like crime. I've already got the murder at the scrappy's in this week's *Gazette*, I need something juicy for the next edition. All I have so far is a story on some neds trying to kill a swan down at the loch. It's not going to win me the Pulitzer.'

After I'd persuaded Kaye that I had nothing that would be of interest to her readers, we got onto the subject of Joanna and the pregnancy. 'Find me a story, Robbie, and

231

you'll never need to look for a babysitter for all these wee Munros you keep producing.'

One of those wee Munros being still very much in production, it was my proclaimed urgent need to be at my wife's side that allowed me to manoeuvre Kaye to the door. An hour later, having battled through the Friday afternoon traffic, I was trying to find a parking space on Great Western Road. Even after I'd crammed my car into a space a hundred yards from the antique shop, I sat thinking over what Kaye had said about the remarkable Eva Glowacki. Previously I'd consoled myself with the thought that I was only taking the proceeds of the painting before the tax man did. Money that, but for Holliday and me, the tax man would never have got his grasping claws on anyway. Now it transpired that the dying old lady was a Holocaust survivor and her estate destined for charity.

By the time I arrived at the antiques shop, it was almost six o'clock. The lights were off and a steel roller shutter had been brought down over the front window. I walked through an archway at the side of the building that was just wide enough for a car or a small van, and up a dark alley to a solid looking metal door at the rear of the shop. I knocked. No answer. I tried the door. It was locked. I was taking my mobile out of my pocket to phone Holliday, when I happened to notice a metallic green car parked further up the alley where it opened into a small courtyard. I also happened to notice that the car was an SUV: one just like Kim's. It even bore the Hibernian FC crest and the logo of her sponsor on the side and rear. I cancelled the call and squeezed between two wheelie bins bulging with cardboard to look through a small window fitted with thick metal bars. Through it I could make out Holliday's back room. Somewhere within, a dim light illuminated the collection of antique sideboards, tallboys, tables and chairs on display. Cupping my hands for a better look, I could see the carved legs of the old pool table, and two other pairs of legs; human legs. Bare human legs, so close together that it was difficult at first to make out where one pair started and the other finished. One pair of legs belonged to a man, Holliday, I assumed. The other set of pins I was sure I had last seen wearing the pink and black socks of the Scottish women's football team. I backed away, walked to my car and waited there until, through the gathering gloom, I saw the green SUV reverse out of the alleyway and drive past me, Kim at the wheel. I waited a further ten minutes before phoning Holliday to tell him I was on my way.

43

'What do you mean you can't go through with it?'

Elliot Holliday was having trouble understanding English. He'd taken me through to the back room where the pool table stood innocently by.

'It belongs to an old lady,' I said. 'She's selling up and giving everything to charity. I can't take the painting knowing some orphan is going to go hungry because of me.'

'But you said she told you to keep it. Remember?' I didn't need reminding. It was the one fragile straw of legitimacy I'd been clutching onto over recent days. It had since snapped. 'The painting's not hers to give to charity. Do what you want with your share of the money, but I want mine.'

I couldn't accept that Holliday had any more right to the painting than I had.

'You have to see that she only told me to keep the stolen stuff to get rid of what she saw as a strange man at her door. She obviously doesn't know the painting's true value. Come on. You're the man who was scared of a curse put on you by an old lady for having it off with her granddaughter. What kind of bad luck do you think follows the theft of a million quid from an old lady who survived Auschwitz, that should have gone to charity?'

Holliday spun around, kicked an Edwardian sideboard and began to pace the room. I waited. Eventually he marched back over to where I was standing next to the pool table, trying not to touch it.

'This was my big break,' he said. 'Look at this place. It's a glorified junk shop. I barely cover my overheads. I'd have been better off staying in the Army.'

His face hardened. 'And what about my money? I gave you ten grand.'

'I'm going to do a deal about that with the old lady,' I said. 'If she won't listen to me, there's this guy who used to work with her husband. He looks after her. I think I can make him see sense. I'll tell him I've had to buy the painting back for twenty, thirty grand even. We can get our money back with a little on top. How's that sound?'

Holliday punched the solid slate surface of the pool table. Neither seemed to notice. 'Tell this guy we'll go fifty-fifty on it. That's fair. We've done all the work.'

'Seeing how you've mentioned it,' I said. 'Strictly speaking, it's me who's done all the work. It was my client who stole the painting in the first place, it was me who recovered it and I'm the one who's been travelling around Europe to have its authenticity verified. So far, all you've done is chip in some money. Money that I'll see you get refunded before the rest goes to charity.'

'That's bullshit, and you know it.' Holliday threw out his chest and jabbed a finger into it. 'There would be no money for charity if it wasn't for me. No one recognised the painting or its value. If I hadn't come along, it would have remained lost for another five hundred years. Somebody owes me.'

It was true. If he hadn't come along, the painting would probably never have been discovered. What was bothering me most, though, was why he had come along? It was something I hadn't really thought about until now.

How had Holliday learned of the painting? Was it really all down to a WhatsApp group for second-hand furniture dealers? One that Ding Dong Davie Bell had belonged to?

Despite what I'd witnessed earlier, I'd thought it only right I should come and tell Holliday in person. Now that I was alone with him in the back room of his shop, with nobody knowing where I was, I began to wish I'd phoned from the car and broken the news that way. Maybe I'd been hoping he'd change my mind like he had the last time, but the more I'd thought about it, the less I could see an argument in favour of doing a charity out of a million pounds.

'I'm sorry, Elliot,' I said, 'but you must know it's the right thing to do.'

'Where is it?' He walked over to me and said, quietly, but firmly, 'Where's the painting?'

'Safe,' I said, which was more than I felt right at that moment. 'But I'm taking it back to the rightful owner. I'll sort something out to see you get your money back.'

The brrring of a bell. A candlestick telephone, sitting on an old mahogany nightstand. I'd noticed it already and hadn't realised it was functional. Its ring was enough to divert Holliday's attention for the split-second I needed.

'Come back!' he called to me, as I turned and walked smartly to the door. 'We had a deal!'

"Had" being the operative word, for I was breaking the deal, and my heart in the process.

44

'You can't tell him.' Joanna seemed quite certain about that. 'I know he's your brother, but it's got nothing to do with you, and, anyway, it's not like Malky's never two-timed anyone before.'

'So, two wrongs make a right, is that it?'

'They are both adults. We don't know what arrangements they've made about seeing other people.'

It wasn't his girlfriend seeing other people I thought Malky would be most bothered about. It would be the rolling-about-with-her-pants-down-on-pool-tables-with-other-people that he wouldn't like.

'All I know is that I'd want to know if it was you,' I said.

Joanna heaved herself out of her chair and came over to where I was standing next to the fireplace, warming my back. The good thing about having a country property was having a log fire. Unfortunately, having to get up in the morning to light it also made it the bad thing about having a country property.

'Give me a cuddle,' she said. I did. There was a lot of her to cuddle now. 'Would you really want someone to tell you if it was me?'

'Yes . . . no . . . I don't know . . . No wait, I do know. Of course, I'd want someone to tell me.'

'And what would you do if you found out? Would you forgive me?'

237

'Have you got something you want to tell me?'

'Of course not.'

'Then why ask?'

'I'm just interested to know what you'd do.'

'Well, you'll never know because it will never happen – will it?' I said.

'No,' Joanna said, 'but—'

'Then stop changing the subject. Speaking as his brother, and knowing him as I do, I think Malky would—'

'Malky would what?' Fresh from his Friday night five-a-sides, Malky dumped his kitbag on the sofa and walked straight through to the kitchen, returning moments later twisting the top off a bottle of beer.

'I thought you were doing Sober October?' I said.

He took a swig of beer and looked down the length of the green bottle at me. 'I am,' he said, after a long drink, wiping foam off his lips with the back of a hand.

'But that's beer you're drinking,' Joanna said. Six weeks' maternity leave hadn't dulled her razor-sharp powers of observation.

'I know,' Malky said. 'I've decided that Sober October can't mean absolutely no alcohol, or else it would be called Dry October. So, I think Sober October must just mean no getting pished for a month. Which, by the way, Joanna, isn't hard if you keep getting in these wee bottles of Italian fizz-water for Robbie.'

It was Italian fizz-water I had bought myself and not yet been able to sample.

Joanna wasn't finished with him. 'But a lot of people don't get pished, Malky – not ever. What you're doing is what those people would call Normal October. I'm not sure why you deserve to be sponsored for being normal.'

My brother concealed his deep interest in my wife's

remarks with another swig and a burp before changing the subject to the one I thought we'd successfully steered him away from. 'Anyway, what was that you were saying when I came in, Robbie? What would I do?'

'Where's Kim tonight?' I asked.

Joanna nudged me somewhere soft with a hard elbow.

'I think she's with her teammates,' Malky said, returning the bottle of beer to his lips.

'Are you sure?' I asked.

Slowly he lowered the bottle.

'I saw her tonight,' I said. 'Just an hour or so ago. With another man.' Malky didn't understand. 'They were being . . .'

'Being what?'

'Affectionate.'

'How do you mean being affectionate?' he asked.

'I mean . . . You know . . . They were . . . It's hard to describe . . .'

'They were having sex, Malky,' Joanna said. Malky spun around to face the opposite wall. Joanna walked over to him, took the bottle that was now gripped tightly in his fist, set it down on the coffee table and put an arm around him. 'Robbie saw them. They didn't see him. You could just pretend it never happened. I know Robbie would never say anything. I'm sure that in time, Kim will come clean about it and ask for your forgiveness. There's most likely a whole set of circumstances we know nothing about, and that will explain everything. What do you say we just forget the whole thing ever happened?'

But my brother wasn't inclined to go down the forgiveness route. 'I'll kill him.' Freeing himself from Joanna, he marched over to me. 'Tell me who this guy is, Robbie, and where I can find him.'

Joanna wasn't for letting up on her attempts at conciliation. 'It was probably all just a terrible mistake,' she said, as though there was still a chance that Kim and Holliday had accidentally bumped into each other, losing their clothes in the process, before tripping up and landing on the pool table. 'Talk to Kim. See how she feels about it.'

Malky seemed to prefer the I'll-kill-him solution to the problem.

'Let it go,' I said. 'It's not like you have trouble attracting women.'

'I want to know who this guy is,' he said.

'Why? He hasn't done anything wrong,' I said. 'It's Kim you should be—'

'What Robbie means . . .' Joanna interjected, 'is that you shouldn't be killing anyone, but if anyone is to blame, it's Kim. On the other hand, are you telling me you haven't had it off with someone else's girlfriend in the past?'

'That's different,' Malky said, not justifying the statement further.

'Anyway,' I said, 'the man concerned might not be so easy to kill.' Hadn't Elliot Holliday learned to play pool in the army? And I was prepared to bet the blade he carried was sharp enough to slice through more than just cardboard boxes. Uncalled for the image of my dad and the rolling pin leapt into my mind. Genghis McCann and Davie Bell, the two people in possession of the painting before me, had both been murdered by someone handy with a knife. A wave of nausea washed across my insides and broke as a cold sweat on my brow. I rushed into the hall and grabbed my coat.

'Where do you think you're going?' Joanna called to me.

'Out,' I yelled back. 'Malky, stay here, and keep the doors locked.'

45

I should have known that pitching up unannounced at Mrs Glowacki's door, half-eight on a Friday night, was only going to be effective as a means of attracting the neighbours or having her call the police. After a few un-answered knocks at the door, the big guy from across the way came over to see what was going on, the small white fluffy dog tagging along in its usual state of hysterical excitement. I didn't think it would help to say that I had a valuable work of art to return to the old lady, but first of all, I'd like to negotiate a finder's fee of twenty or thirty grand. Still, the man was pleasant enough when I explained to him who I was and that I was there to speak to Mrs Glowacki on an urgent legal matter. Unfortunately, even his attempts to have the old lady come to the door were fruitless.

'All I can think is that you talk to Reuben Berlow,' the neighbour said. 'He's Mrs G's husband's old business partner. You might catch him at the shop, though he doesn't work so late on a Friday now that the nights are drawing in, and I'm afraid I don't have his home number. I don't even know where he lives. What you should do is come back tomorrow afternoon. He'll be here around lunchtime. It's the Jewish Sabbath, and he always brings a roast for Mrs Glowacki.' He crouched to pat the fluffy little dog that was weaving in and out his legs. 'Frosty is

241

a big fan of his. He's always got a bone or something nice for her.'

I thanked him for the information, though I didn't want to wait that long. Who knew what Holliday was going to do? He'd already tried to phone me three times since I'd left him at the antiques shop. What to do? I needed to return the painting. There couldn't be that many businesses locally that had the name Glowacki. A quick check on the internet and I found one. I called. It was an answering machine. I left a message asking if Reuben Berlow worked there, and if he did to give me a call, adding that it was important without going into detail.

Back home, Malky was watching TV in the company of Joanna, Tina and four empty beer bottles. He removed my daughter from his knee and stood up when I came in. He'd calmed down and there was no more talk of murdering anyone.

'You're back at last. Can you give me a lift to the pub?' he said.

'Where have you been?' Joanna asked. 'Someone called for you. One of your clients. A Mr Holliday. He said he'd been trying your mobile. I told him you were out, and he asked when you'd be back.'

'What did you tell him?'

Joanna sat up from a reclined position in the big armchair, shifting a cushion and straightening her back. 'There's something funny going on, isn't there?' she said, wincing, and pressing a hand against her bump.

'Are you all right?' I asked.

'It's nothing,' she replied. 'Don't change the subject. You're up to something.'

'Long story,' I said. 'I'll explain when I get back.'

I dropped Malky off on the High Street and was about

to pull away when my phone buzzed. I didn't recognise the number.

'It's Reuben Berlow. You called and left me a message. You said it was important.'

'I've got Mrs Glowacki's property,' I said. 'I went around to try and talk to her, but she wouldn't answer the door. I need to speak to somebody about it.'

He sighed. 'It's Friday night, Mr Munro. I'm glad you've found the stuff, but I'm at home with my family right now. I'm sure it can keep until Monday. Why don't you give me a call then?'

'I'd rather get things started now,' I said.

'Started? What do you mean, started? Why don't you take Mrs Glowacki's property to her house tomorrow evening? I'll meet you there. It'll only take you five minutes. Does that sound okay? Fine, then. Bye—'

'If I do, I think it could place Mrs Glowacki in danger,' I blurted.

'What? Have you gone to the police about this?'

'Not yet. It's difficult to explain over the phone. How about I come and see you tonight?'

'No thanks. That's not happening.'

'Then how about we meet at Mrs Glowacki's?'

'I'm not disturbing her at this time,' he said. 'She'll be in her bed. Where are you?'

'Linlithgow High Street.'

'Okay, go to my shop and I'll meet you there. But this better be good.'

'Good,' I said, 'is putting it mildly.'

46

Reuben gave me directions to a shop that wasn't really a shop. From the outside, it looked more like a garage. It consisted of a single storey building, wide, with a low roof and a sign bearing the Glowacki name fixed above a bottle green roller-shutter door that was set in a brown pebble-dash wall. A set of heavy wrought iron gates lay open, giving way to a large forecourt. As the headlights of my car washed over a familiar small blue van, I saw Reuben alight.

'This really better be important,' he said when I joined him on the concrete surface that was scattered here and there with straw. There was a distinct smell of dung about the place.

'Trust me, it is,' I said.

'So, where's Mrs Glowacki's property?'

'I haven't brought it with me. It's too dangerous.'

'What do you mean, dangerous?'

'Not dangerous. Well, yes, possibly dangerous. I think . . .'

'You're not making any sense,' Reuben said. People had told me that before. Most of them had been wearing horsehair wigs and staring down at me from the bench at the time. I tried to explain, without traumatising the poor guy. 'I have reason to believe that there is someone who knows about the painting, and is prepared to go to any lengths to—'

'What are you talking about? What painting?'

'The painting that was stolen from Mrs Glowacki's home along with all the other stuff. It's extremely valuable.'

'Then why haven't you gone to the police?' he said, as I thought he might.

'We may have to,' I said. 'But later. For now, we need to agree on something.'

'Why? Why can't you just give Mrs G her property back, and if there's a problem let the police handle it? Who is this person anyway?'

'I'd rather not say.'

'But I thought you said they were dangerous?'

'Possibly dangerous. I don't know for certain. It's more of a . . .'

'Hunch? A dream? The work of your overactive imagination?'

'Let's say it's a reasonable inference I've drawn from various threads of evidence,' I said. 'And, leaving that aside, there are a couple of other reasons I can't just give the property back to Mrs Glowacki.'

'And they are?' he sighed, looking at his watch.

'For one, she won't let me speak to her.'

'You don't have to. You can speak to me.'

'Okay, then. The second reason is that I want to come to an arrangement so that I'm refunded for locating her property, including the picture.'

Reuben grunted, reached into his inside jacket pocket and removed a small black wallet. I caught a glimpse of a couple of ten-pound notes inside. 'How much?'

'Twe . . . thirty thousand pounds,' I said.

'What! Are you out of your mind?' Reuben snapped

the wallet shut, shoved it back inside his jacket and took a step back. 'Oh, wait a minute. I see what this is.' He smiled as though now understanding everything perfectly. 'It's a scam. You read in the paper that Mrs G is selling up and giving everything to charity, and you thought what a good time to skim some cream off the top.' He rammed a hand into a trouser pocket and removed a set of keys. 'I'm going. I've heard enough.'

As he turned, I pulled him back by the shoulder. 'The painting is worth a million pounds.'

He froze, turned slowly to face me again. 'That's ridiculous.'

'No,' I said, 'it's not. I've had it professionally valued.'

'Well, you had no right to.'

'And, in the process, I've spent a lot of time and money establishing it is what it is. For that reason, I'm prepared to return the painting to Mrs Glowacki upon receipt of a finder's fee.'

Reuben stroked his beard. 'If what you say is true, it's your own fault you've spent that money.'

'If I hadn't had the painting valued, nobody would know its worth. It would have been sold for a few quid, until years from now someone found it up their attic or at a car boot sale, and meanwhile Mrs Glowacki's charities would have been deprived of hundreds of thousands of pounds.'

'Okay,' Reuben said smugly. 'I'll tell you what we'll do. You give me the painting, I'll have it valued and, if what you say is correct, I'll recommend to Mrs G that you're paid a finder's fee – though I can't guarantee how much she'll be prepared to pay.'

'It's thirty thousand or nothing,' I said.

'Then I'll call the police. I'll tell them you're holding stolen property.'

'What stolen property is that?' I asked. 'Did you not give a statement to the police saying nothing was stolen from Mrs Glowacki's home? I bought this painting fair and square from a respectable second-hand furniture dealer.' It was the best obituary Ding-Dong Davie Bell was ever going to get.

'But you know fine well it was taken from Mrs G's house,' Reuben said.

'Can you prove it?'

'Mrs Glowacki can.'

'Come off it. Once the news of this painting breaks, there will be people crawling out of the woodwork to say that the painting's theirs. Have you never heard the expression possession is nine-tenths of the law?'

'But it was stolen! You know that.'

'No, I don't. You told the police it wasn't stolen, the person accused of stealing it is dead, and so is the person I bought it from.' That could have been expressed better.

Reuben glanced around at the darkness of the courtyard and backed away even further.

'Don't panic,' I said. 'I didn't kill them. But, unless it's a huge coincidence, I think there is someone out there who is prepared to kill for that picture.'

Reuben didn't come any closer. 'If what you're saying is true, it seems to me that now you're in danger, you want to foist the painting onto Mrs G and get as much out of it as you can.'

'When I've been paid my finder's fee, I'm happy for Mrs Glowacki to tell the police. She can tell the world. The more people who know about the painting, the better, and the sooner it's taken to an auction house, the safer everyone will be.'

'That's very handy for you, isn't it?' Reuben said. 'You

247

get your finder's fee up front, Mrs G gets her own property back and then she discovers the painting is worthless. She's a sick old woman, but she's not senile. I say we call the police, have the painting properly valued under their protection and then Mrs G can decide if you should be rewarded.'

There was a big problem with that suggestion: if the police became involved before I'd come to a binding agreement with Mrs G, I'd have no chance of getting any money. I couldn't prove I'd shelled out twenty grand having the painting valued. The money had been paid in cash. There was no vouching. As for Holliday being the murderer of Genghis McCann and Davie Bell, what actual evidence did I have? If anything, my dealings with Holliday only made me look like an accomplice.

'Okay, how does this sound?' I said. 'I return the picture, Mrs Glowacki signs a contract saying that she will pay me a small percentage of whatever the painting raises at auction, say three per cent. That way if the painting is worthless, I'll get a fraction of nothing. If it's worth what I say it is, then everyone's a winner.'

Reuben tugged gently at his beard while he mulled that over. 'What about the police?'

I put out a hand to shake his. 'As soon as Mrs Glowacki signs the deal, she can dial 999.'

47

I spent the rest of Friday night at home with all the doors locked and a claw hammer under the bed. Saturday morning, I was getting Tina ready for her return to the fun-four-a-sides when my dad arrived, offering to take her along to what he described as, 'the field of dreams', though I wasn't sure who dreamt of muddy pitches and traffic cones for goalposts.

'You'll be pleased the wee one's going back to the fitba,' he said, looking down at Tina in her little red football strip, socks pulled up over her shin-guards to the knees, boots laced-up all by herself in knots that would have sent Alexander the Great looking for a sharper sword.

I wasn't particularly bothered whether it was football or dancing, I just wanted my daughter to have fun.

My dad found that hard to understand. 'You don't want a dancer for a daughter.'

It wasn't immediately clear to me why not, so I let him continue because I knew he'd explain. 'Dancers are the sort of women those sex pest guys you read about like to harass. The women end up feeling they can't get a job without . . .' he looked further down the kitchen to where Tina, on tiptoes, was filling a water bottle at the sink. 'You've heard of the casting couch, haven't you?'

If my dad thought I was sending my seven-year-old

daughter to any auditions with strange men when I wasn't there with her, he was gravely mistaken.

'I'm not talking about while she's a wean. I'm talking about when she's older,' he said. 'Football will toughen her up. I'll bet you no sex pest would try it on with Kim.' From what I'd seen the night before, I wasn't sure they'd have to. 'Learn to be tough on the pitch and you learn to be tough off it. None of that *Swan Lake*, dying duck, standing on your pointy-toes carry on. That's for big girls of both sexes.'

'Dad, what are you talking about? Ballet training is one of the toughest physical regimes there is. And who cares what Tina does so long as she has fun? Isn't that right, Tina?'

Tina trotted over, nodding. 'I like football the best now.'

'And football can be a graceful sport too,' I said, pressing home my point. 'It doesn't have to be all about tough tackling, and—'

'I like barging people over and scoring goals,' Tina said. My dad patted her on the head. 'That's my girl.' He picked up her kitbag and they set off to do battle.

On the way, they passed Kim coming in through the front door.

'Have you seen Malky?' she asked. 'I haven't seen him since Belgium. He disappeared after the match. We were supposed to be going for a meal with some of the girls in Rotterdam and he never showed. He sent me a text saying he'd call me after his five-a-sides last night, and I've still not heard a cheep.'

'Oh, well,' I said, forcing a laugh. 'You know what Malky's like. The only thing reliable about him is his unreliability.'

'Well, I wish just for once he'd stick to an arrangement.' Kim was getting herself quite worked up. 'He's always dashing off somewhere or forgetting to phone me. Talk about forgetful? He makes you look like a memory man. Have you seen him?'

'He was here last night, but I had to go out urgently and I asked him to stay with Joanna and Tina until I came back.'

'So, it's your fault?'

'No. It's not Robbie's fault.' Joanna appeared in a dressing gown. The spoon she was using to scrape an empty jar of Ovaltine wasn't the only thing she was holding, she also had a firm grip on the wrong end of the stick. 'He did what any brother would have done in the circumstances.'

I took the jar and teaspoon from Joanna's hands and attempted to guide her through to the kitchen.

With a neat sidestep, Kim shimmied in front of us, blocking our path. 'Hold on,' she said. 'What did Robbie do?'

Now Joanna looked puzzled. 'Told Malky about you and . . .' Joanna looked up at me, realisation dawning. 'Anyone like a cup of—'

'Me and who?' Kim demanded.

'Robbie saw you last night . . .' Joanna said. 'At it,' she added, for the sake of clarification. 'With another man.'

Kim stood there, eyes wide, mouth opening and shutting but emitting no sound. Eventually she managed to come back with, 'It was a one-off. A mistake . . . And . . . If you must know, it was your husband who introduced me to that other man in the first place.'

'Why did you do that, Robbie?' Joanna asked.

Finding myself in the crossfire, I had to at least try and

defend myself. 'Yes, I introduced Kim to him,' I said, giving Kim my best accusing stare, 'but I never told her to get jiggy on a pool table. Joanna, would you mind making us a cup of tea while I explain a few things to Kim?'

By the look on her face, Kim wanted an explanation about as much as my wife intended to make us all a nice cup of tea. What an indignant Kim wanted now was her money back. She said so. Loudly.

'What money's this?' Joanna asked.

'The money I gave Robbie to buy that painting,' Kim said. 'I want it back and I'm not waiting until the end of the month.'

'Painting?' Joanna turned to me. 'Robbie, do you have money belonging to Kim?'

Attempts to steer my wife into a nearby armchair were ineffectual. 'Let's not get hasty,' I said, as she pushed me aside. 'Kim's invested some money with me. She knows it's not due to be repaid yet. She'll get it back later – as agreed.'

'I'd better,' Kim said, 'or I'm reporting you to the police for defrauding me out of five thousand pounds.'

With that and a toss of her ponytail, Kim marched out, slamming the door behind her.

'Five thousand pounds!' Now Joanna did sit down. 'Why did you borrow five thousand pounds from her? Just give it back.'

'That's not going to be all that easy, Joanna,' I said. 'Not at this precise moment in time.'

'If Munro & Co. has cash flow problems—'

'When doesn't it?'

'Then pay her back from our money . . .'

My facial expression was enough to send Joanna leaning back, the heel of a hand pressed against her forehead. 'You've spent that too, haven't you?'

As a means of communication, I was finding facial expressions useful. After a moment or two of heavy breathing, Joanna stood up again. 'I want to know what's going on. Whatever you've got yourself into, we're in it together, understand? No secrets, remember? We promised each other that when we got married.'

I did remember, and I'd stuck by that promise. I kept no secrets from my wife – other than, obviously, the things I didn't want her to know. I sat her down again and brought her a second-dip-of-the-teabag cup of tea.

'It all started with a dog . . .' I said.

48

Two heads are better than one. Especially if the other head is smarter than yours.

I explained the whole story to Joanna and although for a moment I thought I'd brought on early labour, she sat listening, quietly on the most part, absorbing the information she was being fed, processing it, allowing her trained legal mind to form a cold, objective and informed opinion on the situation.

'You're an idiot,' she said. 'And a promise-breaker.'

Those facts established, we moved on to more practical discussions, albeit choosing to depart from the standard dictionary definition of discussion, in that it was my wife who did all the discussing. She was still discussing in quite a loud voice when my dad and Tina came back from Saturday morning football.

'We're going to have to involve the police. What do you think, Alex?' Joanna asked, after Tina and Bouncer had gone off to re-enact my daughter's match-winning hat-trick in the back garden. My dad sat down on the sofa and allowed me to bring him a mug of tea. Joanna had filled him in on the details by the time I returned from the kitchen. It seemed they were both of one mind when it came to resolving my predicament.

First of all, and non-negotiable, was the return of the

painting to Mrs Glowacki for the benefit of her chosen charity.

'After that, we have to catch the killer, this Holliday guy,' my dad said.

'How exactly do we do that?' I asked. 'And, bear in mind, I don't know for certain if he has killed anyone.'

'Of course he has,' Joanna said. 'Apart from us three and those two art experts, whose silence you have so generously paid for, he's the only person who knows the value of the painting. The person who stole it was murdered, and the person the thief sold it to was also murdered.'

'Using the same commando method,' my dad added.

Joanna continued. 'And you say Holliday is ex-army.'

'Take that to the cops and they'd laugh at you,' I said. 'For all we know, Holliday was sitting down to high tea with a couple of nuns in South Queensferry when Genghis McCann and Davie Bell were murdered.'

'You said you saw him with a knife,' Joanna said.

'I did, but it was a tool. He was cutting cardboard with it. Who in their right mind is going to carry a murder weapon in their pocket and flash it about in public?'

'Hidden in plain sight,' my dad said. 'Your average nut-job gets off on that sort of thing.'

'He'd have to be supremely confident,' Joanna said, 'but then again, he seems confident enough when it comes to women.'

We hadn't told my dad about Kim and Malky. I was prepared to let Joanna's remark sail over his head. Unfortunately, it was a big head.

'What do you mean?' he asked.

'What Joanna means,' I said, 'is that Holliday . . . seduced Kim last night.'

'Where did this happen!'

'On a pool table.'

Imparting that news to coincide with my dad taking his next slurp of hot tea was badly timed, even for me. He showered his trousers and I had to fetch a strip of kitchen roll.

'Does Malky know?'

'We told him last night.'

'Good,' he said, 'I never liked the look of that floozy. Too full of herself because she can kick a ball about a park. Not good enough for your brother. I told him that.'

'When did you tell him that?' I asked.

My dad dabbed his trousers and riffled his moustache with a loud snort. 'I was going to tell him. I was just waiting for the right moment.' He squashed the damp kitchen roll in his fist as if it was a wax effigy of a certain female Hibernian FC centre-forward and tossed it to me. 'We're going to nail that son of a bitch, Holliday. And I know the very man for the job.'

49

According to ex-Police Sergeant Alex Munro, the very man for the job was his protégé, Detective Inspector Douglas Fleming. That Saturday afternoon, Fleming was off duty and digging up potatoes from a raised bed in his back garden.

'What have I done to deserve this,' he said, when he saw me walking down the slabbed path, picking my way through clods of dirt towards him.

I gave him the briefest of summaries. He was a cop. He didn't need much by way of facts to jump to a conclusion.

'You want me to give you a couple of cops for how long?'

'Definitely no more than a week,' I said.

He stabbed his garden fork into the earth. 'A week!'

'Tops. Probably a lot less,' I said.

'Why don't I just go and arrest this Holliday now and save the expense?'

'Because, even you couldn't fit him up on what evidence we have. You'll need to catch him red-handed.'

'I don't like it,' Fleming said. 'Why are you so keen to catch murderers all of a sudden?'

'Holliday knows I have the painting, and I don't fancy ending up on a slab with a cut femoral artery.'

'But you're happy for this old woman to get sliced-up, are you?' Fleming said.

'It's not like that. Once Mrs Glowacki has the painting and been told its true value, the story of the long-lost Rembrandt will be all over the media. I know one newspaper editor who'll jump at the story. If I tell Holliday I'm returning the painting, and who to, he'll have to act fast. The plan is that you stake out the place and catch him bang to rights at the old lady's house with the knife in his pocket.'

Fleming took a toffee from his trouser pocket and unwrapped it. 'Last one,' he said, popping it in his mouth. He chewed for a while then picked up his fork again. 'Nah, I don't like it.'

He rammed the prongs into the earth beneath a potato plant. I put my foot on it, preventing him from lifting the spuds.

'What's not to like?' I said. 'He's already killed George McCann and Davie Bell.'

'That's what I don't like about it. Why would he? Neither of that pair would know an old master if it came up and bit them. What's the point in killing them?'

'The point is,' I said, 'that, if he's going to sell it, there can't be any links to where it came from. If Davie Bell and George McCann had found out they'd let a million-pound painting slip through their fingers, they'd have kicked up enough of a stink that the whole thing would be traced back to Mrs Glowacki, the rightful owner. Holliday needed them out of the way so he could concoct a provenance that makes him the rightful owner. Right now, he doesn't know who the owner is. I've never told him.'

Fleming knocked my foot away with his own muddy boot and pressed down on the handle of the fork. A handful of brown nuggets broke through the earth. 'Then how did he hear of the painting?' he asked, stooping to collect them.

It was a good question. One I'd thought long and hard on. 'Davie Bell told me he'd sent a text round a few of his regular customers. He told me he had someone interested. I can only think that was Holliday, and, realising what Davie had in his possession, killed him and McCann to cut any ties to the real owner. Unfortunately for him, he was too late because, meantime, I'd already recovered the stolen property myself.'

'Holliday hasn't tried to kill you,' Fleming said. 'Why's that, do you think?'

'He tried to do a deal with me. Fifty-fifty. Probably thought it safer that way. A murdered lawyer would attract more attention than a couple of well-known crooks.'

'And I suppose he could rely on you to keep your mouth shut,' Fleming said, tossing the spuds into a plastic pail that was already full. 'Why didn't you go along with it? Must have been tempting – all that money.'

'It wasn't my property. And I'd sort of promised to get the stuff back for Mrs Glowacki.'

'Kind of you,' Fleming said. 'Too kind. Come on, what was in it for you?'

'Nothing. I had to shell out thirty quid to Davie Bell.'

Fleming yanked the fork out of the dirt and rammed it under the potato plant from a different angle. 'You know what it sounds like to me? A scam. For all you know, this old Glowacki bird could be in on it too. I'll bet she offers to sell it to you at a knock down price, and you'll be daft enough to take out another mortgage and buy it.'

Up until now I hadn't mentioned the money Holliday and I, not to mention Kim, had outlaid to have the provenance of the painting verified. I could understand why Fleming was suspicious, but no one knew of my meeting with Bridget Goodsir and, on her opinion alone, I was satisfied the painting was real. All I wanted was Mrs Glowacki to sign up to a finder's fee so I could at least cover my outlays. That was a side of things I didn't think necessary to divulge to the cops until the old lady had put pen to paper.

'Would you stop speculating and look at the actual evidence for a moment?' I said. 'Holliday is ex-army. Royal Marines. My dad says that the MO for the murders of George McCann and Davie Bell is classic commando training.'

Fleming stopped digging. 'Your dad knows about this?'

'Who do you think sent me?' I said. 'He was going on about how you were the very man for the job. Those were his exact words.'

'He said that, did he?' Fleming wiped a filthy hand across the stubble on his chin, while he thought some more. 'If this Holliday person is covering his tracks, don't you think you'll be first on his list?'

'No, I don't. Once I tell him I've given the painting back to Mrs Glowacki, he'll have no time to waste with me. I might be second on his list, but you'll have arrested him by then, won't you?'

'When were you planning to set this up?' Fleming asked.

'I'm going to contact Holliday tomorrow and give him Mrs Glowacki's address.'

Fleming bent to take a carrier bag from a bundle that was lying at the side of the vegetable path and handed it to me. 'Fill that with some spuds for your dad.' He started digging again, the cold white air streaming from his mouth. 'Tell him I'll have a couple of cops watch the old lady's house, but for three days, no more.'

'Thanks for doing this,' I said.

'I'm not doing it for you,' he said as I started to fill

the bag with potatoes. 'And it's three days maximum, understand?'

'Starting when?'

'Tomorrow do you?' he asked.

Tomorrow would do perfectly. Tonight, I had other plans.

50

'So, it's another great Robbie Munro plan that can't possibly go wrong, until it does.' Joanna had been feeling tired and nauseous, that is to say downright crabbit, most of the day. After tea, she went for a lie down and was now on the bed reading a book to Tina. Bouncer lay beside them, wagging his tail languorously, more engrossed in the story than my daughter who was using Joanna's iPhone to watch pop videos on YouTube under the covers.

I pulled the painting from beneath the bed. It was covered in a protective layer of bubble wrap and mummified in silver duct tape. I'd dropped into my office to collect it from the safe after my visit to Dougie Fleming's vegetable plot.

'That's me away,' I said. 'Won't be long. Just an hour or so.'

'You think you've got it all worked out, don't you?' Joanna didn't look up from the book. Not keen on the idea of me taking any of the money that was destined for charity, neither did she like the idea of us being in debt. Accordingly, she had adopted a grudgingly neutral stance on my arrangements to restore a financial equilibrium to the Munros' shaky household finances. 'Seriously,' she said, 'do you think I should come with you? It might help if she saw another woman, and I don't want you doing something daft and landing yourself in trouble.'

'You're the only person in trouble around here,' I

said, and went over and gave her a kiss. 'Now rest, finish reading Bouncer the rest of his story, and I'll not be long.'

'Have you remembered your mobile?'

I fished it out of my pocket and held it up to her.

'Good.' Joanna put the book down by her side, plumped up a pillow and lay back. As she did she winced and rested her hands on her bump.

'Still kicking away?' I said.

'Like a chorus line.'

'Are you sure you'll be okay?' I asked. 'You don't think it's the baby this time?'

'No, I think I'd know all about it if I was having contractions. I've still a couple of weeks to go before the due date.'

'How does the baby come out of your tummy, Mum?' Tina asked. Having run down the battery in Joanna's phone, my daughter was suddenly interested in what was going on, and, in particular, matters obstetrical. It was the perfect time to leave.

'I hope you know what you're doing, Robbie,' Joanna called after me.

Of course, I did. What could possibly go wrong? In the manner of all the best plans, mine was elegantly simple. At the meeting with Reuben the night before, I'd arranged for him to come with me to Mrs Glowacki's home. That way, he could act as an intermediary; otherwise I'd never get over the doorstep. Once she was settled, I'd break the good news to the old lady and have her sign a contract agreeing to pay me a percentage of the sum received at auction as a finder's fee. Hopefully, that would be enough to recoup my losses, pay back Kim and, depending on the situation with Holliday, I could even settle my debt to him – that is, if it turned out he wasn't the crazed murderer I suspected him to be.

Mrs Glowacki was safe for the moment. Holliday knew

an old lady was involved, but had no idea where she lived. I'd never told him about the painting's owner, and there was no official record of it having been stolen. All he'd had to go on, I was sure, was a WhatsApp photo message from Davie Bell showing some second-hand whisky collectables for sale. Presumably, he'd asked Davie who he'd sold the box of bric-a-brac to, and Davie had pointed him in my direction. But the fat man preferred to remain hazy as to where much of his stock originated. The most he could have told Holliday was that he'd got it from Genghis McCann, and what could Genghis tell him? The night of his death Genghis had been drunk on prime single malt whisky, and, in any case, he'd got lost and gone to the wrong house in the first place. That's what had started it all.

Holliday's ignorance gave me a fleeting window of opportunity. I'd have the old lady sign the contract tonight, then phone Holliday first thing on Sunday, giving him the details of the painting's whereabouts. I'd tell him that Mrs G was going to talk to the press the following day. That way he'd have to act fast. We could move the old lady out of the house and Dougie Fleming's troops in. I doubted if they'd have to work more than one night shift.

If, on the other hand, Holliday did nothing, then that was also fine by me. I'd let Kaye know about the painting. That way, she could have an exclusive, Mrs Glowacki's charity would get a nice surprise and, unless he was extremely vindictive, there would be no reason for Holliday to kill me or anyone else. After that it would be down to the police to catch the murderer of Genghis McCann and Davie Bell.

It was a great plan, even though I thought so myself, and so, leaving my family, present and future, sprawled across the bed, I set off into the night.

51

We'd arranged that I'd walk to Mrs Glowacki's. It wasn't that I'd made Reuben completely paranoid, or that he believed my tales of murder, but it was only a mile or so as the crow flew and it made us both feel safer that, by walking down the country tracks and lanes, it prevented anyone from following me by car.

Halfway there, my phone buzzed. Holliday. I didn't answer. He phoned another twice in close succession and I bumped those calls too. When he tried a fourth time, I switched the phone off. I'd call him tomorrow to let him know where the painting was. The cops could take things from there.

Reuben's blue van was parked outside Mrs Glowacki's house. The curtains were closed, and the only light came from the neighbouring property a distance away. A dog barked, and someone shouted at it to be quiet.

Reuben answered the door. 'I'm just back from work,' he said, explaining his brown lab coat over a white apron. 'Is this going to take long?'

I held the package up to him, placed a sheet of paper on top and said, 'How long does it take Mrs Glowacki to sign her name?'

Reuben took the sheet of paper and read it over. 'Her executors and assignees whomsoever . . . What does that mean?'

'It means that even if Mrs Glowacki dies before the value of the painting is realised, I'll be paid from her estate.'

'Lawyers . . .' he snorted, still reading, stepping back to let me in out of the cold. 'Two per cent? You really think that's going to be worth thirty thousand pounds?'

I didn't. I thought it might be more like twenty; enough to cover my outlays, and a lot less than the auctioneers would take.

Reuben rubbed a hand down his beard. 'I suppose it's good of you, but you realise how it looked to me at the beginning when you came demanding all that money for a dirty old painting.' He gave me back the contract. 'Wait there and I'll get Mrs Glowacki. In fact, come through to the study.' He led me down the long hall, to a door at the rear of the house and pushed it open. 'Your client broke in through there.' Reuben pointed to a boarded-up window on the other side of the small room. 'The place hasn't been touched since the police were here. I keep telling Mrs G that I'll tidy up, but never seem to find the time. Don't move, I'll be back in a second.'

He left and closed the door, leaving me to look around at lumps of furniture covered by heavy sheets. Beneath my feet was a thick layer of polythene. It wasn't like the cops to be so thorough when investigating a break-in. Normally, a homeowner would be lucky if a cop flicked some fingerprint powder around and left a Victim Support leaflet. Even the pictures on the walls were draped with old towels. Strange that Genghis would have taken the only valuable painting. I lifted the corner of a towel draped over a frame on the wall, half-wondering if it might be another long-lost work of art; a Van Gogh or Picasso. It wasn't. It was a framed black and white photograph of a much younger Mrs Glowacki and a large man I took to be her husband. He looked to be receiving some kind of an award from a small man with a large beard, a black hat on his head and a white shawl across his shoulders. I let the towel fall back over the picture. What was keeping the old lady?

I put down the package, took out my phone and switched it on. I didn't like leaving it off too long in case Joanna called. It buzzed into life and straightaway the screen brought up notification of five missed calls. Two more from Elliot Holliday, and, more importantly, three from home and a text: "Hurry. We're having a baby." I phoned the house. There was no answer. My next call was to Joanna's mobile. It went straight to answering service. I tried my dad. The call also went unanswered. I had to go. I walked to the door to see if there was any sign of Mrs Glowacki. All I'd wanted was to have the contract signed, hand over the painting and get away. If the old woman hadn't been housebound, and I hadn't been so worried about Holliday, we could have done this in my office during business hours, and not on a Saturday evening. We could have done it that very afternoon if Reuben hadn't been working. It was too late now. I had to find out where Joanna was.

I stopped with my hand on the door knob. Reuben working? Why was Reuben working on a Saturday? Wasn't that the Jewish Sabbath? My phone buzzed. Holliday again. What was going on? My mind was racing. I should never have left Joanna and Tina alone. I punched the receive button.

'Is that you, Robbie?' It was Kim sounding worried. 'I'm with Elliot. He's in hospital. Someone attacked him. He's been stabbed.'

'What? When did this happen?'

'About five. He was closing the shop and some nutter was waiting for him in the alley. He's lost a lot of blood. He was lucky. If I hadn't driven up at that moment, he'd have died. I used his belt as a tourniquet and the hospital is only half a mile away.' Holliday had been lucky all right. Unlucky to have been stabbed, but lucky to have been stabbed in Glasgow. It was Scotland's best city to be stabbed in because it was also Scotland's most likely city to be stabbed in and trainee A&E doctors cut their teeth on knife wounds. 'He's conscious now and said I was to call and warn you.' A noise in the hallway. I rammed the phone back into my pocket, backing away from the door.

Reuben entered, smiling, still in his working clothes. The clothes of what? A butcher? A slaughterhouse man? I felt my insides loosen.

'People know I'm here,' I said.

'No, they don't. No one knows you're here. That was the arrangement. You came here to screw money out of an old lady for a painting you had been trying to steal from her. Why would you tell anyone?'

He raised his own hand from his side. In it was the largest knife I'd ever seen. A long rectangular blade. The thick wooden grip clenched tightly in his fist. The adrenalin surged. Fight or flight? The room was small, the window boarded up. The only way out was by the door. It was ajar. But to get through it, I'd have to go through Reuben. That meant there would have to be fight before any chance of flight. I looked around for a weapon, anything. Reuben shuffled forward, slightly crouched, ready to swing at me with the knife. According to my dad, he'd feint for my throat and then jam the blade between my legs. Would he? The man wasn't trained to kill humans. He was trained to kill animals. Not that it mattered much what method he used; any cut with that weapon could prove fatal.

'Wait,' I said, hands outstretched to keep him at bay. 'Think about what you're doing, Reuben. Think about the mess you've got yourself into.'

But I could tell from his painted-on eyes that Reuben's thoughts were only on ripping open some of my major blood vessels. He inched forward. I grabbed the framed photograph off the wall. It was better than nothing, but not much.

'People know about Mrs Glowacki's painting,' I said. Reuben shook his head.

'Yes, they do. Elliot Holliday's still alive. He's in hospital. You didn't finish the job.' He hesitated. I built on that. 'And I've told the police about Mrs Glowacki's painting. They'll put two and two together.'

Mention of the police sent a ripple of disbelief across Reuben's face.

'No, you haven't,' he said. 'And it's not Mrs Glowacki's painting: it's mine now. I haven't slaved my guts out for this family to be left a part-share in a knacker's yard.'

I continued to back away until I reached the boarded-up window. I slammed my shoulder against it. It didn't budge. Reuben lunged. I slung the framed photo at him as hard as I could. It caught him a glancing blow, high on the forehead. He raised his hand to the scratch it had made, looked at his fingertips, and smiled through his beard. My only weapon gone, I had one chance to land a blow before he got in about me with the knife. I readied myself, on my toes, fists clenched and loaded.

'Dad!'

A child's voice. Not any child's voice – Tina's.

Reuben paused. The knife lowered slightly. 'Dad! Where are you?'

Just as it had all started with a dog, it ended with one too. Actually, it ended with two dogs. The first dog, small, white and fluffy, slipped through the gap in the door and jumped up at Reuben. It was quickly followed by a larger animal that didn't so much slip into the room as crash in. The door flew open and bounced off the doorstop. Reuben glanced around. As he turned to me again, my fist smashed into his face with a strength I never knew I possessed. He reeled backwards. I seized his right wrist with my left hand, using my weight to topple him backwards onto the floor, me on top of him, landing blow after blow, while the fluffy white dog nipped at my ankles and Bouncer wondered what on earth was going on. I kept punching even after my hand was numb and spattered with blood, and I didn't stop until the wrist I was holding went limp and the knife dropped to the floor.

52

Jamie Alexander Munro was born in the living room of Eva Glowacki's large detached country house on the outskirts of town, heading east.

I was present at the birth, just as I'd promised I would be; though I hadn't counted on handcuffs or cops either side of me. It wasn't the surroundings my wife would have wanted for the birth of her first child, but as Joanna's waters had broken on the drive over, and I was busy restraining a serial killer at the time, I thought it would be better if the hospital came to us. As the midwife later explained, my wife was 'a fast-worker' and it was all in a day's work for the paramedics who did a great job and, after delivering my son, turned their hands to patching up Reuben's face.

I was allowed a phone call. I made it to Malky who somehow contacted my dad, and he appeared just in time for the cup of tea that Mrs Glowacki had made everyone. While Reuben had been trying to kill me, the old lady had been in bed reading a book, hearing aids somewhere other than in her ears, and oblivious to what was going on. It was a peaceful evening for the old lady, rudely interrupted by a police officer walking into her bedroom, letting her know that a baby was being born on the sitting room sofa and asking if she had any towels.

Not long after my dad's arrival, Dougie Fleming did too.

Based on our discussions earlier that day, and following a chat with my dad, he ordered my release.

'A lot of folk use their middle name if they're not all that keen on the first,' my dad, chipped in. 'Alex Munro – the second. Got a certain ring to it.'

'One Alex Munro's enough,' Joanna said, passing our son to me for my first hold of him. 'It's Jamie.'

'Jamie Alexander Munro, JAM,' I said.

'He'll never be as jammy as his dad,' Dougie Fleming muttered.

I took my son in my arms. So tiny, so delicate.

Later, after delivery of the placenta, something I knew all about from my antenatal video session and didn't think necessary to watch all over again in 3D, Joanna and the baby were transferred to hospital by ambulance for check-ups, while my dad took Tina and Bouncer home. I stayed behind to give Fleming a statement in which I explained the role of the painting in it all, not thinking it necessary at that moment to mention the money I'd spent having it valued or my hopes of reimbursement. It would only have led to a lot of awkward questions.

After the value of the painting had been explained to Mrs Glowacki, she allowed it to be taken into police custody for safekeeping. When the police had gone, she and I had another cup of tea and a chat. It was the first time I'd spoken to her when she'd had her hearing aids in.

'Jakub always liked that old painting,' she said, stirring two lumps of sugar into a floral-patterned china cup. 'He bought it at the canal market when we lived in Leiden. He liked to collect anything to do with whisky. He didn't drink a lot, not heavily, not until after I got my news. I think it was the drink that killed him in the end.'

'And Reuben? Where does he fit into all of this?'

Mrs Glowacki lifted the teacup shakily and wet her lips before replying. 'After my time in Auschwitz, I could not have children. When we moved here and Jakub started his business, Reuben was just a boy. He was Jakub's first employee. He worked for my husband for thirty years. Jakub always said he was a hard worker. More than that, he was like a son to him. Yes, he liked Jakub a lot. Me?' She waved a hand in front of her face. 'Not so much. The boy had no ambition. Always yes Mr Glowacki, no Mr Glowacki. Jakub sold him a half-share in the business when he retired. Then, after Jakub died, Reuben wanted to buy the other half. I told him I was transferring everything I owned to the Drezner Foundation, and they thought the abattoir was worth more to them as a going concern. He wasn't pleased. We were in Jakub's study at the time. I told him he could take something of Jakub's as a reminder. He said some horrible things – really, such language. He stormed out. Two weeks ago, he came back to apologise. He said he'd like to take something of Jakub's after all: the painting. I told him it was too late. The people from Drezner had been. Everything was inventoried and boxed, ready to take away. I suppose I could have given it to him, but I won't be spoken to that way. From then on, he was never away from here, hanging around like a sick dog. Always he would go on about the painting, how much it reminded him of Jakub. I was going to give the painting to him, but not right away. I used to give him lunch and send him on errands.'

Mrs Glowacki took another sip, set her teacup down and wiped her lips with a tiny handkerchief. 'After the break-in, he insisted on speaking to the police for me. Said a box of bric-a-brac wasn't worth the trouble of going to court.' She shrugged. 'I agreed. I didn't know what a fortune Jakub had been sitting on all this time. I'm so glad it's going to be put to good causes.'

I felt in my pocket for the piece of paper, now slightly crumpled. 'Mrs Glowacki. Before I go . . .'

'What is it, son?'

I removed the contract and gently unfolded it. 'I . . . I don't know how to say this exactly . . .'

'Well, if you're going to say it, say it quickly, because after this cup of tea I'm going to my bed,' she said, taking another drink.

Refolding the piece of paper, I returned it to my pocket and stood up. 'I just wanted to say what a wonderful thing you're doing. It's a fantastic legacy to leave behind. You're going to help a lot of people. I know your husband would be very proud.'

She smiled up at me. 'It's really all thanks to you,' she said wiping a tear from her eye. 'They should give you a medal. I'll make sure the people at the Drezner Foundation send you a thank you letter and maybe a nice bottle of wine.'

I took one of her frail hands in mine. The fuzzy blue numbers stood out on the whiteness of her wrist. I squeezed it gently. 'That would be very nice.'

Half a million pounds, even twenty thousand, it was a lot of money to lose. But not to me. Tonight, I was the richest man alive.

53

'You're officially skint,' Grace Mary announced, Monday morning.

Paternity leave for the self-employed is otherwise known as going out of business. Joanna and young Jamie had been pronounced fit and well and discharged from hospital on Sunday afternoon. When my mother-in-law declared she would be taking up temporary residence at our house, I realised I was surplus to requirements, and so might as well try and make some money.

My secretary set down a wire basket on my desk, fished out a letter and floated it down in front of me. 'It's from the lawyers of that snooker player whose career you saved and reputation you ruined.'

And so it was. A cease and desist letter, telling me not to: *publish or permit or authorise to be made or published or otherwise communicate to anyone in any circumstances any derogatory or disparaging statements whether in writing or otherwise concerning our client or, any group, company or organisation with which he is affiliated, or make any such statement calculated to or which might reasonably be expected to damage his reputation, commercial or private interests.*

And then the clincher in the final paragraph. Their client wouldn't be paying my fee, so I wasn't to bother rendering an account. I crumpled the letter and tossed it across the room. It hadn't even missed the bucket and begun to roll across the floor before I had the telephone in my hand.

'You got the letter then?' Peter Falconer said.

'Oh, I got it all right,' I replied, 'and now I'm looking for somewhere to shove it. The deal was no win no fee. Well, I won and now I want a fee.'

Peter sighed down the line. 'Gutted for you, Robbie, but it's got absolutely nothing to do with me. You need to see things from Oscar's point of view. The way you won . . . I mean to say . . .'

Had he forgotten our conversation at court? What ever happened to, *I don't care what you do, or how you do it, Robbie, just make sure he walks out of here still able to play professional snooker.*

'We had a deal,' I said. 'You and me. I expect you to honour it.'

Peter took a different view. 'No, Robbie. Our deal was that if you lost I'd pay your fee. The deal with Oscar was that if you won, he'd pay it. You're right, you did win, but it's not my fault if he's now reneged. You're a lawyer – sue him. But, I have to warn you, Oscar is really not happy. He won't pay and if you do try and sue him, his libel lawyers will kick the shit out of you as they drag you through every court in the land. Can you handle that kind of aggro?'

I put the phone down, but not before whacking the receiver off the desk several times. Grace Mary made a tactical withdrawal. I thought at first it was to escape my temper tantrum, but it wasn't; it was to receive a couple of visitors. Just in case anyone had thought my day could only get better, Kim walked in to my room with Elliot Holliday limping behind her.

276

'I want my money,' she said.

'The deal was the end of the month,' I said.

'I don't care. It's close enough. I want six thousand pounds and I want it now!'

What could I do? I dashed off a debit slip. 'Take this through to my secretary and she'll write you a cheque.'

I handed the slip up to her. She didn't take it. 'I gave you cash. I want cash in return.'

Holliday grimaced sheepishly in the background. He looked pale and drawn and I wondered if he should really be up and about so soon. Then again, ten thousand pounds would be worth the effort.

'Grace Mary will write the cheque,' I told Kim. 'Bring it back to me and I'll open it so you can present it at the bank for cash.'

Kim thought about that for a moment, then snatched the slip and marched out of the room. I could imagine my secretary's reaction as she took the cap off yet another red pen.

'I'm glad to see you up and around,' I said to Holliday. 'I expect you've come for your money too. I'm not sure my overdraft facility will stretch—'

'I don't want it,' he said.

I didn't understand. 'It's ten thousand pounds.'

'I know. We were both in on the deal and we both lost out. That's how it goes.'

'But . . .' I said, unable to prevent myself from arguing on my client's behalf and against my own interests. 'You wouldn't have lost it if I'd let you keep the painting.'

Holliday shrugged. 'You had your reasons. It's not what I'd have done. You did the honourable thing.' He winced and gently rubbed the inside of his right leg. 'Forty-eight stitches and a transfusion of five units of blood.

I discharged myself. I'm not hanging about hospital to catch a superbug. I'm supposed to be resting, but when Kim said she was coming to see you, I thought I'd tag along and say thanks.'

'Thanks? Thanks for what?'

'Saving my life. Reuben Berlow was out to kill me, like he was killing anyone who knew about the painting. I was supposed to die on Saturday night, and I would have if Kim hadn't turned up when she did. I didn't even know she had trained to be a nurse, and she wouldn't have been there at all if you hadn't introduced us.' He came over and sat down gingerly. 'All those years ago, that old witch said all my luck would be bad luck and I'd die bloody.' He grabbed my arm and squeezed it. 'You're my good luck. I might need you to save my life again and I'm not risking it for the sake of a measly ten grand.'

Kim appeared in the doorway. She walked over to my desk and slapped a cheque made payable to herself for six thousand pounds in front of me. I signed it, wrote across it, "please pay cash" and added my initials.

Kim tucked the cheque away in her handbag. 'Let's go, Elliot,' she said, tugging at the sleeve of Holliday's jacket. Holliday struggled to his feet. Reaching across the desk, he shook my hand then hobbled out of the door after her.

54

'What was *she* wanting?'

No sooner had I sunk back into my chair than Malky strolled into my office.

'Some money I borrowed from her,' I said.

'That the new guy? Flash git. Where did she meet him?'

'So, what brings you here?' I asked, not wanting to go into detail over who had introduced the old love of his life to the new man in her life.

'Good news,' he said.

Grace Mary came in. 'Can I bring you anything, Malcolm?' she asked, in a voice she never spoke to me in. 'Cup of tea? Coffee?'

Malky settled for coffee and into the seat opposite. 'There'll have to be changes,' he said.

As with most of my brother's statements, I had no idea what he was talking about.

'Here. This place. It's a dump.' I could hardly take issue. 'Everything's got to go. The desk, your chair.' He stood up and kicked the base of my nearly-leather recliner. 'Especially your chair.' He strolled across the room and slapped my big filing cabinet. 'This monstrosity . . .' He came over and tugged at a withered leaf on my rubber plant. 'This as well . . . Whatever it is, it's for the out. And as for—'

'Thanks, Malky,' I said, 'but when you said everything

had to go, I did understand the meaning of the word "everything". You don't need to narrate a list. Just tell me why it's all got to go?'

'Because it gives people the wrong impression. No, it probably gives people the right impression, but of you, not of me. I can't be expected to work under these conditions. We'll get in some proper furniture. Modern stuff. Get the place decorated . . .'

Clearing corner kicks had been as good a use of my brother's head as any, but the footballs had taken their toll.

'I've been telling Robbie to smarten this place up for years, Malcolm,' Grace Mary said, arriving with my brother's coffee and a half-packet of chocolate biscuits, the existence of which I'd hitherto been unaware.

'Don't you start,' I said. 'You know I've just gone another six grand into debt courtesy of his cheating ex-girlfriend. I couldn't decorate a Christmas tree without selling a kidney. If one of the clients he sends me ever actually pays a fee, it might be different!'

After I'd told him about the letter from Bowman's lawyers, and my telephone call with Peter Falconer, Malky sat down again, leaned back, crossed his feet on the edge of my desk and wafted a hand at me. 'Calm down. I'll have a word with Peter. As for this place, don't worry, I'll pay.'

'You'll pay?'

'We can take it out of your share of the profits later.'

'What profits?'

Malky sighed and turned to Grace Mary. 'How's business?'

'What's the opposite of a crime wave?' she said.

'There you are.' Malky put his feet down and reached

280

for a chocolate digestive. 'It's time to diversify. Get shot of all those losers you act for. Me and you . . .' He dunked the biscuit and stuffed the soggy bit in his mouth. 'Fifty-fifty.'

I'd have said something at that point if I hadn't been busy trying not to burst the blood vessel in my forehead.

'Anyway, it's nearly five o'clock. I'll leave you boys to it,' Grace Mary said, closing the door behind her.

'Sports agency.' Malky finished the rest of the biscuit and helped himself to another. 'If Peter Falconer can do it, anyone can. What's he got that we don't?'

'A booming business?' I suggested.

'That's what I don't get. Why is it booming? It's not like he's clever. He's not a lawyer. He was a goalie, and not a very good one. He played a handful of games for the Rangers before they punted him up north to play with the sheep. You're maybe not all that smart, but you've got a piece of paper from uni that says you are, and I played five seasons for Rangers, captain for three of them. I scored the winner in the Scottish Cup. I captained Scotland. I—'

'That's all very well, Malky.' I was familiar with my brother's sporting CV. He and my dad reminded me of it frequently. 'But you'd need a one hundred-thousand-pound bond before you could even get started.'

'I know *I* would.' Malky had been doing some research. That's how worrying things were. 'But *you* wouldn't. You're a solicitor. You've got PI insurance.' He drank some coffee. 'Here's how it will go. I'll bring in the clients, you'll do the legal work. What do you say?'

It took me a little time to realise that Malky was suggesting we go into business together. Once the siren in my head had stopped, I began to think that he might actually have come up with a really good idea. How could that have happened? I thought about it some more, while he continued to munch his way through the chocolate digestives. Malky had tons of contacts. Everyone in the game knew him. He'd been a winner. Players would fight for the chance to have Malky Munro on their side. He could front the operation, and I could do the legal work. No more legal aid. My head was spinning at the thought of it.

'I've got us a client already,' he said, through a slurp of coffee. 'Jan Oliver, remember her?'

I didn't. 'Who does he play for?'

'He doesn't. *She* plays for Hearts ladies. Do you not remember the young centre-back for Scotland when we were over in Leuven?'

There had been a defender making her international debut. She'd towered over every other player on both sides and been named Woman of the Match. 'The great big girl?' I said.

Malky nodded. 'That's Jan. Tough-tackler. Good in the air. Definitely one for the future.'

'But is there any money in women's football?' I asked.

My brother thought there would be. 'Just wait until the equality folk get their hands on it,' he said. 'Men and women get paid the same at Wimbledon, don't they? Anyway, it's just a start for us, and it was Jan who gave me the idea. She's been offered a deal by Hearts. There's money involved, not a lot, and she was wondering what I thought about it. She wants to negotiate better terms and was thinking of getting an agent. When she mentioned Peter Falconer, I don't know why, but I told her I was starting up my own agency with you. I said that me being a former top centre-half, I could also give her some coaching advice. She said she'd think about it, and after the game in Leuven, we went to her hotel room to discuss things. I gave her a few pointers. For one thing, she stands far too square to the goal at corners. And that wasn't all I gave her, if you catch my drift.' Malky sucked chocolate off a finger and winked at the same time. 'Yeah, I took one for the team. Our team. Me and you. Like you say, she's a big girl, nice figure, great legs, but, when it comes to make-up: it's not a case of you're worth it, it's more, you need it. Lots of it. To be honest, I still feel a little dirty. But, hey, business is business.'

'You slept with her?'

'Actually, there wasn't a lot of shut-eye involved. Some of those lady footballers have great stamina.'

'You had sex with this Jan Oliver so you could sign her up to your non-existent sports agency, and you did that while you were going out with Kim?'

Malky put up a hand. 'Before you get all uppity, it wasn't like that.'

'It wasn't like sex?'

'Yes, it was like sex, in fact it was very like sex, but . . . I felt I had to do it to seal the deal, or whatever you lawyers call it.'

When it comes to sealing deals, us lawyers usually opted for signing pieces of paper, rather than stripping off in hotel rooms. 'We lawyers call it two-timing your girlfriend,' I said. 'You remember Kim, don't you? The girl you said only days before was "The One".'

Malky selected another biscuit and stuffed it in his mouth. 'Do you have to bring her up?'

I swept away the crumbs with which my brother had lightly sprayed the paperwork on my desk. 'Malky, the agency is . . . possibly, a good idea, but you have to see the danger of having sex with young female footballers. Ten years from now, this Jan will be saying you coerced her

283

into sex because she wanted to join your agency.'

Malky stood up, looked at his reflection in the window, gave his hair a flick and laughed. 'Who'd believe that?'

I thought a jury might.

He stared down at me patronisingly. 'Do we have to go over all of this again?'

'Not your league of good looks theory?'

'Exactly. Nobody has ever complained about being sexually abused by someone hotter than themselves.' He swivelled at the hips for another glance at himself in the window. 'I think I'm safe enough.' He turned and put out a hand to me. 'Now, what are you? In or out?'

55

After much thought and a lot more persuading, I was in.

I didn't tell Joanna. Not yet. She'd find out eventually. She always did find things out, but the news that I had gone into business with my brother could wait – hopefully until we'd made our first million. More likely, until I was representing Malky on sexual harassment charges.

On the Sunday afternoon, Malky picked up my dad, Tina and me to take us to the Women's League Cup final. Kim's promised tickets had never materialised. We were going hospitality courtesy of Malky's radio show. In the week or so since we'd become business partners, Malky had brought in four more female footballers, without, so far as I knew, having to lay his honour on the line. Three of our acquisitions were the spine of the Hearts WFC team. One of them being six-foot-two, eyes of blue, Jan Oliver.

The final took place at Falkirk Stadium, a neutral ground for an Edinburgh derby. With a capacity of around 8,000 it was the perfect venue to give the game some atmosphere, and the artificial playing surface was the finest of its kind in Scotland.

As was usual, wherever he went, Malky was interrupted throughout his pre-match meal by autograph hunters, but as we were digging into our pudding, the shadow that fell over the apple pie and custard was not someone wanting my brother to sign their match programme: it was Peter Falconer.

He took one of my brother's hands in one of his own giant mitts. 'Here to steal some more of my clients, Malky?' he said, his fixed smile a lot friendlier than the tone of his voice.

'I think I've got more clients on show today than you, Peter,' Malky said.

The big man screwed up his face and lowered his voice. 'Women's football? You can keep it. Pocket money. More trouble than it's worth.'

'If it's not worth the trouble, why are you here?' I said.

It turned out Peter was there in his capacity as an emissary for Bet AKQ, who were sponsors of the Cup.

'Honest Al likes it if I show face occasionally and encourage the punters to chuck some money away,' he said.

'Oh,' I said. 'I thought you might have come to steal more food from the mouths of my children.' I lifted Tina's pudding bowl and held it out to him. 'Here, there's still some left.' It was slightly melodramatic of me, but thanks to him I had a bank overdraft that could be seen from the moon.

'How often do I have to tell you?' Peter said. 'You not getting paid was nothing to do with me. I'm just Bowman's agent. He owes you. I don't. End of.'

I stood up and pointed a finger across the table at him. 'I saved the career of your biggest client. You promised to pay me and then welched on the deal.'

Peter shrugged his enormous shoulders. 'Think what you like, but I said I'd pay if you lost. That was the deal. Unfortunately, for you, you won,' he said with a smirk I'd have happily removed with a slap – if I could have reached up that far. The big man leaned across the table, the better to laugh in my face. 'Hope you have better luck in your new career.'

'Don't worry,' I said. 'By the time me and Malky are finished, you'll be lucky if there's a ball boy left for you to represent.'

Peter pushed past Malky and came around the table towards me. He really was very big. My dad got to his feet, napkin still tucked into the neck of his shirt, and stepped in between us. 'You. Sit,' he told me. 'And you . . .' He stabbed a finger in Peter's chest, sort of accidentally bumping his chair so that the edge caught the big man high on the shin. 'You were enough of an embarrassment on the pitch without proving you can be one off it an' all.' Some people at the other tables were looking over at us. Peter didn't move. He squared his shoulders and seized my dad's wrist, a snarl on his face.

My dad wrenched his hand away and moved closer. 'Back in the day, I'd have taken you outside and taught you a lesson.'

'Aye, so you would,' the big man scoffed, thinking it an old man's boast, unaware that, back in the day, my dad would have carried a truncheon and that a couple of whacks to the kneecaps would have brought big Peter down to his size.

It was Malky's turn to get involved. 'Robbie, Dad, would the two of you behave? Peter's my pal. He came to our table to talk to me, not so you could give him a hard time. Come on, Peter, let's go get a drink.' He gave Peter a gentle shove, and, with a parting dirty look at the pair of us, the big man allowed himself to be escorted over to the bar.

'Was that bad man trying to steal my apple pie?' Tina asked.

'Don't worry, pet, I didn't let him,' my dad said, ruffling

her hair as she started on the remains of her pudding again. Tina looked up, crumbs of pastry stuck to her lips with custard. 'I didn't like him. Will you send him to the jail, Dad?'

'I'll see what I can do,' I said. We'd thought it better, at least until Tina was older, not to tell her that my job was trying to keep the bad men out of jail.

Malky didn't return until a couple of minutes before kick-off, when the dining room was empty apart from our little group and the serving staff who were clearing the tables. Tina was doing the wee dance she did when she needed the loo.

'Where have you been?' my dad asked Malky, while I sent Tina off in the direction of the ladies' toilet.

'Smoothing things over with Peter after you two had noised him up,' Malky said. 'Then I went and put a line on. It's more fun if you've got a bet on the game.'

'It's not smoothing he needs,' my dad said. 'It's a good doing for bumping your brother out of a fee. Robbie's got my grandson to raise. If he's going to get crooks out of trouble, he might as well get paid for it.'

'I've got some good news about that,' Malky said.

'You've talked him into paying me?' I said. 'How much?'

'Five hundred.'

'Five hundred!'

'Better than nothing,' Malky said. 'Now come on, I don't want to miss kick-off.'

Tina reappeared, having somehow acquired a packet of sweets along the way, and we took our seats in the main stand. There was a cold wind blowing, the floodlights were warming up and a curtain of drizzle drifted across the park putting a sheen on the emerald surface.

'There's Kim!' Tina shouted, pointing to the centre circle, the only one unaware of the break-up between her uncle and the captain of Hibernian Ladies. The referee blew, and the match was under way, with Kim and her teammates in green immediately on the attack.

'Thanks, anyway,' I said to Malky. 'Five hundred pounds is five hundred pounds. At least you gave it a try.'

He reached across and took me in a headlock. 'I'm your big brother. Looking out for you is all part of the job.' He let go in time for me to see the ball being sprayed out wide, then quickly played back into the middle where Kim, twenty-five yards out, took it in her stride. She steadied herself, pulled her left leg back and might have had a strike at goal, but for the intervention of a giant maroon and white blur.

From a strictly scientific point of view, physicists would have described the clash between the two players, one little, the other extremely large, as an inelastic collision. Kim bounced off Jan Oliver's shoulder like a cue ball from the baulk cushion and was propelled violently several yards back the way she'd come to end up flat-out on the artificial turf. The Hibs' physio was waved on and was soon rubbing Kim's back as, on all fours and winded, she fought for breath.

The referee called the Hearts' centre-half over and reached into his pocket.

'Lucky to be getting away with just a yellow,' my dad said, when the decision was made, to loud boos from the Hibs supporters. We were only seconds into the match and things were heating up nicely.

'A booking inside the first two minutes,' I said to Malky. 'I thought the ladies' game was practically non-contact?'

'Yeah,' he said, poker-faced. 'What were the chances of that happening?'

Tina gave me a nudge and pushed her sweets at me. I took the packet, popped one in my mouth and was about to pass them along to Malky, when I stopped. Chewing slowly, I turned in my seat to see my brother staring straight ahead, his expressionless face a dead give-away.

I swallowed the sweet. 'What *were* the chances?' I asked.

Malky shrugged. 'Thirty-three to one, something like that. Seemed pretty good odds to me . . .' He reached into the pocket of his jeans, extracted a crumpled betting slip and stuffed it into my hand. 'So, I stuck Peter's five hundred on it for you.' Eyes still fixed on the game he relieved me of the sweets, put one in his mouth and crunched. 'Monday morning, we redecorate your office.'

AUTHOR'S NOTE

I'm often asked where I get the ideas for my stories, and the reader will be familiar with the adage, 'write what you know'. It's advice that's often followed up by, 'But if you're going to write what you know, make sure you know something first.'

It's true that a knowledge of the criminal justice system is a great help when writing crime fiction, where the readership expects authenticity, and even to learn something new. But of course, a crime fiction author doesn't need to be a police officer, lawyer or indeed a criminal for that matter, to write about crime. That much is obvious to those of us who wince when we read certain successful authors who drive coach and horses through the law, evidence and procedure, while still churning out an exciting page-turner. Exciting because genre is only a frame into which the author pours emotions like love, hate, revenge, jealousy, fear and, in crime, perhaps most of all, a sense of justice – all feelings each of us knows extremely well from an early age.

No, for me the big advantage of a lengthy career as a criminal defence lawyer (aside from saving time on research and making enough money to raise a family) is the deep well of possible plot lines from which I can draw, with no need to steal other people's ideas or stretch my imagination too far.

I have written about Robbie Munro so often now, I know him like I know myself. I know his wife, his brother, his father and his whole supporting cast. I don't need to wonder how each will react to any given situation, I only need to put them into the situation in the first place. As with most writers, I suspect, my first chapter is all important. For me chapter one is all about winding up Robbie Munro, setting him off and seeing if my two-finger typing can keep up with him.

Most of the plot lines, and certainly every first chapter of all the books, is based on a past experience. Sometimes merely a concept, such as in *Present Tense* where Robbie is given a box to keep for a client without knowing the contents, or *Stitch Up* where Robbie is expected to give advice on how to commit a crime and get away with it. In other books, like *Good News Bad News*, chapter one is more or less word for word what happened. That's also the case with *Fixed Odds*, as regards the encounter with the sniffer dog and my subsequent consultation about the housebreaking and the reason for it (though I spoke with the accused – 'Genghis' McCann in the story – and not to his partner).

Another event I'd been keen to use for some time also found a home in *Fixed Odds*. When I was a young trainee, the senior partner, Sheriff Margaret Gimblett, asked me to see a client late one afternoon because, she said, she was too busy. In fact, so keen was she for me to see him that she allowed me the use of her large room, rather than the cupboard where I spent most of my time. The story of the meeting is pretty accurately set out in the book. The client had been caught in flagrante with a young woman, and cursed by her grandmother, who told him from that day hence, all his luck would be bad luck and he'd die an old man while still young. In support of that, he showed me one or two grey hairs that were beginning to show at the temples. Fairly certain that curse law must have been one of the lectures I skipped while at uni, I went through to see Mrs Gimblett, who told me to get rid of him and when I asked how exactly, she said the best way was to quote an extraordinarily large fee.

At the time my salary was £4,000 p.a. and so I quoted what I thought was the astronomical fee of £600, just to get things started. Without batting an eyelid, the client placed three bundles of notes on the desk and told me to let him know when I needed more. At this point, I left the room on the excuse of fetching the receipt book, but mainly to take further instructions. Mrs Gimblett, not always the most patient of women where young trainees were concerned, asked if I had got rid of the client yet. I told her I'd done what she said and quoted him £600.

'Well?' she said.

I showed her the three bundles of notes. She studied them for a while, then relieving me of them, said, 'I'll take things from here, William,' and brushing me aside, marched off and into her office.

I never saw the client again, though I do know we raised an interdict against the grandmother. What happened after that, and whether any long-lost masterpieces came to light at any stage, I'm afraid I don't know.

www.sandstonepress.com

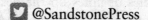 facebook.com/SandstonePress/

@SandstonePress